ACCLAIM FOR THE
PSYCHIC EYE MYSTERY SERIES

"Intuition tells me this book is right on target—I sense a hit!" —Madelyn Alt, author of *Home for a Spell*

"Abby's inner monologue is always entertaining."
—*Publishers Weekly*

"If you like to mix a bit of witty banter with suspense and a touch of mysticism, this series is for you."
—Examiner.com

"Natural pacing and humor." —*Kirkus Reviews*

"Believable . . . [and] complex." —*RT Book Reviews*

"The story line captures your attention and doesn't let go until the final pages. . . . Don't miss this one."
—Monsters and Critics

"Abby Cooper is a character I hope will be around for a long time." —Spinetingler Magazine

"It doesn't take a crystal ball to tell it will be well worth reading." —Mysterious Reviews

"An edge-of-your-seat mystery." —Darque Reviews

"A fabulous who-done-it." —The Best Reviews

continued . . .

"Readers will understand the meaning of 'mission impossible' when they try to put the novel down."
—Genre Go Round Reviews

"Plenty of surprises and revelations in the exciting story line." —Gumshoe

"Full of plots, subplots, mystery, and murder, yet it is all handled so deftly." —The Mystery Reader

"Victoria Laurie has crafted a fantastic tale . . . giving the reader a few real frights and a lot of laughs."
—Fresh Fiction

PRAISE FOR THE *NEW YORK TIMES* BESTSELLING M. J. HOLLIDAY, GHOST HUNTER MYSTERIES

"Victoria Laurie is the queen of paranormal mysteries." —BookReview.com

"Reminiscent of Buffy the Vampire Slayer's bunch, Laurie's enthusiastic, punchy ghost busters make this paranormal series one teens can also enjoy."
—*Publishers Weekly*

"Laurie's new paranormal series lights up the night."
—Elaine Viets, national bestselling author
of *Checked Out*

"A bewitching book blessed with many blithe spirits. Will leave you breathless."

—Nancy Martin, bestselling author of the Blackbird Sisters Mysteries

"Filled with laugh-out-loud moments and nail-biting, hair-raising tension, this fast-paced, action-packed ghost story will keep readers hooked from beginning to end."

—Fresh Fiction

"[A] fun, suspenseful, fast-paced paranormal mystery. All the elements combine to make this entry in the Ghost Hunter series a winner."

—The Romance Readers Connection

"A lighthearted, humorous haunted hotel horror-thriller kept focused by 'graveyard' serious M.J."

—Genre Go Round Reviews

"Ms. Laurie has penned a fabulous read and packed it with ghost-hunting action at its best. With a chilling mystery, a danger-filled investigation, a bit of romance, and a wonderful dose of humor, there's little chance that readers will be able to set this book down."

—Darque Reviews

The Psychic Eye Mystery Series

Abby Cooper, Psychic Eye
Better Read Than Dead
A Vision of Murder
Killer Insight
Crime Seen
Death Perception
Doom with a View
A Glimpse of Evil
Vision Impossible
Lethal Outlook
Deadly Forecast

The Ghost Hunter Mystery Series

What's a Ghoul to Do?
Demons Are a Ghoul's Best Friend
Ghouls Just Haunt to Have Fun
Ghouls Gone Wild
Ghouls, Ghouls, Ghouls
Ghoul Interrupted
What a Ghoul Wants
The Ghoul Next Door

FATAL FORTUNE

A Psychic Eye Mystery

Victoria Laurie

AN OBSIDIAN MYSTERY

OBSIDIAN
Published by the Penguin Group
Penguin Group (USA) LLC, 375 Hudson Street,
New York, New York 10014

USA|Canada|UK|Ireland|Australia|New Zealand|India|South Africa|China
penguin.com
A Penguin Random House Company

Published by Obsidian, an imprint of New American Library, a division of
Penguin Group (USA) LLC. Previously published in an Obsidian hardcover
edition.

First Obsidian Mass Market Printing, June 2015

ISBN 978-0-451-46925-0

Printed in the United States of America
10   9   8   7   6   5   4   3   2

For my amazing editor, Ms. Sandy Harding.
Abby wouldn't be Abby without you. ☺

Acknowledgments

Jotting down the acknowledgments is always my favorite part of any book. And not because by the time I get around to writing them the manuscript is just about finished and I'm feeling pretty good, riding those "Whoooo! I'm DONE!" vibes. Okay, so it's mostly that. ☺ But it's also because I'm afforded an amazing gift in that I get to publicly state how grateful I am to all those people who help make my stories into books—actual *things* that you can hold in your hands, see in a bookstore, check out from the library, or download to your gizmo. Without these vitally important souls, all these stories that I've written, these worlds that I've created, these characters I've loved and made live, and, yes, even killed off (my favorite part) would simply sit idle in a file on my computer, and they and I would be deprived of *your* delightful company, and where's the fun in that? So I think that thanking these folks is pretty crucial to the process. I'm doing it to serve the higher good . . . that I benefit greatly from. But still, serving up some GOOD!

So! Without further ado, lemme get to those thank-yous!

First, I'd sincerely like to thank my amazing editor, the divinely sublime Ms. Sandra Harding. I often rave about Sandy. I suspect that all of her authors rave about Sandy. She's supremely talented, insightful, smart, charming, and utterly delightful, and in addition to being a schmabulous editor, she's also a wonderful person. I hearts her. ☺ Abby really wouldn't be as daring, bold, or human without Sandy's fabulous guidance and support. I think the very best books in the series have been written under her cool, calm, impeccable guidance, and for that I'm oodley grateful. You rock, Sandy. Thank you very much for all you do.

Next, I'd like to thank my literary agent, Jim McCarthy. I'mma be honest here and say that I'm running out of nice words to say about Jim. Like, *every single book* I just roll through all those adjectives, trying to fully describe how awesome he is and now, after a bajillion books together, it's finally happened . . . I got nothin'. Hence, as I've already used up all the good words to describe Jim, I'm left with only one option: I will now be forced to make up new words to express my devotion and gratitude. So, here goes: ahem . . . ahem . . . Jim, you're amazereat. No, really, you're fabredible. I can't fully express to you how wonderlar and specable you really are! So please, don't ever change. You're fantacerful just the way you are and I adorve you. ☺

Moving on, I'd like to thank the rest of my NAL

team and they are: Elizabeth Bistrow, Kayleigh Clark, Danielle Dill, Clair Zion, Michele Alpern, Sharon Gamboa, and Monika Roe. These divinely talented women work so hard behind the scenes. They are my unsung angels and I'm so lucky to have each and every one of them along for the ride.

Last, but certainly not least, I'd like to thank my friends and family, who continually assert their love and support for me even when my blood-sugar levels drop to the danger zone. (Don't mess with me when I'm hungry, motherfinkers!) Brian Gorzynski, Sandy Upham, Steve McGrory, Mike and Matt Morrill, Katie Coppedge, Karen Ditmars, Leanne Tierney, Nicole Gray, Jennifer Melkonian, Catherine Ong Kane, Drue Rowean, Nora, Bob, and Mike Brosseau, Sally Woods, John Kwiatkowski, Matt McDougal, Dean James, Anne Kimbol, McKenna Jordan, Hilary Laurie, Shannon Anderson, Thomas Robinson, Juliet Blackwell, Sophie Littlefield, Nicole Peeler, Gigi Pandian, Maryelizabeth Hart, Terry Gilman, Molly Boyle, Martha Bushko, and Suzanne Parsons.

You may not all be related by blood, but you're my family all the same. Love you.

Chapter One

My eyes popped open just after three a.m. I'm not sure what woke me except that I had a bad feeling the second I sat up in bed and looked around. My hubby, Dutch, was sleeping peacefully next to me, the sound of his light snoring filling the room.

Instinctively I reached for my cell phone, which was facedown on the nightstand and turned to silent. I always mute my phone before I go to bed because anyone calling after eleven p.m. usually has only bad news to share, and in recent months I've had all I can handle in the bad-news department.

Focusing on the phone's display, I saw that my best friend and business partner, Candice Fusco, had just called—and she'd left a message. I pressed play and held the phone to my ear.

"Abby!" the voice mail began, and the urgency in her voice made my back stiffen. "You have to trust me. It's not how it looks."

It's been my experience that *nothing* good ever starts with those words.

Immediately I paused the message and called Candice. It went straight to voice mail. "Shit!" I whispered (swearing doesn't count when you whisper), and tried calling her again, only to get the same result. I looked at the time stamp of Candice's call. Three oh four a.m. It was now three oh six.

I tried a third time to reach her and again the phone went straight to voice mail. Either Candice's phone was turned off or it had lost its charge, because otherwise it would've rung before clicking over.

"Where are you?" I muttered, tapping the phone to go back to that paused voice mail. "You have to trust me," I heard the message repeat. "It's not how it looks. But it's gonna look bad, Sundance. Real bad. Listen carefully and whatever you do, don't share this voice mail with anybody. This is for your ears only. I need you to go to the office the second you get this and do something for me. In the back of my closet is a wall safe. The combination is Sammy's birthday—you remember it, don't you?"

Sammy was Samantha Dubois. She was Candice's older sister, who, tragically, had lost her life in a fatal car crash just outside Las Vegas when Candice was in her teens. Candice had been in the passenger seat at the time of the accident and had nearly died too. She'd pulled through after spending several months in the hospital. I couldn't imagine how difficult that time must've been for her, but I knew it still affected her deeply, because my best friend almost never talked about the accident. Still,

I'd see the deep emotional wound appear in Candice's eyes twice a year on two specific dates: August 5—Sam's birthday—and June 17, the date of Sam's death.

I also knew that in years past Candice had kept a Nevada driver's license with her photo but her sister's information on it. As Candice was a private investigator by trade, she'd confessed to me that the fake ID came in handy on occasion, and it actually had come in very handy on one particular occasion that I could remember.

"Inside the safe you'll find a file," Candice went on, and it was then that I noticed her breathing had ticked up—as if she'd started running. "Take the file and hide it. Don't show it or share it with *anyone*, Abby. No. One. Not even Dutch or Brice. I'll be in touch when I can."

The cryptic message ended there. I replayed it and held the phone tightly, as if I could squeeze more information out of Candice's voice mail. And then I got out of bed and looked around the room, trying to figure out what to do.

After a few seconds I did what comes naturally to me. I flipped on my intuitive switch and tried to home in on Candice's energy.

I'm a professional psychic by trade. I have my own steady business of personal clients, and Candice and I work private investigation cases together. We work so well together that we've nicknamed each other after Butch Cassidy and the Sundance Kid. I'm Sundance, and, as there's nothing butch about Candice, she's just Cassidy. When I'm not working a case with Candice, or busy with my own clients, I also sideline as a psychic for the FBI—although my official title at the bureau is "FBI civilian profiler."

Kinda makes it sound like I have a fancy degree in psychology, doesn't it? For the record, I majored in poli-sci, and there wasn't much fancy about it. As long as nobody asks too many questions when they read my official ID, the Feds are happy.

My husband works for the bureau too. So does Candice's.

Brice Harrison, Candice's husband, is my boss at the bureau. Brice and Candice were married last month, when they eloped to Las Vegas and stayed there for a week and a half on their honeymoon. I wasn't invited to the wedding, but then, nobody else was either. I guess it's only fair, as Candice wasn't exactly present for my wedding to Dutch. And it was probably a little bit my fault that she hadn't gotten married locally. My sister, who'd attempted to orchestrate my wedding extravaganza, was still looking to exercise her wedding planner muscles on someone. The rest of us were just looking to exorcise my sister. She'd been like a woman possessed ever since Dutch and I had gotten engaged, and our wedding had hardly turned out like she'd planned (and planned, and *planned*!).

Still, it would've been nice to watch Candice and Brice exchange their vows. I'm pretty sure she thought the same about Dutch and me, which is why I pretended to be thrilled when she called me from Sin City to let me know they'd eloped. I think Candice knew I was a little hurt, but the weird thing is that ever since she got back from Vegas, she's been different.

Candice has always been a pretty cool cucumber—it's rare to see her lose her composure—but when she came back from her honeymoon, it's like someone turned the temperature of that cool demeanor down another few notches. She's become a little more withdrawn, and a little more—I don't know—*secretive*?

It's not anything I can put my finger on, but lately she hasn't been as open with me about what's going on in that highly intelligent mind of hers. I've been chalking it up to the fact that she and Brice have been busy house hunting and easing into their married lives. But deep down, no matter how I've been trying to rationalize it, I've been worried about her. And my radar has certainly pinged with a sense of urgency every time Candice and I hang out. I kept thinking a big case must be coming our way that just hadn't appeared yet, but now, in light of the voice mail I'd just listened to, I knew I'd completely misinterpreted the signal.

"Abs?" I heard Dutch whisper as I fished around on the floor for my slippers.

"Go back to sleep," I told him. The last thing I needed was for Dutch to get involved in whatever this was before I had a chance to figure it out.

The light on his side of the bed clicked on. "What's wrong?"

I hid my phone behind my back and adopted what I hoped was an innocent smile. "Nothing, sweetie. I couldn't sleep, so I'm just gonna go downstairs and watch some TV."

Dutch rubbed his face and yawned. "Is there any cheesecake left?"

"No," I lied, willing him to roll over and go back to sleep.

Dutch blinked. "You ate six pieces between yesterday and today?"

My smile got bigger and more forced. "Yes. It was too tempting to resist."

Dutch focused on me, his eyes narrowing. Instantly I could tell he knew that (a) I was a liar, liar, pants on fire, and (b) I was hiding something.

"Abs," he said, his gaze traveling to the hand holding my phone behind my back. "What's up?"

"Nothing."

He sighed heavily. "So it's bad, whatever it is."

I opened my mouth to insist that there was nothing wrong when Dutch's phone rang. He glanced at it, then looked back at me as if to say, "I knew you were hiding something."

Heat tinged my cheeks, but I held my ground and motioned with my free hand for him to answer his phone.

"Brice," he said as he picked up the call, and a shiver went down my spine. I knew Brice was calling about Candice, and if Brice was calling Dutch at three a.m. about Candice, whatever was going on was as bad as bad gets.

If I needed any confirmation, the expression on Dutch's face said it all. As he listened, he visibly paled and then his jaw clenched before he said, "When?" followed by, "Where?"

I shoved on my slippers and eased out of the room. Rounding the hallway into our beautiful new kitchen, I didn't even bother to click on the lights. I just navigated the darkness the best I could, muttering the occasional "Dammit!" (swearing doesn't count when you bump into furniture in the dark), and making my way toward the counter with the little copper dish that held my car keys.

"Abby?" I heard Dutch call from the bedroom.

I ignored him and hustled to the door leading to the garage, so thankful that I didn't require the use of a cane anymore. I'd had a nasty accident eighteen months before that'd nearly permanently crippled me, but with a whole lot of physical therapy (and maybe some tough love from Candice when I didn't push myself to get off the cane), I'd finally gotten the full use of my legs back.

"Abs?" I heard Dutch call again as I slipped out the door, closing it as quietly as I could behind me. I tapped the button for the garage door opener, then hurried to the car, tucking inside my shiny new SUV with my pulse racing. If Dutch discovered that I was slipping away, he'd grill me for details, and I felt intuitively that I had to get to the office and retrieve that file for Candice because time wasn't on my side.

I backed out of the garage and closed the door, hoping that Dutch wouldn't see me leaving before the door closed. My hubby had coated the garage door with enough silicone to make a Slip 'N Slide look sticky. Dutch liked that it barely made a sound as it moved up and down, and at the moment I was really glad he'd used two spray cans of the stuff on the gears. It'd give me a few extra seconds before he gave chase, and I knew he'd give chase because that's just how Dutch rolled when it came to me.

Crouched over the steering wheel, I navigated the dark neighborhood streets, for once ignoring the beauty and quiet of our lovely suburban Austin community, and drove to the office I shared with Candice. My phone rang through the SUV's Bluetooth a couple of times, but I ignored the calls from my husband, focusing instead on getting to the office as quickly as I could.

Once I was within sight of the building, I circled the block, hoping to spot Candice's yellow Porsche nearby, but there was no sign of it. I parked in the alley between two buildings a couple of blocks down from the office, guided by my intuition, which was sending me lots of "Danger, Will Robinson! Danger!" signals, and, after looking around the all but deserted streets, I got out and trotted toward our building.

Along the way, I paused once or twice to listen and look, every nerve tingling with trepidation, and at last made it to the front door. I peered through the glass, looking around, but the place was so dark that I couldn't see anything inside.

It took me a minute to fish around my key ring for the right key—no way was I going to risk using a light to find the key—and when I finally had it, the sweat from my palms made fitting it into the lock tricky.

At last I gained entrance and practically ran to the elevator, pressing the button a dozen times until the elevator doors opened. After selecting the fourth floor, I pressed the DOOR CLOSE button another dozen times, then tapped my foot anxiously as the elevator climbed its way up. "Should've taken the stairs," I muttered.

The second the doors opened, I squeezed through and rushed down the hallway to our suite. The corridor was dimly lit—the main lights wouldn't come on for another two hours or so. Still, it was enough light to see by and I had no trouble getting in the door this time. The first thing I did was call out Candice's name on the slim hope that she was there, hiding. I felt my phone vibrate in my back pocket and I took it out to look at the display.

It was Dutch. Again. Trying to reach me for the sixth time.

I clicked the call over to voice mail and called out again. "Candice? Honey, it's me. Are you here?"

There was no reply and the office was eerily silent. The hair on the back of my neck stood up on end and goose pimples lined my arms. I realized I was alone and vulnerable.

Turning back toward the door, I checked to make sure it was locked, then squared my shoulders and got on with it.

Candice and I have shared the suite of three private offices and one central lobby for nearly two years. We had a similar setup even before that when we both lived in Michigan. The arrangement of sharing space together worked really well for us.

Like me, Candice had her own set of private clients— the easy adultery cases or background-check stuff— and she and I tackled the more difficult missing persons and such cases together. It was a wonderful partnership, as we each brought something different to the investigation process. Candice had a wealth of PI experience, smarts, and a handy assortment of deadly weapons. I had my intuition, my sunny disposition, and a cache of colorful expletives I'd been saving just in case of emergency.

Candice's office was just to the right of the front door, and my two smaller offices were to the left. Anxious to follow my best friend's instructions and get the hello Dolly outta there before anyone was the wiser, I headed to the right of the tiny lobby and found Candice's door closed. I tried the handle, but it was locked. "Son of a bitch!" (Swearing doesn't count when your best friend doesn't tell you she's locked her office door and you need to get a secret file from the back of her closet before the poop hits the fan.)

Standing back from the door, I thought for a second, then remembered that I had a spare key to her office hidden somewhere in my desk drawer. We'd exchanged keys just in case of an emergency right after we'd signed the lease, but I hadn't seen the key since I'd moved in.

Grumbling to myself, I moved back through the lobby to my office and over to the desk. Once there, I risked turning on the little lamp at the edge of my blotter and began rummaging around in the drawers when I felt that same prickly tension creep up my spine again.

I stopped rummaging and turned off the desk lamp, listening for any sound that might suggest I wasn't alone. The seconds ticked by without incident, but instead of feeling less anxious, I began to feel even more nervous.

Turning around, I moved to the window and peered

outside, and that's when I saw a patrol car ease its way down the street. "Shit!" I hissed. (Swearing doesn't count when you're creeping around in the middle of the night and you think the cops may be about to rain on your parade.)

As my heart rate ticked up, I swiveled back to the desk and used my phone to shed some light on the drawer, frantically pushing at all the odds and ends I'd shoved into my desk over the past two years. And then, miracle of miracles, I found the key. "Eureka!"

Clutching it to my chest, I hurried out of my office and back over to Candice's door. The key slid easily into the lock and I let myself in, then tapped at my phone to listen to her message again. ". . . In the back of my closet is a wall safe. . . ." I paused the message and moved to the small closet to the right of the desk, pulling open the door. Candice had a large filing cabinet in the closet, which took up almost the entire space and would neatly conceal anything behind it. Still, seeing it there was enough to make me groan. "*Really*, Candice?" With a sigh I pulled at the back edge of the filing cabinet, but it was extremely heavy, and trying to twist it out of the way was much harder than it looked.

It took me a minute or two of pulling, twisting, and shoving to get the cabinet to turn sideways so that I could wedge myself inside the closet and have a look behind it. I saw the wall safe midway down, just like Candice had said. What struck me, though, was that when we'd first looked at the space two years earlier, I was certain there'd been no safe inside this closet. Candice must've had it put in without telling me.

Why she'd done that I couldn't guess, but it bothered me because I was Candice's BFF and we weren't supposed to keep secrets from each other.

Still, my radar was telling me I didn't have a lot of time to dwell on such things, so I hunkered down and stared at the dial. Putting the phone back to my ear, I listened to the next part of the message again. "The combination is Sammy's birthday—you remember it, don't you?"

"August fifth," I muttered, but then my breath caught. I didn't know the year. "Crap, Candice! What year was your sister born?"

In desperation I tried calling Candice's cell again, but now, instead of going straight to voice mail, a recorded voice told me that the voice mailbox was full. I had a feeling Brice might be responsible for filling it up, because if Candice wasn't taking my calls, I doubted she was taking Brice's calls either. That could only mean she was in *serious* trouble.

Frustrated, I stared at the dial for a few seconds when I realized I could probably come up with the answer on my own. I started to spin the wheel toward the digits I did know—eight, five—then talked the problem of the remaining digits out loud. "Sam was four years older than Candice and Candice was fifteen at the time of the accident, so that would have been in nineteen ninety-five, I think. . . . Ninety-five minus nineteen equals seventy-six. So, right again to nineteen, then left to seventy-six."

Just as the dial landed on that number, I heard a noise from somewhere in the building. I froze and strained my ears to hear more. Faintly I could just make out the sounds of activity in the building and my pulse quickened yet again as my radar sent a little ping of warning. Crossing my fingers, I pulled at the handle to the safe and it popped open. "Thank God!" I gasped, and shone the light of my phone into the interior. There in the safe was a fat wad of cash, one of Candice's spare handguns, and a manila file without a label to indicate what it might contain. I snatched the file and the cash. "Leave the gun, take the casholi," I whispered, thinking that if Candice contacted me, she'd probably need the money. Then I closed the safe door and spun the dial to lock it.

Standing up again, I wedged myself back out of the closet and shoved the filing cabinet with my shoulder. Under the fuel of adrenaline, the cabinet moved back into place without nearly the trouble it'd caused me a few minutes earlier. I closed the closet door and hustled back out of Candice's office.

Risking a few extra seconds to lock her door again, I made sure to keep the key close, tucking it into my pocket before darting to the small window in the lobby overlooking the street. There were two patrol cars parked at the curb.

I didn't even pause to utter an expletive; instead I whirled around and ran for our front door. Putting my ear to it, I listened, but didn't hear anyone out in the hallway, so I undid the lock and eased the door open a crack. Putting my eye to the crack, I peered out and that's when I heard the faint ping of the elevator. "Time to go," I whispered, ducking out into the hallway. I paused only long enough to reach back and lock the handle on the door before closing it softly, then dashed off in the opposite direction from the elevators. There was a maintenance elevator at the rear of the building and I didn't slow down until I'd reached it. I thought of using the stairs, but the door triggered the fire alarm, and I rather liked the fact that no one knew I was here in the building . . . yet.

As I waited for the service elevator, I could hear voices back down the hallway, and I knew the cops had made it to our office. I wasn't totally convinced yet that they were looking for Candice, but I had a bad feeling all the way around and the last thing I wanted was to get caught up in some hot mess before I even had a chance to figure out what kind of trouble I was about to be swept up into.

The elevator finally arrived and I ducked in, pressing B for basement. The good thing about using the service elevator was that it didn't ping when it arrived like the central elevators. It simply did its work quickly and quietly. "Thank you, service elevator," I said once I was safely on my way down.

Once the elevator had stopped, the doors opened and I peered out. I'd been down on the basement level only twice, but I thought it a good idea tonight to avoid the lobby. There was a stairwell that led up to street level and out into the alley, but I knew that door was likely locked. I could only hope that my key for the front door worked on the rear door lock; otherwise, I'd be stuck.

It took me a little bit to find the stairwell door—the basement was a maze of corridors—but at last I was in front of the exit and with a little prayer I inserted my key. The lock turned and I wanted to whoop. Tucking through the door, I paused on the landing as the cool air from outside enveloped me. I couldn't hear any voices from up top, so I made my way to the street and ran to the alley two blocks down where my car was still parked, hidden behind a Dumpster. I smiled to myself when I spotted it, grateful I had such good radar. I knew that if my car had been parked in the street, the cops would've definitely run my plates. Here at least I was fairly certain they hadn't noticed the SUV.

I wasted no time slipping back behind the wheel and starting the engine, but I wasn't about to turn on the headlights until I was well away from the building. I could only hope the cops didn't look out one of the windows and see me inching away.

As I drove west headed toward home, I tried to figure out the best hiding place for the file and the money. At first I considered hiding them at my place, but I didn't yet know what Candice was up against. Whatever it was, it was bad enough for Candice not to want to tell Brice about it—that'd been made clear by her choice to call me to retrieve the file and not her husband.

I had to conclude that whatever was going on, it was illegal, and Candice didn't want Brice involved, and if it was truly that bad, then I sure as hello Dolly didn't want to get Dutch involved either. I was totally willing to go to the mat for my BFF, but I wasn't willing to suck Dutch into something sticky if I didn't have to. Therefore, I concluded, hiding the file in the house where Dutch could find it was out.

That left me with few options, though, because obviously the office was also out. I considered my car, but again I had to nix that idea because wouldn't that be one of the first places my hubby or my best friend's hubby, or some other law enforcement officer, might look?

And then an idea struck me and I tapped at the steering wheel nervously while I considered it.

Our next-door neighbors, the Witts, were out of town on a two-week getaway to the Greek isles. They'd asked Dutch and me to watch the house for them, and I had their garage code for garbage day. Because Dutch had to work late, I'd been the one to pull in the Witts' cans two days earlier, tucking them neatly back into the garage, thinking of all the brownie points I was racking up. But now I was thinking that the Witts wouldn't be home for another ten days and who would think to look in their garage?

After considering all the angles, I decided that my neighbors' garage was clearly the best short-term option and as long as I could sneak in there without Dutch noticing, I'd be home free until I heard from Candice.

When I got to my subdivision, I took the long route around the north end so that I could approach the Witts' from the west instead of the east, as most of the windows I knew Dutch would be peering out as he waited for me to get home were at the other end of the house.

It was still dark out and I cut the lights on the car again as I came around the bend, parking between two houses midway down the street. As I cut the engine, I looked around, listening and watching for any sounds of approaching cars.

The sub was blissfully quiet and after waiting a few

more seconds just to be sure, I opened the door and hopped out. Jogging along the sidewalk, I lifted my gaze to the upstairs windows of the houses I passed, nervous and jittery about being seen. At last I made it down the Witts' driveway and lifted the little panel of the garage door keypad before consulting my phone for the Witts' garage code. "Six-two-seven-four," I recited, punching in the code and hitting enter. The door lifted and I sighed in relief at the fact that they also had a wonderfully quiet garage door. (Maybe Dutch and Scott Witt had compared silicone notes?) I tapped my foot impatiently while the door rose, then ducked under it and hurried to the back to punch the button to close the door again before it fully opened. I didn't want anybody to see me fishing around in here. Still, when my phone vibrated in my back pocket, I jumped. Deciding it might be best to pick up the line before Dutch put out a BOLO alert, I answered the call with a cheery, "Hey, sweetheart!"

There was a pause, then, "You okay?"

"Terrific."

"Wanna tell me where you are?"

I poked around at some yard supplies on the Witts' back shelves. "Not particularly."

"Is Candice with you?"

I sighed. "No."

"Are you lying to me right now?"

Pulling at a small bag of potting soil next to the shelves, I said, "Not this time. Pinkie swear."

There was another pause, then, "You sound like you're in a cave."

I eyed the large three-car garage. I knew Dutch was trying to figure out where I might be. "I had something to take care of, but I'll be home very soon."

"How soon is soon?"

I smiled. "Sooner than you think."

"Good. The police are on their way. I'd turn that soon into quick if I were you."

My back stiffened. "Noted. See you in a few."

I hung up with Dutch and tugged again at the potting soil. There was a big terra-cotta flowerpot behind it that was large enough to conceal the file and the money, so without further delay I shoved the goods into the pot, then put the bag of dirt on top for good measure and punched the button for the door again.

I made it back to my car thirty seconds later but had to resist the urge to start the car and head straight home. If I arrived too early, Dutch would know I'd been very close by when I picked up his call, and I wouldn't put it past him to connect the dots—after all, he'd been with me when the Witts had asked us to look after their place.

I waited three full minutes before pulling into our driveway, and immediately noticed Brice's black Volvo at the bottom of the drive. "All right, Candice," I muttered as I got out of the car, "let's see what you've gotten yourself into this time."

Dutch greeted me with an arched eyebrow. "Is there coffee?" I asked, ignoring the eyebrow.

"In the kitchen," he said. "Brice is in there."

I walked ahead of Dutch to the kitchen and the second I saw Brice, I came up short. He looked stricken, like he'd just lost his best friend, and more out of instinct than anything else, I went straight to him and gave him a hug. He stiffened against me—Brice isn't exactly the warm and fuzzy type—but then I felt his arms encircle me and he hugged me back hard. "Have you seen her?" he whispered as he let go and stepped back.

I shook my head. "No."

Brice's lips thinned and I could tell he didn't believe me. "Do you know where she is?"

I looked him in the eye. "No. I swear. I don't even know what's going on."

"You don't?" he said, looking surprised.

I shook my head and decided to be honest with him. Well, partly honest. "I got a voice mail from Candice at three a.m. She asked me to take care of something for her. That's why I went out, but I haven't heard from her or spoken to her since then."

Brice's gaze was searching my face for clues, and I could tell he suspected I knew more than I did. "Brice, I swear, I don't know where she is and I don't know what's happened. But obviously you do, so please tell me."

Brice continued to stand there and assess me, and I started to grow frustrated until Dutch moved to stand next to me and I felt him nudge my arm. When I looked down, I saw he held a cup of coffee. "Sit," he said.

I took the coffee but held my ground. "I think I want to stand."

"Dollface," he said gently, "trust me on this. You'll want to sit down."

I took a deep breath, and more to get on with it, I

took a seat at the counter, cupping the warm mug with both hands as I'd suddenly gotten a chill.

For a long moment neither Dutch nor Brice spoke, but something seemed to pass between them and at last Brice said, "Candice didn't come home last night."

My eyes widened. "She didn't?"

"No. She called me yesterday around five to say that she had to work late and wouldn't be home for dinner and that she might not be home until close to midnight. She said she'd call me again around eight or nine, but I never heard from her. I figured she was running surveillance on somebody, and I wasn't too worried about it. I fell asleep on the couch and woke up around two a.m. She wasn't home and she hadn't called or texted, so I reached out to her."

"Did you talk to her?"

"No. Her cell rang, but she didn't pick up. I was about to head out to track her down when an APD detective showed up at my door looking for Candice. She wouldn't give me any information until I flashed my badge and then she told me what Candice had done. . . ." Brice's voice trailed off at that moment and I saw disbelief in his eyes.

"What Candice had done?" I repeated, looking from Brice to Dutch. "Guys . . . what'd she *do*?"

But Brice didn't seem able to say anything more, so Dutch reached for his iPad and handed it to me. "Brice was able to get a copy of the tape," he said.

My brow furrowed. "What tape?"

"Surveillance tape from a parking garage at the airport. I should warn you—it's bad."

I took another deep breath and tapped at the screen until it lit up and displayed a frozen image of a nearly empty parking garage. The camera was angled down—it'd probably been mounted to the corner of the building—and for the first five seconds or so there wasn't much to look at, but then a yellow Porsche came into view and parked in the space almost directly across from the camera. I recognized Candice's car right away. As soon as she parked, a man came into view at the opposite end of the screen. He seemed to be walking straight for the car, pulling his luggage with one hand and holding a phone in the other. As he got to within a few feet of the car, the door opened and out stepped Candice. I recognized the new Burberry white coat she'd brought back from Vegas, as I'd greatly admired it the first time she wore it to the office.

Candice stood next to the car and the man continued to approach. It seemed he was quite happy to see her. Or maybe he was relieved. The quality of the tape was good—much better than the grainy images one usually sees—and I was about to ask who he was when Candice reached inside her coat and withdrew a gun. In the next second there was a flash and a terrible spray of red as the man's head snapped back, and then he dropped like a sack.

My hands came up to cover my mouth as I gasped in horror. And then my best friend in the whole world calmly lowered her arm, got back into the car, closed the door, and backed out of the space. She drove away without even looking back.

The tape continued to run for several more seconds

and all I could do was sit there in stunned disbelief as a pool of blood formed all around the man lying flat on his back, so obviously dead. Toward the very end of the tape a security guard came running into view. He knelt by the victim, then reached for his cell to call it in. That's when the tape ended.

I opened my mouth to say something, but my vocal cords seemed paralyzed. I tore my gaze from the screen and looked first at Brice, who was staring hard at the floor, and then at Dutch, whose face was pinched with concern. And that's when I knew how truly bad this was. Dutch's cop face is made of granite. He's impossible to read even in the worst of scenarios because he closes down all emotion and it's "just the facts, ma'am." But here he was looking like he'd just been punched in the gut, much like I was feeling, and his expression said more than anything that our lives had all just permanently changed.

"It's a mistake," I rasped, willing myself to say something, anything, to reject what I'd just seen.

"It's no mistake," Brice said, so softly that I almost didn't hear him. "That's Candice's car. Her coat. Her gun. It's her."

I turned my attention back to the video, blinking hard as I rewound the tape to just before the car door opened. I let it play and squinted at the screen. I watched the door open, and out came her left leg. I recognized her boots. They were new just like the coat. White calfskin Ferragamo boots. I'd drooled over them just the day before in fact. I'd seen Candice briefly in the morning when I'd gone into the office to pay some bills and schedule a few appointments. I hadn't had any readings, but I'd stopped to chat with my BFF before leaving and I'd taken note of those gorgeous boots.

I'd mentally noted that Candice seemed to have spent a good deal of money in Vegas, but I hadn't thought it was anything to be alarmed about because Candice had been left a small fortune by her grand-mother, and truth be told, she was doing pretty well as a PI here in Austin. I knew for a fact that the shopping in Vegas was amazing, and it hadn't surprised me that she'd taken advantage of all the designer-label stores on the Strip.

Besides, Candice always looked good. She wore nothing but the best—stylish without being overly flashy—something I'd always admired because, left to my own devices, I'd live in Lululemon yoga pants and hoodies.

So even more than the coat and the boots, the way she exited the car so smooth and catlike convinced me that my BFF had been the woman in the video. The woman who'd just murdered an unarmed man in cold blood. It left me stunned, and breathless. I turned to Brice again, imagining what he must be feeling. He looked gutted. Just gutted by the magnitude of what was on that video.

"Brice, I—"

"What did she say on the voice mail, Abby?" Brice interrupted before I could say anything more. "What did she want you to do for her?"

I bit my lip. Brice wasn't asking. He was demanding. And I couldn't tell him. As damning as that video was,

I wasn't ready to throw away my faith in my best friend, the woman who'd saved my life on more than one occasion. "She wanted me to lock up her laptop."

Brice's eyes narrowed. "Lock up her laptop?"

I nodded. I hadn't seen Candice's laptop when I'd entered her office. If she didn't take it with her, she always locked it in the top drawer of her desk, and that's where I assumed it might be.

"Did you?" he asked. "Did you lock up her laptop?"

I licked my lips nervously as both my boss and my husband eyed me closely. For the record I'm a terrible liar. Also for the record Candice can turn lying into an art form. She'd taught me that the secret to telling a lie is to pepper it with a little truth. So that's what I did. I peppered. "When I got to the office, I didn't see her laptop. It wasn't on the desk or anywhere else in the office that I could find."

Dutch crossed his arms. I thought he might be on the fence about believing me. "Did someone take it?"

I shrugged. "I don't think so. The place was neat as a pin, just like she usually keeps it. Nothing had been disturbed that I could tell."

Brice's gaze shifted to Dutch. "What could be on the laptop?"

"Don't know. But my guess is once APD is done tossing your place, they'll move on to the girls' offices."

My eyes bugged. "Tossing what, now?"

"That APD detective who came looking for Candice also came with a search warrant. I heard her on the phone ordering a patrol car to head to your offices and stand guard until she could get there to serve out the rest of the warrant."

My mind flashed to the two squad cars outside our office building. I figured I'd barely escaped their notice. At that moment the doorbell rang and I jumped.

"That'll be them," Dutch said.

"Them?" I repeated. "You mean the cops?"

Dutch nodded.

"They'll want to talk to you, Abby," Brice told me as Dutch turned toward the front door. "They're looking for Candice and they'll leave no stone unturned." And then something flickered in his eyes and his gaze moved to my cell phone, which was on the counter next to me. "They'll ask you if you've heard from her. If you tell them about the voice mail, they'll want to hear it." And then Brice gave me a meaningful look before turning away to go over to the coffeepot and pour himself some more coffee.

I didn't stick around for another hint. I grabbed my phone and hustled to the bedroom.

Chapter Two

After closing and locking the door, I ran to the master bath and closed and locked that door too. Then I tapped at the screen of my iPhone until I'd pulled up the voice mail, but suddenly realized that deleting the message wouldn't permanently remove it from the phone's hard drive. I'd seen the bureau's tech forensic specialist recall all sorts of deleted material off phones before. Still, I thought that might buy me a little time, so I went ahead and got rid of it and for added measure I turned the phone off completely. Then I looked around the bathroom for a hiding place. Opening the cabinet door, I got down on my hands and knees and angled my cell up to wedge it between the sink and the cabinet, then quickly backed out, stood up, flushed the toilet, and ran the water for a minute before opening the door. Entering the kitchen from the living room, I saw Dutch bringing in a woman with long black curly hair, wearing a blue blazer and dress slacks. I'd put her in her mid-thirties. She walked with confidence and there was an intelligence in her eyes that I knew I shouldn't underestimate.

Self-consciously I ran a hand through my hair and stepped over to Brice. "Good morning," she said, flashing her badge. "I'm Detective Grayson."

I shook my head and blinked. "Detective Grayson?" I repeated.

"Miss Cooper, I presume?" she said, a slight smile to her lips. "Or should I say Mrs. Rivers?"

I blushed in spite of myself. Although I'd only spoken to her on the phone, Detective Grayson had assisted Candice and me with an investigation into a series of suicide bombings that'd plagued the Austin area several months before. The case had very nearly blown up in our faces—literally—and although Grayson's assistance had been rather minor, it'd still proven to be a crucial piece to the puzzle. To think she'd be the one leading the investigation into the Candice mess seemed a crazy coincidence.

"It's nice to finally meet you, Detective," I said, sticking out my hand to shake hers. "And thank you again for helping us with the bombing case."

Grayson's grip was sure and strong, and I knew she caught the fact that my palm was sweaty. "I read all about what happened to you in the paper," Grayson said. "Sounds like it was quite an ordeal for you, and on your wedding day to boot."

I shrugged. It'd been the worst experience of my life, but I couldn't let myself be distracted by that awful day now. I was still reeling from what I'd seen on the tape, and wondering how much I should reveal to Grayson. "It wasn't my best day, that's for sure."

Grayson nodded like she understood completely. I'll admit I was a little thrown by her demeanor. She appeared far too congenial given the situation.

After letting go of my hand, she nodded to Brice. "Agent Harrison. I assume you've informed Mrs. Rivers of the events of this evening involving her business partner?"

"Her business partner and *my wife*," Brice said, his tone a little sharp. "She's aware of the situation, Detective Grayson."

Grayson's congenial manner never wavered. "Good," she said. "Then we can get down to brass tacks. Mrs. Rivers—or is it Ms. Cooper? Which do you prefer?"

I felt Dutch's gaze land on me. This was a stupid bone of contention between us. I'd kept my last name because I was the independent, modern-woman type, and he really wanted me to take his last name because he was the traditional, caveman type. Right now, however, was not the time to pick a fight, so I settled for a happy medium. "We're all friends here," I said. "How about you call me Abby."

"Okay," Grayson said. "Abby, when was the last time you saw or talked to your business partner, Candice Fusco?"

"Yesterday morning."

Grayson pulled out a sleek silver pen and began writing in a notebook that looked dog-eared and filled with other notes. "I see," she said, laying the notebook on the counter for easier writing. And then she seemed to notice the countertop. "Wow. I love this granite."

Dutch and I exchanged a look of surprise. "Thanks," I said. Maybe this wouldn't be so bad. Maybe I could be all friendly-like and dodge most of the incriminating questions.

Grayson focused back on her notes. "You say yesterday morning was the last time you spoke with your business partner?"

"Yes."

"How did she seem?"

I shrugged. "Fine."

"Fine?"

"Yes."

"Define 'fine,'" Grayson said, those intelligent eyes squinting a bit.

I shrugged again. "She seemed unfettered. Normal. Business as usual."

"Are you two friends outside of work?"

"Yes."

"How close are you?"

"Close."

"Besties close?" she pressed.

I sighed. She'd find out sooner or later. "Yes. Candice is my best friend and she's also my business partner."

Grayson tapped her pen, and behind her I could see Brice scowling. He didn't like her easy-breezy manner. I could hardly blame him given the circumstances.

"And what time was this meeting you had yesterday?" Grayson asked next.

I scratched my head. "It wasn't a meeting," I said,

irritated that she seemed to be reading into my words. "I went to the office to catch up on some paperwork, and Candice was there. I poked my head in to say good morning and we chitchatted for a little bit before I left the office around eleven a.m."

"And you're sure that's the last time you saw or heard from her?"

I swallowed hard but stuck to my guns. "Yes. Positive."

Grayson cocked her head. "I see," she said. "You didn't meet up with her somewhere within the past hour or so?"

My brow furrowed and I felt my palms start to sweat again. "No."

Grayson set down her pen, that easy-breezy manner becoming more serious. "The hood of your car is warm, Abby. It's a cool night out, so I can only assume the engine was running not long before I showed up."

Out of the corner of my eye I saw Dutch edge a little closer to me. I knew he'd have my back no matter how I played this out. "I went for a drive," I said.

"In the middle of the night?" Grayson asked.

"Yeah. I get insomnia and sometimes a car ride helps me relax enough to be able to get back to sleep."

Grayson cocked an eyebrow. She didn't believe a word of it. "Where'd you go?"

"Around."

"Around where?"

I shrugged for a third time. "I like to drive in the hills. The view is nice."

Grayson blinked. "At four a.m.? What view can you see before dawn?"

I felt a blush touch my cheeks. "The houses are usually lit up. There're some really beautiful homes in this hood."

Grayson smiled, but it wasn't an "I totally believe you" smile. It was more "Nice try, Miss Liar-liar-pants-on-fire."

"What do you know about the vic?" Brice asked, and I was grateful for the redirection.

Grayson glanced his way and said, "All we know so far is that the vic was a sixty-three-year-old white male and a resident of Palm Springs, California."

"That's it?" Brice pressed.

Grayson looked at Brice in a way that suggested she wasn't sure how much to tell him. True, Brice was FBI, but he was also married to the suspect in a murder investigation. At last she seemed to make up her mind and said, "No. That's not it. He was also an MD."

My breath caught. Candice had killed a doctor? Up to that moment I had afforded my BFF some license in this whole murdering-a-man-in-cold-blood thing. I mean, I trusted Candice with my life because she was perhaps the smartest, most capable, most dependable person I'd ever known. There were even secret parts of me that thought I might perhaps trust her more than my own husband. And if she'd really shot someone in cold blood, well, then I was willing to believe she'd done it for a very good reason. Like the guy was a serial killer. Or a child molester. Or a hit man who'd been contracted to kill Brice. Or a serial-killing, child-molesting hit man who maybe also abused puppies and kittens. The point was that I knew my best friend, and she wasn't a loose cannon. If she shot to kill, it was for a damn good reason.

But what reason could Candice have to kill an unarmed doctor from Palm Springs? My eyes searched Brice's face for an explanation, but he seemed as troubled and confused as I was.

Then Grayson pointed to me and Brice and said, "Does the name Dr. David Robinowitz mean anything to either of you?"

I shook my head. I'd never heard of the guy. Brice shook his head too. "What was his specialty?" Brice asked.

"We're not sure," Grayson said. "My team is still trying to track down his next of kin, but we may have to wait until midmorning our time before we can find someone who's awake in California."

"Candice hasn't been to California in years," I said, knowing this all had to be one giant misunderstanding. "How would she even know of this doctor from Palm Springs?"

Grayson wiggled her pen. "According to the doctor's itinerary, he came into town on a direct flight from Las Vegas. His plane landed at eleven forty p.m. yesterday and he was shot at approximately twelve oh two this morning on an upper deck of short-term parking at ABIA."

A chill went through me as I remembered something from the previous morning's conversation with Candice. We'd been talking about our schedules and I'd asked Candice if she might like to catch a movie with me later that evening. She'd declined, saying that she had a busy night of work lined up and that she had to pick up a package at ABIA for a client.

I hadn't thought anything of it. Candice worked plenty of cases without me and lately she'd been working all of her cases alone. I'd assumed we were working fewer investigations together because my BFF was pulling back on accepting the more dangerous cases for a while to give us both a break, and I hadn't complained because I'd been settling into married life and building up my own private client list. The past six months had been a lovely vacation from all the mayhem and murder of previous years. I'd even been ducking my duties with the FBI because I just needed to step back and feel normal again. My routine had devolved into reading for private clients four days a week and puttering around our beautiful new home the rest of the time. It was wonderfully relaxed if also a bit dull.

"Abby?" I heard Grayson say, and I realized she'd asked me a question while I'd been thinking about the conversation with Candice the day before.

"Come again?" I asked.

"I said, were you aware that your business partner was meeting someone at the airport last evening?"

"No," I answered truthfully. I mean, I knew she was going to the airport, but I didn't know she was *meeting* somebody there. Somebody she was going to shoot at point-blank range.

"And you've never heard of this Dr. Robinowitz?"

"No. I swear. I've never heard of him. And I have no idea what his connection could be to Candice."

"And she hasn't been in contact with you since yesterday morning?"

Uh-oh. We were getting into tricky waters here. "I already told you," I said. "I haven't spoken to her since yesterday morning."

"No texts or phone calls either?" Grayson pushed.

I had a feeling she'd ask that, so I made a big show of going to my purse and digging through it. "If you don't believe me, you can check my phone. Wait. Where's my phone?" I dug through my purse with a little more urgency, then dumped all the contents out on the counter and fished around like I was frantic to find my cell. Then I looked up at Dutch and said, "Honey, have you seen my phone?"

There was a flicker of recognition in his eyes and he said, "Can't say I've seen it since yesterday, Abs."

"Hmmm. Maybe it's in the car," I said, and began to head for the door.

Grayson stopped me by calling out my name. "That's okay," she said. "You can check it later. Right now I have one or two more questions for you."

Those "one or two" questions turned into something closer to fifty and it was another two hours before Grayson finally wrapped up her interview. She'd asked me all sorts of questions: how Candice and I had met, what I knew about her family, where she might have gone in the hours since the shooting.

And that was the question that bothered me the most. I had no idea where Candice might be. And I could tell that Brice didn't know either. In parting, Grayson said that our offices were currently being searched, but the warrant didn't extend to my half, which was a relief. Still, the detective asked my permission to look through my suite, and I immediately declined. I'd seen enough search warrant aftermaths to know that tidiness and leaving things as they found them wasn't a priority. Plus, I had no idea what kind of incriminating evidence might show up in my suite. Candice had access to both of my offices. She could easily have attempted to hide something on my side of our shared space.

Grayson also said that we should be aware that a BOLO alert for Candice had been issued, along with a press release about the crime that named Candice as a person of interest. The police and citizens of Austin were warned to be on the lookout for a woman fitting Candice's description, who was armed and extremely dangerous, driving a yellow Porsche. The public was urged to dial 911 immediately if she was spotted.

When Grayson finally left, I felt sick to my stomach. Brice looked white as a sheet, and even Dutch seemed shocked and troubled. "What do we do?" I asked into the long silence that followed Grayson's exit.

Brice moved over to the kitchen table and sank into one of the chairs. "What was she thinking?" he asked.

"There has to be an explanation," I insisted.

"She left you a message, right?" he asked. I nodded. "Get your phone and let's listen to it."

I bit my lip. "No," I said. When Brice's brow lowered to the danger zone, I added, "Brice, you have to trust me—it's for your own good."

My boss tapped his finger on the counter impatiently and then he tried a different tack. "Fine, then at least tell us the gist of what she said, other than asking you to lock up her computer." Brice's tone was sharp. He wanted answers and he wasn't going to be put off.

I glanced at Dutch, and saw that he was studying me closely. He'd let it be my call as to what I told Brice. I decided to confess the less important parts. "She started off by saying that it wasn't how it looked."

Brice's brow furrowed and in his eyes I saw a hint of hope. "She said that?"

I nodded. "Yeah. She asked me to trust her. That it wasn't how it looked, but she knew it looked bad."

Dutch motioned with his chin toward the iPad on the counter. "How else *could* it look?"

I shook my head. "I don't know. But Candice would never assassinate someone in cold blood."

"What did she say *exactly*?" Brice asked next.

"Well, like I already told you, she wanted me to go to the office because she was worried about her computer. Maybe she thought she left it out, or maybe she thought that someone might try to break in and take it."

"Candice usually takes that computer everywhere she goes," Brice replied. "I haven't seen it out of her reach in months."

"Well, maybe she had to leave it behind for some reason and couldn't get back to lock it up." I had no idea whether Candice had her computer with her, but it was a good decoy and cover story that I badly needed the boys to buy into so that they wouldn't press me for details of the rest of Candice's message. She didn't want me to show that file to anybody, and Candice was still my BFF. Until I had proof that she wasn't who I thought she was, I'd believe in her and help her any way I could.

"What else?" Brice asked.

I shrugged. "Nothing, really. It was short and sweet."

"What time did her call come in?" He wasn't gonna let me off the hook so easy.

"Just after three a.m."

"So, she shoots this Dr. Robinowitz at midnight and then lays low for the next three hours until she decides to reach out to Abby?" Dutch said. "That doesn't make sense. She had plenty of time to go back to the office and lock up her computer. What'd she do during those three hours?"

Brice shook his head. "She didn't come home. That's all I can tell you." Then he looked back at me. "How did she sound?"

"Sound?"

"Yeah. Was she anxious? Upset? Scared?"

I closed my eyes recalling the message. "None of those, really. I mean, even when Candice is freaked-out, you'd never know it. But there was . . ."

"What?"

"I don't know. There was this note of . . . I guess . . . alarm, and maybe something else. Her voice sounded strained, like she was upset, or alarmed or stressed-out, and she was trying really hard to keep it together, but there was something uncharacteristic there too. It's hard to tell with Candice."

"Did she say where she was calling from? Or where she was going?"

I shook my head. "I know she was outside—"

"How do you know she was outside?" Harrison asked.

I closed my eyes to concentrate on the memory of Candice's message again. "I could hear the wind," I said. "As she was talking, I could hear the wind. And also, toward the end it sounded like she was running."

I opened my eyes to see Brice staring at me with that same stricken look on his face. "She was running?" he asked, and I nodded. "From whom?"

I sighed. "I don't know. There were no other voices or footfalls in the background. Just Candice."

Brice's gaze dropped to the floor, but I could clearly see the worry in the set to his shoulders. "Abby, please, let us listen to the voice mail," Brice said next.

I shifted on my feet. "No, Brice, you can't." When his gaze lifted back up to me, I added, "I'm sorry, but I've already deleted it."

Brice's expression turned angry. "Why the *hell* would you do that, Cooper? Don't you realize you've just destroyed a key piece of evidence? There could be something on that voice mail that you missed! It could be the way to finding her! What were you thinking?!"

I took a step back. Brice had never lost his cool with me like that before. Okay, maybe once when we'd first started working together, but that was before I actually *liked* him. Back then I thought he was a serious douche bag and he thought me a serious fraud.

Dutch held up his hand and said, "Hey, lay off, Harrison. She's trying to help."

Brice's anger subsided, but only a fraction. He glared hard at Dutch, then back at me; then he seemed to settle for looking meanly at the floor again.

For a minute I debated coming clean with both of them. I mean, I'd done as Candice asked before I knew she'd murdered someone in cold blood. I just couldn't shake the image of Dr. Robinowitz walking up to my best friend looking so trusting and happy to see her. And that sparked a thought and I said, "Brice, in the video the doctor seems to recognize Candice. Did you ever hear her mention anything about this Robinowitz guy?"

Brice shook his head and sighed. "No. If she knew him, then she didn't mention him to me."

"Did she ever bring up the name to you, dollface?" Dutch asked me.

I racked my brain for any memory of Candice mentioning a doctor from Palm Springs. I came up with nothing. "Maybe it would help if we could figure out what kind of doctor he was," I suggested.

Dutch reached for his iPad. After a minute or two of tapping he said, "Robinowitz retired his practice in Palm Springs six months ago. The old site says he was a board-certified plastic surgeon."

"Why was he coming into Austin through Vegas?" I asked.

"Connecting flight?" Brice suggested.

Dutch shook his head, continuing to tap at the screen. "I don't think so. Looks like he might've moved to Vegas four months ago. I found a condo listed under his name there. And I think I know why Grayson is confused about his residence; from what I can see, he's still listing his address in Palm Springs because it hasn't sold yet and he probably wanted the tax write-off until he off-loaded it."

I rubbed my temples. None of this was making any sense. "Why would Candice want to kill a plastic surgeon?"

"Why would Candice want to kill anyone?" Brice replied.

"The answer could be on that computer," Dutch said, referring to my decoy and cover story.

"If she left it at the office, APD would've confiscated it by now," Brice said.

"Does she back it up to a cloud?" my hubby asked.

Brice's brow lifted. "Yeah. I think she does."

I said nothing. For the record I knew that Candice only backed up certain things to the cloud like her address book and calendar. My BFF was intensely personal and perhaps a weensy bit paranoid, so she kept a lot of what she was up to off the grid. Still, it was a direction for the boys to go in and it would allow me time to figure out what the heck to do next. And, luckily, I already had a plan forming.

I left the boys to the task of trying to track down Candice's cloud account, and headed back into the bedroom for a shower and some much-needed think time. I knew that the first step was going to be to abandon my cell phone. I'd have to get rid of it altogether because Brice wasn't about to let me get away with the "I erased the voice mail" excuse. I had a pretty good feeling that the minute my head was turned, he'd lift it out of my purse or off my person and claim to know nothing about its whereabouts while ushering it down to bureau forensics to see what they could recover.

While the water was heating up, I retrieved the phone

from its hiding place and eyed it moodily. I loved my phone and it was practically brand-new. I wasn't due for an upgrade, so replacing it was going to be expensive, but what choice did I have? If Brice discovered that Candice had entrusted me to retrieve and hide a file for her, he'd never let up until I handed it over.

Also, I wasn't exactly sure when I'd last backed up the phone, but my computer was at the office and I couldn't risk taking the phone there and have it become part of the search warrant. I knew Grayson was a little ticked that I wasn't cooperating by allowing her to check my side of the suite, but no way did I want APD snooping through my stuff. I had a feeling she'd be working to find a way to extend the search, and I didn't want my phone caught in the middle. The Austin PD had computer forensics people too.

With a sigh I turned the phone on one last time to see if Candice had called, and when I saw that she hadn't, I took the phone into the shower with me. It took only thirty seconds under the spray to completely fry the hard drive. The only thing the phone would be good for now was a paperweight. True, the forensics guys might still be able to retrieve something, but it'd take them that much longer, and time to help figure this thing out was something I knew I needed to fight for.

After I'd gotten myself together, I went to the door, opened it a crack, and listened. I could hear Brice and Dutch talking. My hubby was asking Brice some pointed questions.

"This guy had a condo in Vegas. Do you think she could've met him on your honeymoon?"

There was a pause, then, "I don't know, Rivers. It's possible. There were at least a couple of days where I played two rounds of golf while Candice was out shopping. If she met this guy on one of those days, or had some other encounter with him, she didn't make me aware of it."

"How did she seem in Vegas?" Dutch pressed.

I heard Brice sigh heavily. "For the first couple of days, she seemed great. Happy. Relieved even that we'd taken the final step. But then something changed."

"What?"

"I don't know. I thought maybe she was missing Abby, and having second thoughts about eloping without her best friend in tow. Abby's the only person besides me that counts as family in Candice's eyes. Hell, sometimes I think she trusts Abby more than she does me."

I winced. I could tell that it bugged Brice that Candice had called me and not him, and that what he'd just said was undoubtedly true. But I'd known Candice longer, and we'd saved each other's lives a number of times. Bonds forged in life-or-death situations ran deep. Deeper even than marriage vows.

"So something changed in Vegas and you thought it was that she missed Abby, but now you think it could've been something else?"

"Given what's on that video, it was definitely something else."

"Candice was born just outside Vegas—you knew that, right?"

"Yeah. She told me about her life there. Her sister's car accident. Her mother dying of cancer and her dad's heart attack three years later. Poor woman was an orphan before she was twenty."

"Did she tell you about her first husband?" Dutch asked next. It rubbed me a little wrong that he was airing all of Candice's dirty laundry.

"She mentioned being young and falling for a guy who trained her as a PI, then helped her get her license. Candice never talked much about their split, only that she was naive and trusting and it took her a few years to wise up."

"Did she tell you about the fake driver's license from Nevada?" Dutch asked next. I felt increasingly defensive of my best friend and I wanted to march out there and tell him to shut it.

"You mean the one with her sister's info on it? She didn't pull it out for my inspection, but she did say that she had an alternate identity and the name on the fake ID was her sister's. Why? You think maybe Candice is using the fake ID now?"

"If I were her and I wanted to disappear, that's the tactic I'd use."

"Okay," Brice said. "I'll set up a trace on her license. Maybe she used it to open up a credit card or book a flight and we'll get a hit on her location."

There was a long pause. Then Dutch said, "Why don't you let me work on finding Candice?"

"You?" Brice said, his tone hardening. "She's *my* wife, Rivers."

"Exactly my point, buddy. Given the circumstances, what do you think Director Gaston is gonna say to utilizing the bureau's resources to find your wife, who's now the primary suspect in a murder investigation by the APD?"

Brice sighed again. "I have a conference call scheduled with him later this morning. I don't even know if he's heard yet, but you're right. Once he finds out, he'll order me not to get involved. Which means I'll have to order you to butt out as well."

"I can call Milo and have him work it off the grid," Dutch suggested. Milo was Dutch's best friend and business partner in the private security firm my hubby had started many years ago, and which, in recent years, had provided us with a pretty cushy lifestyle. Milo still lived in our old neighborhood back in Michigan while he waited for his youngest son to graduate from high school; then he had plans to move down to Austin and work at the security firm from here to be closer to Dutch. I wondered what he'd say when he learned about what'd happened.

"Isn't Milo still in Michigan?" Brice asked.

"Yeah, but he has sources. And I can make discreet inquiries."

I cocked an eyebrow. My hubby was known for his discreet inquiries.

"What about Abby?" Brice said next. My other eyebrow joined its twin at the top of my forehead. "We haven't even asked her to use her radar yet."

Aw crap. I'd purposely withheld giving any intuitive insight into what was going on because I didn't want to give the boys anything useful until I had a chance to assess the situation. But as soon as Brice asked Dutch about it, I knew his next move would be to knock on the bedroom door and ask me to come back out to flip that intuitive switch and start spilling.

So I did the only mature, reasonable, well-thought-out thing I could. I gently shut the bedroom door, locking it, before heading to the window to slide it open, knock out the screen, and shimmy into the backyard. "Thank God for a master bedroom on the first floor," I said after wiping my hands and cruising around to the far side of the house. I let myself out of the gate and trotted to the car. I figured I had maybe fifteen seconds before Dutch doubled back and poked his head out the front door. Luckily for me, it took less than ten to exit the driveway.

Once I was on the road, I took a look at the clock on the dashboard. It wasn't even seven a.m. I didn't quite know what to do or where to go first, but luckily my stomach decided for me. With a little grumble it reminded me that I hadn't eaten in nearly twelve hours.

I drove to a favorite spot of mine—coincidentally it was a place Candice had introduced me to—and easily found a secluded spot to sit and order coffee and a breakfast burrito. I'm a *huge* fan of breakfast. And burritos.

After polishing off the delicious meal, I dug through my purse for a pen and the small notebook I kept for grocery lists and the like. I then closed my eyes and took some deep breaths, willing myself to relax. Then I flipped on my radar and let the impressions unfold.

I don't think most people realize that there is no garden-variety psychic. We're as varied as any profession that has a multitude of specialties. For my private clients, my specialty is predicting the future, but for the Feds, I'm just as adept at peering into the past.

Specifically, when I'm working a case, I think of time like a ribbon stamped or punctuated by events. Some events are mutable. They haven't happened yet, but in the ether they are likely to take place. This could be something like, if I were to see jail bars, I know that eventually the suspect will be brought to justice. Other events, however, are immutable; i.e., they've already taken place and all I have to do is focus on them to get a feel for what actually happened.

If I have a starting point, I can look into the ether and talk in detail about those events at that specific point on the ribbon, like who was there, how the event unfolded, what led up to the event, and best of all, sometimes I'll even discover some lost clue or unnoticed fact that can help my investigative team home in on a suspect.

My track record is pretty good—it'd have to be to work with the Feds—but there are limitations. I don't tend to see things unfolding my mind like a movie. If I'm able to describe a suspect, it's often in the sketchiest of terms, like the suspect has dark hair, dark eyes, pale complexion. If I'm really lucky, sometimes I'll even have an inkling as to how he or she relates to the victim. I don't get names, addresses, or phone numbers, and I don't think I've ever been able to definitively say that Colonel Mustard did it in the library with the candlestick, but I can often point my team in a direction that helps move the case forward. So I was fairly confident that I'd be able to get something off the events in the parking garage from the night before.

What I found in the ether troubled me greatly. I felt strongly that Candice knew the victim prior to his murder. I also felt strongly that she'd meant to meet up with him in that parking garage. I could sense that she'd had some sort of appointment with him, that they'd agreed to meet. Why she'd murdered him eluded me, but there were traces of other troubling things in the ether too.

Hoping that perhaps the good doctor wasn't so good after all, I homed in on his energy—maybe Candice had had a very good reason for shooting him—but what I came back with was that he'd been a fairly decent man.

I kept getting this feeling like Robinowitz had been the victim of a betrayal. Like he'd been trying to make amends or do something good to atone for something else, and he'd come to Austin to fulfill that promise, but it'd all blown up in his face. Literally.

And the betrayal ran deep. I made a notation on my pad that there were other players involved and I could sense a strong connection back to Vegas. The more I looked, the bigger the picture seemed to get and the more confusing. There was another woman at the center of all this; everything seemed to swirl around her. It wasn't Candice that I was picking up on; it was another female, unknown to me. All I could tell about her was that she wasn't to be trusted and that she had dark hair and light eyes. She felt attractive to my senses, and I was convinced that this woman turned heads when she was in public.

She was linked to Candice, but the oddest thing was that I couldn't say for sure that Candice knew her.

Every time I tried to focus on what happened to Dr. Robinowitz, this woman's energy popped up as the root cause.

After nearly half an hour of jotting down my impressions and going back over the clues in the ether, I finally laid down my pen and rubbed my temple. I had a headache from trying to make sense of all the discordant parts.

"Cassidy," I muttered, using Candice's nickname. "What the hell have you gotten yourself mixed up in?" (Swearing doesn't count when your BFF is accused of murder and you have no idea how to help her.)

Pushing past the throbbing in my temple, I tried to find Candice in the ether. My BFF hums a little low, and by that, I mean that her energy—or her essence, if you will—isn't very "loud."

A small minority of people vibrate on high, and finding them in the ether is like suddenly hitting on a nearby radio station. The transmission is loud and crystal clear; there's no static or guesswork. The majority of people, however, have a medium sort of vibration—you can find them, but it may take searching the airwaves for the perfect dial setting. Since Candice is in the low-vibration category, she's hard to find. You have to hunt. And she's usually on the AM dial amid a sea of static.

I've shared this observation with her before. On her birthday every year I've given her a personal reading and to prep her I always say, "Okay, now remember, when we sit together, you've got to open yourself up." What I mean by that is that Candice has to come to the session with a willingness to be read. She has to allow me in past those walls she's had up since the car accident that took her sister. That's hard for her, I know, but if she doesn't come to the reading with the right frame of mind, I have to work extra hard to pull even the smallest details out of the ether.

And my BFF is a wily one. I know for a fact that she sometimes puts my limitations with her energy to the test. In other words, if Candice doesn't want me to find her, she usually gets her wish.

So I wasn't surprised when I barely registered her pulse on my radar. "Damn you," I muttered as I focused all my intuitive ability right at her, trying to pick up any clue I could. But it was pretty pointless. All I could tell was that Candice was for the moment safe, but where she was I hadn't a clue.

I then tried to read her emotions and what I found was that she seemed alarmed and upset. But not the weepy kind of upset—more the "I'mma kill you" kind of upset. With her track record of the past twenty-four hours, I found that super worrisome. She seemed intent on getting even, but for what or with whom I couldn't even scratch the surface. I mean, hadn't she already brought the hammer down on Robinowitz? What havoc was she going to wreak next?

Taking a break from focusing on her energy, I sat back and considered that the answer might be hidden in that file she'd had me take out of her safe, and now that I'd already been interviewed by APD, I figured maybe I could take a peek at the contents of the file without committing perjury. But there was no way I could go back to the Witts' to retrieve it in broad daylight. I'd go later that evening when it was dark again. I didn't quite know how I was going to fill the whole day, but I did know that I needed to get a new phone, so after leaving enough to cover the bill and a generous tip on the table, I headed out.

I dozed off in the car waiting for the cell phone store to open and when I woke up, there was a note under my windshield. I blinked to clear the bleariness and got out to inspect the note.

Reaching out the window, I lifted the folded piece of paper out from under the wiper and, when I opened it, saw that it revealed a sequence of numbers. That's all, just a set of ten numbers. I turned the paper over, but nothing else was written there.

Looking up, I glanced around the parking lot to see who might've left it, but there was no one around and mine was the only car in the lot. I looked back at the note and muttered, "What the hell is this?" (Okay, so that probably cost me a quarter.)

Puzzled, I glanced at the clock on the dash. It was just before nine. I got out, locked up, and approached the double doors of the store, hoping they were open, and saw an employee walking toward me holding up a set of keys. She undid the lock and as I entered, I said, "Did you happen to see anybody around my car a few minutes ago?"

Her brow furrowed. "Around your car?" I pointed to the only one in the lot. "No," she said, shaking her head. "But I just got here about ten minutes ago myself. My car is out back. Why? Did someone hit you?"

"No," I said. "Just someone left a note on my windshield, but I'm not sure who."

"What'd it say?" she asked, then covered her mouth. "Oh, sorry. I don't mean to be nosy."

"No, don't worry about it," I said. "It's cool. Here, look at this. It's just a set of numbers, but I don't know what it's supposed to mean."

The girl leaned forward. Her name tag read TANISHA. "That could be a phone number."

I squinted at the digits. They began with 702. "If it is a phone number, it's not local."

Tanisha shrugged. "If it is a number, it starts with the area code for Las Vegas."

My head snapped up. "It does?"

Tanisha nodded. "My mom and my grandma both live there. That's their area code."

I felt tingly with excitement. "Tanisha, I'll need to purchase a new phone today. As quick as possible. I'm not due for an upgrade, but I brought my husband's credit card, so what do you have in the latest iPhone? I'm a bit partial to the gold one."

Once I had my shiny new gold phone in hand, I raced out of the store and back to my car. I could hardly wait to plug it in and call the number. I just knew it was Candice.

When I got to my car, however, there was another folded piece of paper on my windshield. I grabbed it greedily and opened it. There was a printed word there. It read, *Text only*.

Hustling into my car, I plugged in my phone and typed out the following message:

> Cassidy, where are you?!!!!

I watched the display for a good five minutes, which felt like fifty. Finally a new message came in.

> Did you get the file?

I sighed. I was almost afraid to reply because once I did, she'd have no reason to text me until she wanted that file back. Which gave me an idea.

> I have it. Did you want me to bring it to you?

Again I waited over a minute for her reply.

> No. Tell no one about it, or that we communicated. Delete these messages and get rid of the notes.

I typed back, desperate to have her trust me enough to help her:

> Candice! Where ARE you?!!!

But after waiting fifteen minutes, I knew there'd be no additional response. "Dammit," I muttered. (That one probably counted too.)

Candice was being particularly cagey, and I couldn't say that I blamed her, but I was her best friend and if she was going to trust someone to help her, then it had to be me or Brice. I didn't know whether she'd contact him or not, but I doubted it.

It was risky enough contacting me, but he was a whole other kettle of fish. Brice had ways and means of finding someone once he put his mind to it. If Candice wanted to remain on the lam, then the last person she could contact was Brice.

Thinking about that made me feel bad for him, because I knew he was crazy worried. And then I thought of a way I might be able to tell him she was okay without letting him know that I'd spoken to her.

I'd have to be careful, though. Brice wasn't to be underestimated, and neither was my husband. I had no doubt that the two of them would double-team me just to try to figure out where Candice was. Still, I owed it to Brice to try.

Putting the car into gear, I sped out of the parking lot, hoping my plan didn't turn into a trap.

Chapter Three

I found Brice and Dutch huddled over Brice's desk in his office. Their jaws dropped a little when I walked in. "Morning, fellas," I said casually, sashaying my way over to the small conference table.

"Where ya been, Edgar?" Dutch asked just as casually, as if he'd only just noticed I wasn't around. I wasn't buying it for a second.

"Here and there," I said, taking a seat.

"We've been calling you," Brice told me.

I tried to look confused. "Really? That's weird."

"Your phone is going straight to voice mail," Dutch said. "Is it off?"

"I think I left it at home." (In the shower.)

"Huh," the boys said together.

"Why not check your purse?" Dutch suggested, nodding his chin in the direction of my handbag like he just *knew* I was a big fat fibber. "I noticed a new charge to the Verizon store on my credit card this morning."

I smiled tightly. "Okay, okay, you caught me." I dug into my pocketbook and retrieved the brand-new phone. "Isn't it pretty?" Dutch frowned. "I'll pay you back," I promised. Dutch added a skeptical eyebrow to the frown. I could hardly blame him. I owed the swear jar close to a grand, so he probably had good reason to doubt my creditworthiness.

"We noticed this morning that you went out the back way," Dutch said next, referring to my hasty exit out the back window.

I squirmed, but just a little. "Sorry about that. I had to check something out."

"What?" they both said together.

"It's not important. What *is* important is that I had a little ping on the old radar about Candice."

"A little ping?" Dutch repeated, his eyes narrowing. He had great lie detector skills and he wasn't even psychic.

I stuck to my story. "Yeah. I've been trying to get a bead on Candice all morning."

"And?" Brice said anxiously.

"And I feel she's safe." For emphasis, I added a big grin and a nod. "Isn't that great? She's okay."

Dutch came to sit down next to me. "Where is she?"

"Don't know," I told him, which was the truth. "The only feeling I had was that she was tucked away somewhere safe."

"Has she tried to call you again?" Brice asked, just like I'd hoped he would.

I shrugged and placed my new phone in the center of the table I was sitting next to. Putting it on speaker,

I dialed my voice mail and heard that I had six new messages. I clicked through all the ones from Dutch (three) and all the ones from Brice (also three), and then turned up my hands before hanging up the call. "I guess she hasn't called me again."

"What aren't you telling us?" Dutch asked.

Uh-oh. "Nothing, sweetie," I said, my voice cracking.

Brice came over to sit down too. And then he did the most unexpected thing. He reached out and put a hand on my arm and as I looked at him, I saw that his eyes were a bit misty. "Abby," he said softly. "I don't know what's going on with her, and it's killing me. Please. Tell me what you know."

My gaze fell to the tabletop. I didn't want to look at Brice when I lied. "I don't know anything more than you do," I whispered. And then I lifted my chin and added, "But I do know that Candice wouldn't shoot anybody unless she had a *very* good reason. Whatever this is about, we only know a small part of the story. There's more than meets the eye, Brice. I'm sure of it."

Brice sighed and let go of my arm to sit back in his chair and rub his face. He looked exhausted. "She needs our help, Abby. I'm not psychic like you, but I can *feel* that she needs our help."

I had a good sense of that too, but there was no way I was letting Brice know I felt that way.

"I need to find out what she might've had on that laptop," Brice said, standing up to pace the floor. "Rivers, what's the name of that detective you've been mentoring at APD? We need to call him and see if he can get us a copy of the file they're building."

"Brice," Dutch said. My eyes widened a little because at the office Dutch never refers to Brice as anything other than "sir."

"Yeah?"

"You can't. If the director finds out you're digging around for intel in the APD investigation of your wife . . ." Dutch didn't finish the sentence.

But Brice didn't seem to want to listen. "What am I supposed to do? Sit back and do nothing? She's my wife, Dutch. *My wife!*"

I had an impromptu impulse and stood up to go over to Brice. I stood in front of him and his expression was just so lost, so desperate, so crushingly agonized, that I stepped forward a little more and hugged him. He stiffened and I hugged tighter. And then he let out a tremendous sigh and hugged me back. While I held on to him, I intuitively assessed his energy. He felt on the verge of panic, as if he was about to do something crazy and drastic. I saw two paths extending out into the future. One had him throwing his career away and a legal element tainting his energy—as if that drastic thing he'd be doing would get him into trouble with the law. The other path felt safer, more discreet, but barely restrained. Next to him on this path was a female with light brown hair. I focused on this second path, because I knew the female with the light brown hair was me, and when I finally let go and stood back, I knew what I needed to do.

"Dutch is right," I began. "You can't get involved. But I can. I just can't do it officially."

"What're you talking about, Cooper?" Brice asked.

He didn't seem impatient, just exhausted and so worried about Candice that he couldn't think straight.

"I can investigate this as a private citizen." Moving over to my purse, I fished around for my official FBI consultant's badge and set it on the table. "I just can't have any ties to the bureau while I do it. So as of right now, sir, I'd like to resign as your civilian profiler."

"Abs," Dutch said, holding his hands in a time-out. I wasn't surprised that he was ready to protest.

"You can't get involved either," I said to him. "Listen, you two, Candice has taught me enough over the years to be able to investigate a case on my own. No, I don't have a PI license, but I can ask questions. And I can use my intuition. I can bring you my findings as hypotheticals—there'd be nothing official about what I'd be telling you, and we could then *hypothetically* figure out a way to help Candice without jeopardizing everybody's jobs."

Dutch frowned and shook his head, but Brice looked like he was considering the idea. The silence stretched out in the room, so I finally said, "What other choice do you guys have? Any other way you slice it, if either of you goes rooting around for info and finds something out that pertains to the case, if you don't divulge it to your superiors immediately, you know you could be brought up on obstruction charges. It'd ruin your careers."

"I could resign and investigate on my own," Dutch suggested. "I make enough to live on with the security firm."

"No," I said. He cut me a look and I glared at him.

"Seriously, Dutch, no. You love this job. If you let it go and we cleared Candice, how long before you started resenting her for giving up the job you love?"

Brice moved to his desk chair and sat down heavily. "I don't like it," he said. "But Cooper's right, Rivers. What other choice do we have?"

Both Brice and I looked expectantly at Dutch. If he said no, then I'd do what I wanted anyway and our house would be tense and awful for the next few weeks. If he said yes, he'd be giving me the inch that he knew I'd turn into a country mile. Poor guy. I felt a little sorry for him.

At last he said, "Sir, would you mind if I had a private moment alone with my wife?"

Brice stood up and walked to the door. "Take as long as you need."

Once the door was shut, Dutch crooked his finger at me and I moved over to him. He pulled me forward to straddle his lap and after eyeing me thoughtfully for a few beats, he said, "To hell with hypotheticals, Edgar. There're things you're not telling us already and I know that you'll keep more to yourself than you'll reveal. Which means that if you get into trouble, we won't know it until it's too late."

I couldn't help but smile. "How about I avoid getting into trouble, then?"

"This isn't funny, dollface."

I let go of the smile. "I don't know what you want me to say. Candice needs help, and I'm the only one who can offer it to her without risking my career."

"Yeah, well, you were right about the fact that I love

what I do, but that pales in comparison to how I feel about you."

My smile returned and I cupped the side of his face. "Sometimes you say the exact perfect thing."

Dutch sighed again and bowed his head forward until it was touching mine. "Abs," he said. "There's something I gotta ask you."

Uh-oh. "Okay. But I may not be able to answer it."

"It's not about where you went last night or that bullshit story about you leaving your phone off. I have to ask . . . do you really trust Candice?"

I pulled my head back away from his. "Do I trust Candice? What kind of a question is that?"

"An honest one. You saw that video. She murdered that guy in cold blood. What's to say that she isn't who we think she is and if you get in her way, she could take you out too?"

I was so stunned that for a moment I couldn't think of a reply. Then, I spoke from the place that I knew to be true. "My gut says I can trust her. And, until it says differently, I'm going to keep doing that."

Dutch nodded. "Okay, then."

"Really?"

My hubby grinned sideways at me. "If I said no, you'd just go do your thing anyway. This way at least Brice and I will be a little more in the loop."

I wound my arms around his neck and leaned in for a kiss. "Like I said. Sometimes you say the perfect thing."

I left the bureau a short time later promising off the record to give Dutch and Brice a report on my findings.

Brice told me that I couldn't use any bureau resources, which bummed me out because, as a civilian, you can only learn so much by asking questions and digging around on the Internet.

Still, I had at least one lead: the file in the Witts' garage. I just needed to wait until dark to retrieve it. I also needed to get a look at my calendar of scheduled clients and see if I could rearrange a few of them to free up the rest of my week.

With that in mind, I headed to the office I shared with Candice and braced myself as the elevator doors opened to our floor. I had no idea what I'd find since the police had searched the place. Moving down the corridor leading to our offices, I saw the building manager standing outside our door. He looked nervous and my radar pinged. This wasn't going to be a pleasant encounter. "Good morning, Mr. Giles," I said.

"Ah, Ms. Cooper. I didn't expect to see you."

Giles appeared nervous, and he was fidgeting with an envelope that he seemed to be hesitating about whether to give to me. "That for me?" I asked, pointing to the envelope.

Giles flushed. "This? Oh, yes, uh . . ."

I held out my hand. I already knew it was bad news; I just didn't know how bad. My landlord handed it over and his blush deepened. I opened the envelope and began to read. Giles said, "It's just that the lease clearly states—"

"What's this?" I demanded. "You're *evicting* us?!"

The building manager cleared his throat and tugged

on his blazer. "You and Ms. Fusco are in violation of your lease."

I stared at him with mouth agape. "We are not! We pay our rent on time each and every month, Giles, and I have the canceled checks to prove it!"

"I'm not talking about your rent," he said, squaring his shoulders. "I'm talking about section five C, paragraph three of your lease, which clearly states that no unlawful business shall be conducted in this building."

"Unlawful?" I snapped. "I'm not violating *any* laws, Mr. Giles. My business is clean."

"I'm not referring to you, Ms. Cooper. I'm referring to your business partner, Ms. Fusco. There's a warrant out for her arrest, and we do not lease office space to felons."

And then I understood. He'd seen the news, and the police in the building serving out the search warrant. "We'll fight you in court," I said. I was so angry I wanted to smack him. "Under the law, Candice is considered innocent until *proven* guilty, Mr. Giles."

"That may well be, Ms. Cooper, but I must inform you that we are more than willing to take this matter to court if you insist. We'd welcome that, in fact."

The little bastard knew he had me. Filing a claim in court would take weeks or months, and to prove that my landlord didn't have a claim, I'd have to provide evidence that Candice was innocent, which I couldn't currently do. "This is bullshit," I told him, crumpling up the letter and throwing it on the ground.

He didn't say anything. He simply stared at me with unfriendly eyes. "You have until the end of the month."

"Two weeks from now," I growled.

Giles shrugged and turned on his heel. There would be no winning the argument with him. I shook my head and went into the office, only to stop short. "What the . . . ?" I gasped.

The place looked like a tornado had hit it. No, scratch that. It looked like an earthquake had struck first, a hurricane second, and a tornado third. There was so much debris littering the area that it was hard to see the floor. And the mess wasn't just contained to Candice's side of the office. It'd flowed all the way over to my side too.

For several seconds I just stood there gaping and blinking at the scene. It was like I was having a hard time registering the totality of it. And then I was in motion, slip-sliding to the left through the paper and broken furniture to my office, where I came up short again. I gasped anew.

My desk had been overturned and every single drawer had been removed and turned upside down. My filing cabinet was on its side on the floor and all my files were strewn about. The oil painting that Dutch had purchased for me the previous summer when we went to an art fair together had been ripped nearly in half and was lying next to my ergonomic leather chair, which had both a handle missing and a large tear right down its middle. And the wedding photo of the two of us staring lovingly into each other's eyes was also smashed and lying broken on the floor.

I felt unbidden tears sting my eyes and I turned away to shuffle through the mess to the room where I read my clients, a fairly small space that I'd so carefully decorated with the softest, most comfortable chairs, a half dozen amethyst, quartz, and citrine crystal geodes placed just so, and little artful touches that wouldn't distract.

But when I reached the doorway . . .

For long moments I simply stood there, my lower lip quivering and tears leaking down my face. And then I couldn't look at it anymore and turned away to go back to my office.

Wiping my eyes, I pulled out my new cell, but then thought better of it. Shuffling through the mess again, I managed to find the phone for the landline, which thank God was still intact, and I called 411. "Austin Police Department, nonemergency, homicide division," I said when the automated recording asked me for the listing.

An hour later Dutch was standing next to me when Detective Grayson showed up. It was hard to tell who was more ticked off between me and the hubby. I think the oil painting was the clincher for him. I'd loved it the second I saw it, but it'd been expensive, and I'd tried to talk Dutch out of buying it, but he'd wanted so much to do something special for me. It was more than just a piece of art to us; it was a sweet moment we'd shared together that now felt ruined.

"Whoa," Grayson said as she came through the door. Turning in a half circle, she looked at us and said, "What the hell happened in here?"

I blinked. I'd had an angry speech all prepared and

Dutch had even contacted our attorney, ready to file suit with the APD for violating the search warrant, but Grayson's reaction to the mess took both of us by surprise.

Dutch recovered himself first. "Don't you know, Detective?" he said angrily. "Your guys completely trashed the place *and* violated the terms of the warrant by tearing apart my wife's half of the office! I've got a call in to my attorney and I should warn you that I plan to personally speak to the chief of detectives."

It was Grayson's turn to blink in surprise. "Whoa, whoa, whoa, Agent Rivers, we conducted a search of the place, but none of our guys did *this*."

Dutch and I looked at each other and I could tell he was as shocked as I was. Turning back to Grayson, I crossed my arms and said, "No one else had access to this place, Detective. You guys were the last people in here."

She scowled at me. "You sure about that?"

"Yes!" I said, looking from Grayson to Dutch. "I had to unlock the door when I entered, and this office can only be locked and unlocked with a key."

"How did you guys access the office to serve out the search warrant?" Dutch asked.

"Agent Harrison provided us with the key, which we returned to him several hours ago," Grayson said, surveying the mess again.

Dutch turned to me. "Who else has a key?"

I sighed. This was so frustrating. "Me and Candice of course," I said, "and you know I keep a spare at home, just like Candice did. But other than the land-lord, that's it."

Grayson stepped back to the door and squatted down to inspect the lock. "No sign of forced entry," she said. "Are you sure no one took your spare?"

I thought about it for a moment. "No, it was in the dish this morning when I fished out my car keys. I'm positive it's still at home."

Grayson stood up again and leveled her gaze at me. "You sure your partner didn't come back here and do this?"

I rolled my eyes. "How stupid do you think she'd have to be to come back here knowing you guys are looking for her?"

"And why would she tear apart her own office?" Dutch said to Grayson.

The detective shrugged. "Maybe she was trying to cover up the fact that she took something out of the office."

"Wait, what?" I asked.

Grayson pulled out her notebook. "We cataloged everything in here," she said. "Down to the number of pens in the pencil holder. If something came up missing, we'd know about it. Maybe Candice wanted whatever she took to get lost in the chaos. Which is why she trashed your side of the office too."

For the smallest fraction of a second I took that in as a possibility. My radar kicked it right back out again. "No way. There's *no way* Candice did this," I said firmly. "And if it wasn't you guys, then somebody else was in here." A creepy feeling then traveled up my spine and I felt goose pimples line my arms. Dutch seemed to sense what I was concluding and he reached out and took my hand.

Grayson sighed. "Okay, so some intruder with access to a key came in here and tore the place up. Abby, do you know if anything is missing?"

I shook my head. "I haven't even looked. . . ." My voice trailed off as I had a terrible thought, and letting go of Dutch, I rushed slipping and sliding on the paper and debris over to my office. Heading around to the other side of the desk, I got down on hands and knees and began to push around in the clutter. "What is it?" I heard Dutch ask as I was frantically searching.

"My laptop! Dutch, it's not here!"

Dutch came over next to me and began pushing aside the mess too. After a few minutes we knew the search was fruitless. I sat back on my heels and used up at least five dollars' worth of swear jar credit.

Once I was done, I heard Grayson on the phone out in the lobby. She poked her head in with her phone pressed to her ear. "I'm calling in a B and E," she said. "I'll have a detective here in a few to take a report."

I nodded, not quite able to say thank you. I was too upset. Dutch helped me to my feet and wrapped me in his arms. "We'll get you a new computer," he promised.

"It's not just that," I said, my voice quivering. "Dutch, you saw what they did to my reading room. They destroyed my sanctuary. I feel so violated."

"But you're safe," he said, squeezing me tight.

"Which is what counts. And all that stuff might be tough to replace, but we'll do it, Abs. I promise."

I leaned against him and let his warmth seep into me. Dutch and I had grown even closer since our wedding and we'd been crazy in love before. There was a deeper, more meaningful level to our relationship now, and it was hard to quantify, but it was like we'd let go of any petty squabbles or hang-ups we'd once carried, and now we just felt grateful every single day to have each other to go through life with. And personally, I noticed that I'd stopped thinking of myself as this independent woman in love with a great guy, and more as a part of something greater than the sum of our individual parts. Dutch was my connection to a wondrously secure, safe, and loving existence. It was hard to breathe sometimes because my chest was so filled up by that love, and I felt a wealth of it pass through me as he held me and told me everything would be okay.

And then we heard Grayson clear her throat. "Abby," she said softly.

I lifted my head away from Dutch's chest and wiped self-consciously at my wet cheeks. "Yeah?"

"Can you come with me for a sec?" Grayson asked.

I looked at Dutch and he nodded. He'd be right next to me.

We stepped carefully out of the room and through the small lobby, following Grayson over to Candice's office. It was in perhaps even worse shape than mine. Candice's glass desk was completely shattered, and large shards littered the debris on the floor. Grayson pointed toward the closet door, which was open, and the large filing cabinet I'd struggled to move only hours before was on the floor, blocking entry to the closet. But that wasn't what Grayson seemed interested in. With a stopping motion she indicated that we should stay put, and she moved over to the closet. Taking out a small penlight from her pocket, she shone the light into the interior. I could see the safe door hanging open.

"What do you know about this safe?" Grayson asked me.

Thank goodness my eyes were already big and surprised. "Uh . . . nothing," I said. "I had no idea Candice had a safe back there." Which was partially true; I hadn't known about it until she called me at three a.m. to tell me about it.

Grayson studied me. I kept my eyes big and innocent.

I don't think she bought it. "No idea what she might've kept in there?"

I shook my head. "None." That was also partially true. I hadn't yet peeked inside the file I'd taken from there. I had no idea what it contained.

Grayson sighed and I saw her jaw muscles clench. "Dammit," she said. "We didn't pull the file cabinet out from the wall, so we didn't know it was back here either."

"Whatever was in there must've been what the intruder was looking for," Dutch said.

Grayson nodded. "Yeah, but I don't think they got their hands on it."

"Why do you say that?" I asked, nervous that she was onto me.

Grayson motioned with her penlight to the disaster that'd been Candice's office. "I think they found the safe, got it open, and when they didn't find what they were looking for, they took it out on the rest of the office. This is rage induced, which tells me two things: One, that you're right; it probably wasn't Candice who did this. And two, that whatever was in that safe was pretty important to somebody."

I nodded again. I knew that to be true. No way would Candice risk my neck if it weren't important. But it also made me really curious about what the hell was in that file.

It was hours later that Dutch and I crawled home. We'd given a statement to another detective, who hadn't held out much hope that anything from the office would be recovered, but he'd given me a copy of the police report so that I could file an insurance claim. He'd then gone to the surrounding offices and asked if anyone had heard any sort of commotion, because causing that kind of damage had to have made some noise. No one reported hearing anything, which told us that the burglar had likely come in immediately following the exit of the police, who'd left after conducting their search at about six a.m.

While I was busy with the detective, Dutch had gone out and come back with some large trash bags and we'd spent most of the rest of the afternoon and early evening sorting through the mess. I'd managed to recover many of my client files, but they'd need to be sorted and put back into alphabetical order. I'd had a moment where I'd smirked a little when I thought back to the lecture Candice had given me about coming into the twenty-first century and putting my client files on my computer. A fat load of good that would've done me with the computer gone.

It was well past seven when we pulled up to our house, and we both saw Brice's car at the bottom of the drive. "Does he know about the break-in?" I asked Dutch.

"Yeah. I called him on my way to get the trash bags."

"Will we have to speak in hypotheticals tonight?"

"Tonight. Tomorrow night. And probably for a few nights after that, dollface. At least until we can make sense of this mess."

Brice got out of his car holding a large pizza box and I wanted to hug him. "God bless you, sir," I said when he handed it to me and the delicious scent wafted up to my eager nose.

While I got plates and napkins, Dutch filled Brice in on the state of the office. The second I sat down, Brice looked at me and asked, "Did you know about the safe?"

The slice of pizza making its way to my mouth paused midflight. "I knew about it," I said, avoiding particulars like *when* I'd learned about it. "But she never told me what was in it." Again, technically true. Until I'd opened it, I hadn't known what was in it. I figured as long as I spoke in the past tense, I'd avoid being sent away to liar-liar-pants-on-fire jail.

Brice shook his head and cursed under his breath. "What the hell would Candice keep in there that somebody would be after?"

I focused on my pizza, ignoring the expectant look Dutch was giving me. "Abs?"

"Mmmff?" I said, carefully chewing the *tremendous* bite I'd just shoved into my piehole.

"Hypothetically speaking, any idea what she might've been hiding in there?"

I held up a finger and continued to chew thoughtfully, buying time. Should I answer that with the truth? Should I tell them about the file? If I told them about the file, would it compromise their jobs or, worse yet, put them in danger? Would it put Candice in danger? Would they demand to see it? Would they forgive me for not telling them about it sooner?

A dozen questions bulleted their way through my mind and at last I swallowed and said, "Did I know what she might've been hiding? No."

Dutch frowned. Turning back to Brice, he said, "What the hell was she working on before all this started?"

Brice shook his head again. "You know her. Candice never talks about her cases. Ever. And neither do I. We leave work at work like the bureau expects us to do."

I saw a slight blush touch Dutch's cheeks. He always talked about his cases with me, because I often was able to give him some intuitive input. It wasn't completely against the rules for us because, until that day, I'd been a consultant for the bureau, but there were some cases I knew he should've kept hush-hush and hadn't.

There was a bit of an awkward silence that followed and I made sure to take another ginormous bite of the pizza. Then Dutch said, "Grayson didn't know about the safe either. According to her, the search concluded at approximately zero six hundred, which means the perp entered the office between that time and zero eight hundred, when some of the other tenants came to work. I think whoever wanted into that office was watching the cops and waiting their turn."

I shivered. It was creepy to think that our offices were being watched by some unknown person violent enough to destroy our workplace when they didn't get what they wanted.

"The other thing that's off about this is the key," said Brice. "I gave my copy to Grayson and she brought it right back, and Abby, I'm assuming you've checked to make sure you've got all your copies?"

I held up my finger again and hurried to the kitchen counter and the copper dish that held all our keys. I found my spare in the bottom of the dish. "It's here," I called, holding it up so they both could see.

"And those are the only copies you've got?" Brice pressed as I walked back to the table.

"Yeah, except for Candice's key and the landlord's."

"It wasn't Candice," Brice said firmly, tapping his fingers against the table.

"What about the landlord?" Dutch asked.

I rolled my eyes. "He served me with an eviction notice when I got to the building this morning. I doubt he'd have the balls to trash the office before serving me that."

Both Dutch and Brice sat forward. "He what, now?" Dutch asked.

I realized I'd been so upset over the destruction of

my office that I'd forgotten to tell Dutch about Giles's eviction notice. After I explained what the notice had said, he and Brice exchanged a look and Brice said, "I'll make the call in the morning, Abby. Don't worry. You're not getting evicted."

It was my turn to sigh. I was so tired I found it hard to focus. "You know what, Brice? Don't bother. Candice and I have been thinking of moving when our lease runs out, and this just makes it easier to make a clean break."

"You sure?"

"I'm sure, but thanks. As soon as we clear this thing up with Candice, we can start looking at new office space to rent."

The room got quiet again and I could tell everybody was thinking the same thing I was, namely, *But what if this never gets cleared up and Candice goes to jail for murder?*

Chapter Four

I never made it back over to the Witts' that night. Exhausted and sleep deprived, I followed Dutch to bed right around nine and slept well past seven the next morning. My hubby woke me a little before eight and said, "Hey, I went online this morning and ordered you a new laptop from the Apple Store. I also scheduled an appointment for you to pick it up around ten, so maybe you should think about getting out of bed soon."

I rolled over and muttered something poetic and sweet to fully convey my gratitude at his thoughtfulness. "Mmmff."

Dutch chuckled and kissed my forehead. "I'll be home around six. Be good and stay out of trouble, you hear?"

"Mmmff."

"Yeah, love you too, dollface."

I sighed and lay there for a bit wrestling with the idea of getting up and making myself breakfast before sneaking over to the Witts' garage, but then I thought that there'd be too much morning neighborhood commuter traffic to risk it.

So I did the smart thing and went back to sleep, only to wake up at nine forty-five, look lazily at the clock on the nightstand, and bolt out of bed. "Ohmigod!" I squeaked as I hopped around the room hunting for clothes, shoes, and a hairbrush—in that order.

Scrambling out of the house only four minutes later, I bolted to the Apple Store and was only five minutes late.

The store itself is located at an upscale, outdoor mall called the Domain, which is an aesthetically pleasing place filled with designer labels and loads of pretentious attitudes. I winced when I stepped out of the car as the memory of having had lunch with Candice there only the week before came to my mind. It'd been an unusually hot day that afternoon, but oddly, when we arrived at the restaurant, we'd found the climate a bit cooler. I'd remarked on the oddity to Candice, who'd smirked in that usual way she had right before she delivered a good line. "Didn't you know, Abby?" she'd said drily. "This place never gets hot because God simply *loves* rich people."

She'd said it loudly while we fought the crowd of wives with too much money and too much time to do anything meaningful, so they filled it with purchasing pretty things. To my eye, most of the women seemed to be giving my beautiful friend the "up-down." You know the look. That bitchy once-over some women make when they perceive a competitor in their midst? Yeah, that one. In all my years of hanging out with

Candice, I've never seen her give another woman the up-down and she's got loads of money in the bank and plenty of style. But even more than that, she's got class . . . in spades. Thinking about that last outing with her made me really miss her.

Still, I was late, so I shook off the melancholy and headed into the store and was shuffled around from "genius" to "super genius" until I got to the guy who would actually hand over my freaking computer. He seemed pretty good as geniuses go, because he helped me recover most of my files from the cloud, including my scheduling calendar, and only an hour later I was on my way back to the office. I had a client at one o'clock and my reading room was still a bit messy.

And I almost made it without incident, except as I was cruising down Highway 360, jamming out to some great tunes, I saw a flash of yellow in my rearview mirror. Immediately I focused on the view behind me, but all I saw was the usual mix of pickups, SUVs, and sedans. And then, I saw it again. A flash of yellow seemed to poke out from behind a big F-150.

I tapped the brakes and moved over to the right lane to get a better view, and as the F-150 came closer, I felt my palms begin to sweat. I'd recognize Candice's Porsche anywhere. Just as the pickup was creeping up on my left fender, I saw that flash of yellow dart over to my right, then all the way over down the exit I'd just passed. "No!" I yelled, seeing Candice race down the off-ramp and out of sight.

Gritting my teeth, I punched the accelerator and raced to the nearest turnaround—but that was a half mile farther south and by the time I got back to the exit, I knew I'd never find her. Still, that didn't stop me from heading up and down the street, looking for her. I gave up after twenty minutes and got back on the highway.

Once I was at the office, I headed to the left side of the suite and paced in front of my desk, frustrated and unable to shake the feeling that Candice seemed to be following me. It wasn't that I minded; it was more that I didn't know why. Did she want her file back? Was she trying to make contact with me?

I'd checked my phone at least a dozen times for a text message, but there was no word from her. So why would she follow me if she didn't want to talk to me?

Was she worried that I'd given the file to Brice? Or to the police? Didn't she know I'd never betray her?

I typed her a message.

> Hey. I still have your file. No one's seen it. If you want it back, just tell me and I'll get it to you.

I tapped my foot impatiently for her reply, but none came. "Fine," I muttered, putting away the cell. "Be that way."

I got busy cleaning up the mess in the reading room. All of my crystal cathedrals had sustained some damage, but happily, most were still okay to display. That's the thing about rocks—they're tough to destroy.

As I was vacuuming and casting anxious glances at the clock, I felt the phone in my back pocket vibrate. Pulling it out, I saw a text from Candice.

Please don't text me about the file again.

I blinked and I could feel a touch of anger settle into my shoulders at the obvious rebuke. I thought up a dozen smart-ass replies and was about to tell her what she could do with her file when another text came in.

But if you really need to mention it, refer to it as my laundry. Please lay low and be safe, Sundance. I'll be in touch when I can.

I stared at her text for a good two minutes, a thousand unanswered questions ricocheting around in my mind. I closed my eyes and searched the ether for her and felt her close but hidden with no hint of where she might be.

And then I did the thing that I'd been afraid to do. I reached out with my forecasting ability to read Candice's future, and what I sensed shocked and frightened me. I didn't per se "see" any tragic event she'd be involved in, but there was something terrible coming.

I opened my eyes again and glanced at the phone. I was seriously tempted to call Dutch and tell him that I'd seen Candice tailing me, but as I was reaching for it, I heard the front door of our office open.

"Hello?" called a female voice.

I muttered under my breath and went out to greet my one o'clock client. I'd have to worry about it later.

In between clients I did a little snooping on my new computer. I'd decided in the car to look into the man that Candice had shot. I still couldn't believe that she'd murdered someone in cold blood for no good reason. Something else was going on and I was determined to find out what.

I found Dr. Robinowitz online, but, like a lot of professional sixty-year-old men, he didn't have much of a footprint on the Web. No Facebook page, or LinkedIn account, and definitely no other social media accounts, but I did find a little bit in the public records search.

Robinowitz had lived in Palm Springs for about thirty years prior to buying his condo in Vegas. He'd had a long-running practice in California, but it appeared that in recent years he'd also had more than a handful of malpractice suits brought against him.

Even more telling was a DUI he'd received around that same time where he'd blown nearly three times the legal limit, and he'd obviously become belligerent with the arresting officer, because there was the tacked-on charge of resisting arrest.

It looked like Robinowitz had managed to avoid jail time, but within the year he had seemingly retired from his practice and put his big house in Palm Springs up for sale. I found the listing online. It was a beautiful place, and had to be worth a few million. It'd been for sale for over six months, though, and I wondered what would happen to it now that Robinowitz was dead.

Other than the stuff I found in public records and snooping around his property, there wasn't anything newsworthy about Robinowitz until his murder hit the airwaves two nights earlier.

From the online story of the murder in the *Austin*

American-Statesman, I pulled up the photo of the doctor and stared at it for a long time. His image appeared flat and plastic to my mind's eye, which always let me know when I was looking at a dead person. "Why?" I asked his photo. "What did you do that inspired Candice to kill you?"

But of course there were no replies or answers forthcoming, so I shut down the computer and got ready for my next appointment.

The rest of the day flew by, as I'd packed the afternoon with clients, and by seven I was wiped out. I realized that I'd never told Dutch that I was working late, so I called him on my way home.

"Hey, dollface," he said when he picked up the call. "Where you been? I've been worried."

"I'm on my way home and I've got a few hypotheticals to run by you, but maybe I should run them only by you and not Brice."

"Understood. I've got a pork roast in the oven. Dinner should be ready by the time you get here and Brice left ten minutes ago. I think he needs some alone time tonight. This thing with Candice is eating him up."

I bit my lip. Poor Brice. "See you in fifteen," I said.

When I got to the house, Dutch was plating our food and he took one look at me and said, "How about we save the hypotheticals until after dinner?"

I hugged him. "You're the best husband ever, you know that?"

He kissed me sweetly. "Just remember this moment if I ever forget our anniversary."

We ate our meal and caught up with each other. He

asked if I'd gotten my computer and I thanked him (properly this time) and told him how great it was. He asked about my day and then I asked him about his.

"It's been tense," he said, pushing his plate aside and setting his napkin on the table. "Brice is distracted for obvious reasons, and the squad doesn't know what to say or think about the situation. They've all got sources at APD, so I know they've seen the tape from the parking garage, and they all know and love Candice, so they're pretty torn up too."

I looked at my husband and noticed for perhaps the first time the pinched corners of his eyes and the worry lines etched across his forehead. Reaching for his hand, I squeezed it and asked, "And how're you doin', cowboy?"

The question seemed to catch him off guard. "Me?"

I nodded.

"I'm fine."

With my free hand I stroked the side of his head. Dutch has the most gorgeous hair, light blond and so soft to the touch. I loved to run my fingers through it. "You're worried about her too," I said.

"It shows?"

"Yeah, but only to me," I lied.

Dutch reached up to cover my hand with his. "You ready to talk hypotheticals?"

I nodded. "Hypothetically, I saw Candice on the highway today."

Dutch stared at me. It took him a second to recover himself. "Where?"

"Not far from our office."

"On Three Sixty," he guessed correctly.

I shrugged. "I think she was following me."

He sat up a little. "Why?"

"I have no idea. But I'm assuming that when she saw that I'd caught on to the tail, she took the next exit and disappeared again."

Dutch's lips pressed together. "I don't like that, Edgar."

"She'd never harm me, Dutch."

"Don't you think Robinowitz thought the same thing?"

That gave me pause. "We don't know for sure that they knew each other."

He rolled his eyes. "Come on, Abs. You saw the tape. He recognized her and was happy to see her."

"I looked him up today," I admitted.

"Looked him up? Who, Robinowitz?"

I nodded. "I found some stuff in a public records search."

Dutch scratched the stubble on the end of his chin. "You mean the DUI and the malpractice suits?"

"You did your own research, I see."

He shrugged. "Nothing in his past is worthy of murder, is it?"

I sighed. "No. It's not. All the lawsuits appeared to have been settled, and his driving record had been clean for two years. And, even if he'd continued to drink and mess up his life, it's still not anything I could ever imagine Candice wanting to kill him over."

Suddenly, Dutch appeared to have a thought. "Abs?"

"Yeah?"

"Candice's sister, the one who died in the accident, was it a drunk driving incident?"

My brow shot up. "You know, honey, I don't know. Candice never told me what caused the accident, just that it was raining really hard that day, which is why she gets a little nervous driving in foul weather."

Dutch scratched at his chin. "What if Robinowitz was somehow involved with that accident?"

I considered that for a minute before I said, "That was twenty years ago, Dutch. You really think Candice would wait twenty years to take her revenge on him?"

"It makes more sense than any other theory we have right now, Edgar."

"We have no other theory right now."

"Which is why it makes sense," Dutch insisted.

"Okay," I said, getting up and moving to retrieve my new laptop. "Let's just vet this theory of yours."

It took us only fifteen minutes to find out that Robinowitz had no connection to the accident that had taken Sam Dubois' life. There had been only a single car—Sam's—on a slick, wet stretch of road where she'd lost control and the car had flipped multiple times. The details were awful to read, but the police report had designated it all Sam's fault, suggesting she was driving too fast for the conditions.

Dutch seemed disappointed to discover his theory for Candice's motive held no merit. "The thing that really surprises me about your hypothetical," he said, referring back to our earlier conversation, "is what the heck is Candice doing driving around on the highway when she knows there's a citywide search for her and that car?"

I frowned. It hadn't even occurred to me how risky that was. Candice's car was flashy, and her face and that car had been all over the news, so why *would* she risk driving around town when she could so easily be spotted? "It doesn't make a whole lot of sense when you know how careful and cautious Candice usually is," I agreed.

Dutch nudged me with his knee. "All of this is totally out of character for her, dollface."

"There has to be something up with Robinowitz," I said. "Candice would never just shoot an innocent man, Dutch. I know her, and she'd never do that."

"Babe," he said soberly, reaching out to take my hand. "Even if he proves to be the lowest scum on earth, Candice still *murdered* him. And even though I've agreed to let you investigate this on your own without protest, I'm worried that you haven't really wrapped your head around the fact that, in the eyes of the law, Candice is a cold-blooded killer. The DA will be looking at murder one, and given the brutality of the crime and the fact that by all accounts Robinowitz was an upstanding citizen, they may even go for the death penalty."

My breath caught because I realized Dutch was right. My best friend had murdered a man in cold blood, and whatever her reasons, none would ever be good enough to justify her actions in the eyes of the law. I blinked hard, but my vision still blurred with oncoming tears. If and when Candice was caught, the best she could hope for was life behind bars. The worst was that her life would end in a prison execution chamber. However I hoped to help her, I'd never be able to erase what she'd done.

Dutch seemed to understand what I was thinking because he pulled me out of my seat and into his lap. "Hey," he whispered as I cried bitter tears. "Edgar, don't cry."

"I don't know how to help her or what to do," I whimpered.

"I know, sweetheart. Me either. So for now, we'll just be her friend, continue to work on the facts, and keep an open mind until we know why she did what she did, okay?"

I hugged him tightly. I hoped he knew how much I loved him for saying that.

At two in the morning I crept out of the house and over to the Witts'. I'd left Dutch snoring away in our bed, and part of me had thought long and hard about leaving his side to come back for the file. The truth was, I didn't want to look in it. I wanted to leave it where it was and never think about it again, because something told me that the second I looked into that file, I'd be falling down a rabbit hole with no easy way out.

The thing that'd finally gotten me to sneak out of the house and over to the Witts' was knowing with an absolute certainty that Candice would never give up on me so easily. So I shrugged on a pair of leggings and Dutch's big hoodie sweatshirt, slipped out the back door, through the gate, and over to my neighbors' garage. For a few seconds I hid by the side of their house while I scoped out the street. Seeing no one else about,

I crept to the house and put in the code. The door opened and the light inside came on. I ducked low and shimmied under the door, then hit the garage button on the inside quickly to lower the door again. Once it was all the way down, I moved to the terra-cotta pot I'd hidden the file and the cash in and retrieved the file.

Finding one of those canvas foldout chairs nearby, I sat down and closed my eyes, still silently debating with myself. At last I opened my eyes again and said, "Down the rabbit hole it is."

I opened the file and took out the first piece of paper. I was quite surprised to find that it contained a DNA test for a Salazar Romero Kato, and an Olive Wintergarden. According to the results of the test, there was a ninety-nine percent chance of a familial relationship.

My brow furrowed. "What the hell is this?" I then caught myself and felt out the pocket of Dutch's hoodie, which had jingled slightly when I'd put it on. He had fifty cents in the right-hand pocket. I'd get that "hell" for free and a bonus swearword if I wanted.

I looked back at the file and saw, behind the DNA results, a sheet of paper that was blank except for an address. I didn't know whether the address was local; there was just a number and a street, nothing more. Puzzled, I looked at the paper behind that and found a signed lease agreement for an apartment in Las Vegas, Nevada, which had been prepaid for a year. The lease was made out to ExFactor LLC, and there was a set of keys taped to the lease.

The last few items in the file were equally mysterious. Behind the lease was an envelope containing a

Nevada driver's license with Candice's somewhat blurry face but her sister's info. It wasn't a secret that Candice kept a fake ID using her sister's name, but I'd never seen it up close until now. I studied the ID; something about it felt off. And then I realized that the height and eye color were wrong. Candice was a few inches taller than me (I'm five-four . . . ish), but the height listed on the ID read five-four. And Candice's eyes were hazel, yet on the ID they were listed as green.

I felt sad as I read the stats, because I figured that Candice was using her sister's height and eye color just to be consistent with her sister's real height and eye color. It was a wonder no one at the Nevada DMV noticed, but then, why would they scrutinize something like that? Behind the ID was a corporate credit card that looked freshly minted. It was shiny with no scratch marks and the back hadn't been signed yet. The name on the card was also ExFactor and there was an additional small scrap of paper with four digits at the back of the file. The digits were 6168. Curious, I called the number on the back of the credit card, plugged in the account number, and when it asked for the last four digits of the primary account holder's Social Security number, I typed in 6168.

"You have a prepaid credit balance of two hundred thousand dollars. No payment is due at this time."

I ended the call and stood up to pace the garage. Nothing in the file made any sense at all and for the life of me I couldn't understand why Candice thought them worth killing for. What did a DNA test, a street address, an apartment lease, and a prepaid credit card have to do with Dr. Robinowitz?

Unless . . .

I stopped pacing and looked at the DNA test. "Maybe Robinowitz was trying to get his hands on the test and maybe the apartment is where these two family members are hiding, and maybe the credit card . . ."

I sighed heavily. I had no good working theory for why Candice would want Robinowitz dead, but at least I had a few names to investigate. I'd start with the address on the sheet of paper. With any luck, the Google search would come back with a listing in Vegas and a piece of the puzzle would slide into place.

With another sigh I closed up the file and moved back over toward the flowerpot. Just as I was about to put it back in its hiding place, however, my radar pinged with a warning. I hesitated and focused on that ping.

What I felt was that it was a bad idea to put the file back in the flowerpot. In fact, I had a feeling I needed to take the file and the wad of cash in the bottom of the flowerpot with me over to my house. But where could I hide them? On the off chance that the cops came to our house with a warrant, they'd find them for sure, wouldn't they?

And then the image of my walk-in closet came to my mind.

Dutch and I had his and hers closets, and in mine, above the top shelf was a return air vent that was missing the screws. Dave, our handyman/builder, had pointed it out to me right before we'd closed on the house, and he'd promised to come over and secure the vent, but three months later he had yet to deliver on that promise. The vent could easily be popped out, I knew, because, not wanting the thing to drop on my head, I'd wiggled it free just to see how secure it was without the screws. It seemed to be a snug fit even without the screws, so I hadn't bothered to pester Dave about it, and now that I thought about the vent, I figured it was at least a decent hiding place for the file and cash.

With my mind made up, I tucked the items into the waistband of my leggings, pulled the sweatshirt down low, and hit the button for the garage door.

Ducking under the door, I typed the code into the pad quickly, and the door never rose above my waist before closing again. I crossed my fingers that no one had seen me as I hurried away from the Witts'.

Slipping back inside the house, I waited by the door, listening for any hint that Dutch might be up and looking for me, but the house was quiet and not even Eggy and Tuttle seemed disturbed by my night-crawling.

Tiptoeing into the bedroom, I didn't relax until I heard the sound of Dutch's soft snores. I took great care not to make any noise as I eased into my closet, closed the door, and flipped on the light. Using the small step stool I kept in the corner, I reached up and pulled the vent cover free, slipped the file and the cash into the hole, and felt like I'd just done the exact perfect thing. It never occurred to me that I'd actually just avoided a disaster.

Chapter Five

Dutch shook me awake the next morning around five thirty. "What's happened?" I said, jerking myself awake. I'd been in a deep sleep.

"It's our neighbors," Dutch said. "They've had a B and E."

"They . . . *what*?" I gasped, blinking furiously to try to shake the grogginess making my thoughts feel fuzzy.

"The Witts," Dutch explained, pulling on his jeans and the sweatshirt I'd worn just a few hours before. "The cops are next door and I got a call from the security company. Someone called in some suspicious activity at their place last night and the cops just arrived."

I stared slack-jawed at Dutch. "They . . . *what*?"

Dutch smirked and kissed my forehead. "Go back to sleep," he said. "I'll find out what's going on and fill you in later."

He left me to sit there and stare about the room, trying to make sense of what he'd just told me. And then I was also in motion. Throwing off the bedcovers, I reached for my leggings again and a sweater from the dresser and ran after him.

I found Dutch standing at the top of the Witts' drive talking to an officer who was taking the report. There were two patrol cars parked in front of our neighbors' house and the front door was open. Inside I could see more cops searching the place and even through the door I could tell the house was a mess.

I let Dutch do all the talking as he explained the Witts were out of town and we were keeping an eye on the place. I learned from the cop that the Witts' security system had been overridden and if not for the call from the neighbor across the street who saw the bounce of a flashlight beam through one of their windows, no one would have been the wiser until the Witts returned home.

I gulped when I thought about the chance I'd taken by using the Witts' garage as a hiding place for the file, and then I had a terrible thought that I wanted to shrug off, but couldn't.

What if the break-in had been related to the one at my office? What if the intruder had been looking for that file?

I turned my head up and down the street, seeing all the hiding places for someone to watch me unnoticed while I slipped into the Witts' garage and came out twenty minutes later. Playing devil's advocate, if I were the person who'd vandalized our offices looking for that file and discovered it gone, I'd stick close to Candice's best friend just to see if she did anything suspicious, and going into a neighbor's house via the garage in the dead of night was certainly worth investigating. I could easily see how the perp had assumed I'd hidden it somewhere on their premises.

Little did he or she know, however, that I'd taken it with me when I came back out. I felt a chill sneak up my spine when I thought about it, because if the perp hadn't found the file at the Witts', would he or she assume it was back at our place?

I looked nervously over at our home. After we'd had a really big scare on the day of our wedding, Dutch had installed top-of-the-line security for us complete with cameras, motion detectors, motion lights, silent alarms, and even a fully stocked panic room. We were as tight as Fort Knox, but maybe the Witts had thought that too?

I hung out next to Dutch for the next half hour as he called the Witts and explained what'd happened. Dina Witt had taken the call and she was quite distraught, asking Dutch to take some pictures of the damage to text to her. I went with him inside the house and it looked a whole lot like my office. Broken and overturned furniture, every drawer opened and emptied, clothing pulled out of closets and bureaus, even the cupboard had not been spared—nor the dishes in the cabinet. The garage had barely been searched, only a few things were out of place there, and I could tell that whoever had been watching me had thought I'd merely entered the home through the garage, and hadn't thought to hide anything there. The flowerpot with the bag of potting soil on top remained where I'd left it, neatly tucked on a shelf.

Heading back inside, given the mess, I couldn't really tell what might've been taken, except of course the obvious empty jewelry case on the floor of Dina and Scott's bedroom.

I heard her start to cry when Dutch called her back and told her about that. He hadn't wanted to send her a photo without bracing her.

Later, we walked back over to our place and Dutch started a pot of coffee. I sat forlornly in a chair feeling huge waves of guilt because I was convinced the robbery at the Witts' and the robbery at my office weren't a coincidence.

It was a few seconds before I realized Dutch was staring at me with his arms crossed and an expectant look on his face. "What?" I asked.

"That's what I should ask you," he said.

My brow furrowed.

"What're you hiding from me, Edgar?"

I pressed my lips together. I didn't want to lie to him anymore, but I couldn't tell him about that file until I knew why Candice wanted me to hide it and why someone was so intent on getting their hands on it. I stared at the ground and shook my head. "Dutch . . ."

"This is serious, Edgar."

I lifted my chin. "Don't you think I know that?"

Thumbing over his shoulder toward the Witts', he said, "That's the same guy that hit your office. I doubt he got the addresses mixed up. The other night you called me from the inside of what sounded like a warehouse, but now I'm thinking it might've been the Witts' garage. What the hell was over there?"

I pressed my lips together again.

"Was it Candice's laptop?" he asked.

I stared him in the eye. "No."

"Then what? What's over there, Edgar?"

I kept looking him in the eye and said, "Nothing. There's nothing there."

"Was whatever you were hiding for Candice taken?" he asked.

I said nothing. Dutch was starting to figure all of this out and I wanted him to stop.

"You're not going to tell me?" he asked after a long silence.

"I can't."

Dutch's jaw clenched. He didn't like that answer. "Okay," he said after another long silence. "How about hypothetically, then?"

I almost chuckled, but he didn't seem like he thought it was funny. "Listen," I began. "Candice asked me to keep something safe for her, and she asked me to promise not to tell anybody what it was, so, until she tells me different, I'm keeping it secret."

"Is it a weapon?" Dutch asked, and I knew he was thinking it might be the gun she had used to shoot Robinowitz.

"No. It's not. I swear. I'm not really sure what it is exactly, but I can tell you that she wanted me to hide it and keep it safe and I've done that."

"Is it bigger than a bread box?" he asked next.

"Stop trying to guess!"

Dutch blew out a sigh and ran a hand through his hair. "Fine. But whatever this thing is, will you at least tell me if you had it over at the Witts' place at some point?"

"Yes. It's not there anymore, but I had hidden it over there."

Dutch got up and began to pace. "Christ, Abs," he said. He didn't sound mad at me per se, but I couldn't blame him if he was. If that burglar had been the same person who'd hit our offices, I was responsible, even though indirectly, for the robbery next door, and the Witts had suffered because of my carelessness.

"I don't know how to make amends to them," I said. When Dutch looked at me, I motioned with my chin toward our neighbors' house.

"It's not your fault," he said. I looked at him doubtfully. "Mostly it's not," he added, his lips quirking at the corners. "The thing that worries me is that someone's obviously watching you. They knew you'd hidden something in that house, and they probably know you've retrieved it by now, so that makes me worry about you and our place."

"Not if I make it look like they didn't find what they were looking for and pretend to take it back," I said, thinking fast.

Dutch cocked his head. "Come again?"

"The odds are probably pretty good that whoever was watching me is still watching me, right?"

"Yeah," he said. "Which is what worries me."

"You're missing the point."

"Okay, go on. They're still watching you—so?"

"What if right after the cops leave, you and I go back over to the Witts' and enter through the garage and then we'll come out a few minutes later and you could . . . I don't know, have something tucked up under your jacket, and then you could immediately get in your car and drive off. Whoever was watching us would then assume you had the thing that Candice was trying to hide."

"And where would I go with this pretend thing?" Dutch asked me.

"Straight to the bureau offices. If you head there, no way would anybody risk a break-in to retrieve the ffffah . . . er . . . thing. The thing."

Dutch arched an eyebrow. "The ffffah—thing?"

I waved impatiently. "Leave it alone, cowboy. I'm not going to tell you what it was. Anyway, once you leave, I could follow after you at a discreet distance, and if I see anybody tailing you, I could call you and let you know, and then we'd nail this son of a bitch!" (Crap, there went the other free quarter I'd lifted from Dutch.)

Dutch eyed me with heavy lids. "*Or* I could call Brice, fill him in on what's going on, and *he* could tail me to see if anybody's following."

I put my hands on my hips. "Why him and not me?"

"Because he knows how to shoot a gun."

"I know how to shoot a gun!"

"His aim is better. He can actually hit what he's aiming at."

"Ah. Good point. But wait—if we fill him in, won't he demand to see what it is that I've hidden?"

"The ffffah—thing?"

I cut Dutch a look.

He smirked. "Yeah, he might."

"Will you back me up if I refuse to show it to him?"

"I might."

"You might?" I said, glaring a little, because I totally knew where this was heading. Why did marriage always have to come with so much compromise? "You might cover for me if what? I do the dishes every night for a month?"

Dutch offered me a lopsided grin. "I might if you *promise* to call me the second things get dicey, and by dicey I mean you see Candice tailing you in your rearview mirror, or anything even remotely similar to that, you call me. I don't like this one bit, Abs. You don't have anybody to cover your ass if things escalate, and that makes me nervous."

"I'll be okay, honey," I said.

"How can you be sure?"

I tapped my temple. "My crew always lets me know when I'm in trouble."

"Yeah, but you almost never listen to them either."

"Ah. Good point. But this time I will. I promise."

Dutch nodded. "Okay, but I'm gonna need more from you than your usual pinkie swear."

"Like what?"

"If I catch on that you lie to me about being followed or withholding more than you know you should, then you have to show me this ffffah—thing, whatever it is."

I nodded. "Yeah, okay. That's fair. You have yourself a deal. Now call Brice and let's get this show on the road!"

It took us both an hour to calm Brice down. He was furious with me for withholding the ffffah—thing, and I wouldn't even hint at what it was that Candice had asked me to hide. He demanded to see it. When I wouldn't, he threatened to arrest me. When both Dutch and I leveled a look at him, he threatened to call Detective Grayson and have her arrest me. I finally got up and headed to the kitchen. Brice followed me, shaking his finger the whole way. I ignored him and got down some pancake mix.

"What the hell are you doing?!" he yelled.

I turned to face him. "You seem crazy stressed-out, Brice. And you look like you haven't eaten a decent meal or slept in three days. When I'm stressed, hungry, and tired, I always want pancakes. So, how about you sit your damn ass down, and wait for some pancakes so you can feel better and then we'll have a reasonable discussion." (Swearing doesn't count when your boss is being a li'l cray-cray.)

Brice glared at me, but I stood my ground—whisk in hand. At last Dutch patted Brice's shoulder and said, "Come on, buddy. Let's park it over here and get you some coffee while Abby makes us breakfast."

Reluctantly, Brice allowed Dutch to shuffle him over to the table. He collapsed in a chair and we got him coffee, then a nice heaping stack of pancakes and bacon.

He didn't talk much through the meal, and he ate like a man who in fact hadn't had much to eat in a few days. At last he pushed his plate away and said, "Thanks. Sorry for yelling at you, Abby."

"It's cool," I said, and Dutch nudged my knee affectionately under the table.

"I still want to know what it is that Candice asked you to hide for her," Brice said.

"I know. But until she tells me it's okay to let you see it, I can't. My loyalty is to her, Brice."

"So is mine, Abby."

I sighed. "I guess we're at an impasse, then."

"Hey," Dutch said to get our attention. "For now I think we should focus on flushing out whoever's trying to get their hands on this thing—whatever it is—and once we've caught him, maybe we'll have more of an idea what prompted Candice to shoot Robinowitz."

Brice flinched. I could see that it pained him greatly to be reminded that Candice had murdered a man in cold blood. I knew exactly how he felt. "Yeah, okay," he finally agreed. "What's the plan?"

We went over the details and as we did so, I realized that I finally had to come clean and confess that the "fffah—thing" that Candice had hidden was a fffah-ile. A file containing something that I wouldn't even hint at. The only reason I finally let on that it was a file, and not her computer, or a weapon, or Jimmy Hoffa, was that I wanted whoever was watching me to know that I was turning over the goods to the bureau. It was the only way to keep me, Dutch, and the pups safe from an attempted home invasion.

Once we had our plan in place, Brice left, but he was only going as far as the bottom of the sub to wait for Dutch to drive past and then he'd follow him at a discreet distance to the bureau offices.

Dutch then headed out the front door with Eggy and Tuttle—he was going to pretend to be walking the dogs while rather indiscreetly watching the front of the Witts' house—and I headed out the back. I crept along the side of our neighbor's house and spotted Dutch at the top of the Witts' drive with both pups sniffing around their mailbox.

My hubby sent me a nod and I moved around to the front of the garage, punched in the code, and went inside.

Again I was a little surprised to find the garage in much the same state as I'd left it the night before. Only a few paint cans and storage boxes had been moved around from the far left wall. "What kind of an idiot destroys the whole house looking for a file but doesn't even think to fully check out the garage?" I muttered as I pulled up the canvas chair and sat down. I needed to make it look like I'd hidden the file someplace really good, so Dutch and I had agreed that I'd spend three minutes inside the garage before coming back out again.

I kept an eye on the clock on my new phone. . . . Three minutes takes a long time to pass when you're simply waiting for it to go by. And then I got up, folded up the chair, and headed out the garage again.

Dutch was walking the pups up the street a little and I waved at him as I trotted up the drive. He met me by the mailbox and handed over the leashes while I pulled out a plain manila folder with nothing but blank paper inside. I handed that to him and he made a show of looking around before tucking it into his coat and kissing me on the cheek. I left him to walk over to his car while I went in our front door and put the pups in their crates, set the alarm, and grabbed my keys.

Now, following after Dutch and Brice hadn't been part of the plan, but I'd never been the kind to follow directions. I'm more of a make-it-up-by-the-seat-of-my-pants kind of gal. So, I jumped into my SUV and took off to try to catch up to them.

I wanted very much to apprehend the guy who'd caused so much mayhem at my office and at the Witts', and I also wanted to grill him about what he knew about the file, and I figured that tailing Brice, who was tailing Dutch, was a pretty good insurance plan. If the perp caught on to the fact that Brice was tailing my hubby, he would probably be too focused on Brice to notice me. I figured it doubled our odds of finding him.

I didn't catch up to Brice until he was entering the freeway, and I got stuck at a yellow light behind a car that refused to make the turn. Grinding my teeth while a ton of traffic passed us before the guy in front of me *finally* moved, I whizzed around him and raced to the on-ramp.

Weaving in and out of traffic, I scanned the road ahead for any sign of Brice's car. At last I spotted his black Volvo and breathed a sigh of relief. Easing up on the accelerator, I tailed him for a few miles at a nice comfortable distance when I noticed that Brice was picking up the pace.

I sped up too and kept speeding up to maintain my tail. We blew past seventy-five, eighty, ninety, and I realized that Brice wasn't just speeding; he was chasing after another car.

In front of Brice was a black SUV very similar to mine, but that one had some zip to it. It cruised ahead and Brice stuck with it. I wove in and out of traffic and white-knuckled the steering wheel just to keep up. Then Brice flipped on his strobe lights and it was game on.

The SUV raced down the highway and Brice raced after it. About a mile down I saw Dutch's car had slowed and now both of them were giving chase. I bit my lip anxiously, trying to decide if I should continue to keep up or back off because we were exceeding a hundred miles an hour now and while I'm a good driver, I'm not an idiot. Common sense took over and I slowed down to eighty-five. My heart still felt like it was going well over a hundred and anxiously I searched ahead for any signs of the boys, because I'd lost track of them.

At last, way ahead I spotted a group of cars all pulled over on the side of the highway. I squinted and could just make out four cars in total—Brice's sedan, the black SUV, and Dutch's car, along with an APD patrol car with its lights flashing. I breathed another sigh of relief and checked my rearview, ready to move over to the right lane and pull up behind them on the shoulder, when I spotted a flash of yellow about five cars back. My breath caught and I focused on the yellow Porsche. It was definitely tailing me. I couldn't see Candice clearly—she was too far back—so I focused on the road ahead for a second and realized I was closing in on the four cars on the side of the highway. Between me and them, however, was an exit, and I just *knew* Candice wouldn't whiz by Brice in her car. She was gonna take that exit, but if I took it first, I risked having her skip it and accelerate down the road to the next exit, which was only a quarter mile away.

So I checked my left side mirror and luck was with me. No one was behind me. I then checked the rear-view one last time and Candice was still behind me, a few cars back. When I was almost to the exit, I darted out to the next lane on my left and hit the brakes hard. Cars on my right flew past me including Candice's Porsche. "Aha!" I shouted as I punched the accelerator again. "I've got you now, Candice!"

Just as I'd predicted, Candice flew down the exit ramp and I was right behind her. At the bottom of the exit was a green light, but then it went to yellow and I hissed through my teeth. Candice accelerated and flew through the light just as it turned red, and I was too far back to drive through safely. "Dammit!" I yelled, hitting the steering wheel. (Swearing doesn't count when your BFF keeps ducking you.) I watched her car cruise away and out of sight with mounting irritation, so the minute the light turned green, I was off like a bullet. I was hoping to catch her at the next intersection, but there was no sign of her. I cruised down the street farther, my head turning back and forth looking for any hint of that yellow Porsche, but there was nary a yellow car in sight.

Pulling over at a gas station, I took out my phone and sent her an angry text.

Really?????

I waited, staring at the display for her reply, but none came. Finally I sent her another text:

I don't like this game you're playing, Cassidy.

Then I tossed my phone on the passenger seat and headed back toward the freeway.

It took me a good ten minutes to work my way back to Dutch and the boys. I had mixed feelings about telling him that I'd had another Candice sighting. Our deal was that I had to let him know, but I had a pretty good loophole, namely, that I couldn't be absolutely one hundred percent *positive* that it was Candice's yellow Porsche behind me. I mean, it *could've* been someone else's car. Austin was a big place. Candice couldn't be the *only* person in the city to drive a yellow Porsche, so . . .

Anyway, I decided not to fill Dutch in just yet. If it happened again, I'd totally come clean (maybe). What I really wanted was to figure out why the heck she was tailing me. I mean, if she wanted to know what I was up to, all she had to do was text me and I'd fill her in, and I knew she knew that, so why the tail?

While I was thinking on that, I came close to the group of cars pulled over on the highway, and I saw that there were now considerably more cars, most of them the black sedan or SUV variety.

Instead of pulling over and adding mine to the mix, I passed by and took in the scene. There were a number of men there, all in suits, except for the patrol officer, who appeared to be having a heck of a time trying to keep the peace. One guy in a suit was in handcuffs, and Brice stood behind him, with Dutch on his left, but there were three other men all yelling at Brice, who looked mad enough to throw a punch at someone. "Yeesh!" I said as I flew by, and ducked when I saw Dutch's head snap in my direction. "Ruh-roh," I muttered.

Not really knowing where else to go, I headed to the bureau to wait for whatever was going to come next.

What came next was Director Gaston, looking so angry my breath caught. Gaston had been the director for a few years, and what I really liked about him was how cool under pressure he always seemed to be. He never got ruffled no matter what the situation, so to see him seething with anger was terrifying. I immediately regretted my decision to come to the office and wait for Dutch and Brice.

Gaston spotted me and walked right over. I'd been sitting at Agent Oscar Rodriguez's desk, chatting with him, when Gaston walked in. The second Gaston parked himself in front of us, his eyes pinning me to my seat, Oscar cleared his throat and muttered, "Think I'll get some coffee." And he hustled away.

I gulped. "Sir," I said.

"Abigail," Gaston replied smoothly, his voice belying the fury in his eyes. "May I speak to you in Agent Harrison's office?"

"Actually, I'm sorta late for an appointment," I said,

reaching nervously for my purse. No way did I want to be locked in an office with Gaston. He was shrewd, cunning, and intuitive in his own right. He'd have me confessing all in a matter of seconds.

"This won't take long," Gaston said firmly, and I knew his request wasn't so much a request as it was a direct order.

I gulped again. "Yes, sir."

I followed after him to Brice's office and he closed the door, then shuttered the blinds, and I will admit to being so scared I almost peed a little. He took a seat then and simply stared at me intently for a few beats.

I tried not to squirm and failed miserably.

"I know you've resigned your position as civilian consultant," Gaston said. I didn't say anything, because I knew there was more coming. "I'm very disappointed with that decision, Abigail."

"I . . . I thought under the circumstances it was the right thing to do, sir."

"Under what circumstances?"

I blinked. "Uh . . . the Candice-being-accused-of-murder circumstances, sir."

Gaston sat back and studied me again. "Do you know where Ms. Fusco is?"

I felt claustrophobic. Even though I've had tons (and tons) of practice, I'm not a great liar, especially not with an exceptionally gifted interrogator like Gaston. "No, sir."

"Have you heard from her?"

Crap. He'd asked a question I didn't want to answer. "I don't think I can comment on that, sir."

"Why not?"

"On the grounds that I might incriminate myself."

"Incriminate yourself?" Gaston said, his brows raised in surprise. "Did you participate in the murder of Dr. Robinowitz?"

"No! No, sir!"

"Then how would you be incriminating yourself by answering a simple question?"

"I'd just prefer not to, if it's all the same to you. Respectfully. Sir."

Gaston got up and turned his back on me, and that made me feel really bad. The director had put a great deal on the line when he'd hired me; in fact, he'd likely risked his reputation and career by insisting that I be hired on as a consultant. As a general rule, the FBI does not hire psychics. Even completely reputable ones. To my knowledge, I was one of only two or three on their payroll, and I knew that Gaston often got flak for that, even though I'd proven myself to be a valuable asset many times over.

So I could understand why Gaston was pissed off. Essentially, I'd betrayed him and possibly made him look the fool by resigning.

At last he turned back around and said, "Agent Harrison has been suspended."

My jaw dropped. *"What?"*

"And your husband has been reassigned to the San Antonio bureau."

I added a gasp. *"Why?"* I demanded. "They've done nothing wrong!"

Gaston came back over and took his seat again.

"Agent Harrison arrested another federal agent today even after that agent presented him with credentials. His ability to separate his personal life from his professional life has come into serious question, and I've temporarily relieved him of his duties. He'll be suspended with pay until Internal Affairs finishes their investigation."

I sat there slack-jawed and bug-eyed as Gaston spoke. Clearly I'd missed a great deal when I'd exited the highway chasing after Candice.

"As for your husband, I'd prefer for his career not to go up in flames like Agent Harrison's, so I've temporarily reassigned him to the San Antonio branch. He'll have a long commute if he chooses to remain in Austin, but it's the best I can do to protect him for now."

"Sir!" I exclaimed. "I think there's been a huge misunderstanding!"

"And as for you, Abigail," Gaston said, as if I hadn't spoken, "if you were still on my payroll, there is much I could've done to protect you too. But as you've clearly resigned so that you can assist your best friend in her efforts to remain a fugitive, there is little I can do for you. You should have come to me before making a decision like that."

"I'm *not* assisting her!" I yelled. "I'm trying to *find* her!"

My admission seemed to surprise Gaston. "You truly don't know where she is?"

"I swear to God I don't know, sir!"

Gaston seemed to weigh my sincerity before he said, "Well, then, Abigail, for your own safety I suggest you stop looking for Ms. Fusco." At that moment there was a knock on the door and Gaston turned his attention away from me. "Yes?"

The door opened and a stranger stood there; tall and beefy, the man was well over six feet with a thick neck and bullet-shaped head. He looked like he'd probably played football at some point in his life. He was certainly big and intimidating enough to have played in the pros.

"This her?" he asked Gaston.

"It is," the director said, getting up. Turning to me, he said, "You have the right to have an attorney present, Abigail. It might even be a good idea."

I felt the blood drain from my face. They must've discovered the file and they were here to arrest me for obstruction. I stared a little desperately after Gaston as he moved to the door, and the big beefy dude clearly wasn't pleased by the director's advice to me.

"Am I under arrest?" I managed to squeak out.

"Not yet," said Big Beefy. "But the day's still young."

Chapter Six

The second Big Beefy sat down, I stood up. "I want to speak to my attorney. I won't answer any of your questions unless he's present."

He eyed me with irritation and tapped his fingers on the tabletop. "Fine. You can use this phone. But the minute your lawyer gets here, we're gonna talk and you *are* gonna tell me what I need to know."

"I don't even know who *you* are," I snapped. I don't much like being intimidated.

"I'm Special Agent Frank Oppenheimer, Ms. Cooper."

He said that like it should mean something to me. It didn't. "I've never heard of you."

He snickered. "Yeah? Well, I've heard of you."

"Color me flattered."

Oppenheimer got up and pointed to the phone. "Hope your lawyer's a good one," he said as he walked out the door.

I sat down and dialed Dutch's cell. It went to voice

mail. I left him an urgent message to call me and waited nervously for him to call me back. After fifteen minutes the door opened and Oppenheimer stuck his face in. "Where're we at, Cooper?"

"My husband isn't answering his phone," I said.

"You were supposed to call your attorney."

"My husband has our attorney's phone number on his cell."

"I can look him up," Oppenheimer suggested, pulling out his smartphone.

"That's okay," I said. "I'll wait for my husband to call me back."

Oppenheimer seemed totally annoyed and he shut the door again. I got up to pace. Finally, a half hour later my cell rang. "Dutch?"

"You okay?" he asked.

"No. There's an agent named Oppenheimer here and he wants to interrogate me. Gaston suggested I have an attorney present."

"Dammit," he swore. "I figured they'd want to talk to you, but I didn't think it'd be this quick. I'll send over Calvin Douglas. He's good. Sit tight until he gets there."

"Thanks, but could you come too?"

There was a pause; then Dutch said, "Where are you?"

"In Harrison's office."

"I'm in the conference room, and I'm about to be interrogated myself. My union rep is on the way, and I'll meet with him before these Feds from Vegas start grilling me."

"Honey?"

"Yeah?"

"What guys from Vegas are we talking about? I thought Oppenheimer was IA?"

"Oh, sorry, dollface. I forgot you weren't in the loop about what's happened since this morning."

I clutched the phone tightly. "What's happened?"

Dutch sighed. "Brice noticed a tail on me this morning as I left the subdivision. We managed to get him to pull over, and we were in the middle of arresting him when he claimed to be a Fed. That's when Brice lost it. I don't know what got into him, but he refused to let the guy show us his ID and slapped some cuffs on him. Then he was a little rough getting him into the car. I tried to talk him down, but I think this thing with Candice has shaken the sense out of him. He wouldn't listen to me, and he wouldn't listen to the guy he arrested, and then a whole fleet of Feds showed up and I realized we'd arrested a fellow bureau boy."

"Whoa," I whispered.

"You said it. Anyway, it took a call from Gaston to get Brice to stand down, and even then he was giving the other agents lip. Turns out they're a group from Vegas, and normally they're supposed to let us know when they're in town as a professional courtesy, but under the circumstances, they kept their arrival on the down low. And now we've got two divisions angry as hell at each other."

"Why is the Vegas bureau here?" I asked. I'd actually had a rough time with some Vegas boys a few years back. If Oppenheimer was from that office, we definitely weren't gonna get along.

"They'll fill you in," Dutch said. "Listen, let me get off the phone and get Cal over here. You'll like him, Abs. But don't talk until he gets here. And tell the Feds the truth about Candice asking you to retrieve her computer, okay?"

I blinked. Dutch had said that so firmly that I knew he was trying to help me cover up the fact that I'd retrieved a file from Candice's office.

"Tell them exactly what happened," Dutch went on. "That Candice left you a voice mail asking you to retrieve her computer, which you never found, and that after your offices were broken into, you suspected you were being watched, so we set up a ruse to draw out whoever was surveilling you."

"Yes," I said to him. "Yes, you're right. I'll come clean and tell them the truth."

"Good girl," he said, but I hardly felt better. "I'd be in there if I could," Dutch added, like he was reading my mind. "Call me the second the interview is over."

I hung up with Dutch and went back to pacing the room. What did the Vegas bureau want with me? I could only speculate that they were here investigating Dr. Robinowitz's murder, but even that seemed odd, as the jurisdiction should've fallen to the Austin Police Department. What were the Feds doing getting involved in a doctor's murder?

I had quite a while to ponder that question, because Calvin Douglas, my attorney, didn't show up for two more hours. Dutch texted me after an hour and a half. He was through with his interrogation and had been ordered to go home. He wasn't allowed to set foot in the Austin offices until further notice.

I felt even more scared and vulnerable knowing he was out of the building. Just before one o'clock the door opened again and in walked a man of medium build with red hair and wire-rimmed glasses. "Hello," he said, extending his hand. "Mrs. Rivers?"

"Hi," I said, shaking his hand. "You can call me Abby."

"I'm Cal," he said, sitting down and opening up his briefcase to pull out a legal pad and a pen. Motioning with his chin toward the door, he added, "They're itching to get started, but I told them I needed twenty minutes to confer with you. Your husband has retained me and I'll be representing you through this interview and also through the possible arrest—"

"The *what*, now?"

Calvin put his pen down. "Sorry," he said. "But typically when I show up at a federal office and sit with a client through an FBI interrogation, it almost always ends in arrest."

I felt dizzy and realized I was panting. "I haven't done anything!"

"Okay," he said, picking up his pen again. "Let's start there. What is it these guys think you've done?"

I bit my lip. I knew I could trust Calvin not to breathe a word of anything I told him given attorney-client privilege, and I was nervous about lying to him, but remembered Dutch's subtle warning and thought Cal might be the perfect person to practice my lie on.

"I think the Feds believe I'm hiding evidence, Mr. Douglas."

"Call me Calvin," he said kindly before adding, "And what evidence do they believe you're hiding?"

"On the night that Dr. Robinowitz—do you know the case?"

"The doctor from Vegas who was shot at the airport?"

"Yes. On the night he was shot, I received a voice mail from my business partner, Candice Fusco-Harrison—the woman currently accused of that crime. In the voice mail Candice asked me to go to her office and get her computer for her. I've known Candice for years, and I trust her, so I followed her directions and went to the office, but her computer wasn't there. I didn't know if it was locked in her desk, and I didn't have keys for it, so I went back home. The next day, the office I share with Candice was burglarized, and many of our belongings were either stolen or damaged beyond repair. I went home later and felt super paranoid, and that's when I swore I saw someone lurking around our neighbors' house. They're out of town and Dutch and I have been keeping an eye on the place, so I went over and entered through the garage, but I don't have their alarm code or a key to the house, so I simply sat in the garage with my ear pressed to the door, listening for any sign that someone might be inside. When I didn't hear anything, I left and went back home.

"The very next morning Dutch woke me and said there'd been a break-in next door. When we went over to see what was happening, we both noticed that the

Witts' house had been burglarized in the same manner as my office, and I mentioned to Dutch that it seemed too familiar to be a coincidence. I told him that I'd gone over to the Witts' to make sure their house was secure, and he thought maybe we were being watched, so we set a trap to make it look like I was trying to hide something over there, and that's when Dutch and Agent Harrison arrested the Fed who was tailing Dutch."

Calvin was scribbling furiously over his legal pad and after he finished, he picked his chin up and said, "Okay. Let me see if I understand this: Your business partner murdered a man in cold blood at the airport three nights ago, and shortly after that murder, she called you and asked you to go to her office and retrieve her computer?"

"Yes, but at the time I didn't know that she'd been involved in a shooting. She just left me a message that said, 'It's not how it looks.'"

"And what did you take that to mean?"

I blinked. "Uh . . . I don't know. I think I took it to mean that something bad had happened and Candice was caught in the middle."

"Something bad."

"Yeah."

"Like what?"

I shrugged. "I don't know, like maybe one of the people she was running surveillance on caught on and some sort of an altercation had taken place."

"Did she ever mention Dr. Robinowitz to you?"

I shook my head. "Never."

"Do you still have the voice mail?"

I felt a blush touch my cheeks. "I dropped my phone in the sink. It's dead."

Cal's brow furrowed. I could tell he thought that was suspicious. "Do you have the phone?"

I reached into my purse and pulled out the dead phone. I knew I had to hand it over or risk being arrested for obstruction. Cal attempted to turn the phone on, and when it didn't respond, he pocketed it. Then he eyed his notes and said, "Okay, so what were you going to do with Candice's computer if you got your hands on it?"

I shrugged again. "I was going to give it to her."

"Where did you think to meet her?"

"Uh, probably at her condo. Remember, I didn't know she was on the run at the time."

"Have you spoken to Candice since that night?"

"No." That wasn't a lie. We hadn't spoken; we'd texted and I'd deleted all of those. True, the Feds could retrieve the texts through the phone company, but I knew from personal experience that those records would be very slow to come in. I could only hope Oppenheimer asked me the question about hearing from Candice the same way.

"All right," Cal said. "When Agent Oppenheimer comes in, I want you to keep your answers short and to the point. Don't elaborate even if they don't respond to your answer. They'll try to draw information out of you by asking a broad or general question, wait for your answer, then wait a little longer to see if you'll elaborate. Don't. Answer only the question they pose, nothing more, and don't explain more than you have to."

"Got it," I told him. I was plenty wise to the ways of interrogators.

Cal then eyed me as if he wanted to ask me another question but was hesitating.

"What?" I asked.

"Your husband mentioned that, until recently, you were a consultant for the bureau. He also mentioned that you're a professional psychic."

"Yes, that's true."

"Why did you quit consulting for the bureau?"

"It's this thing with Candice," I said. "It really upset me, and I just needed a break for a while." That wasn't the truth, but there was no way I was letting on to anybody but Brice and Dutch that I'd quit to try to track down Candice without it being a conflict of interest.

"Fair enough," Cal said. "And as for that second part, would you mind, Mrs. Rivers, giving me a demonstration of your abilities?"

"Why?" I asked. I get irritated when people look to me for freebies. I mean, would these same people walk into a bank and ask for free money? Or a doctor's office and ask for a free exam? Why am I any different? Readings are how I make my living, and it ticks me off that people put such little value on my abilities that they think nothing of asking to get one for free.

Cal smiled. "You get asked for free readings a lot, don't you?"

"Probably even more than you get asked for free legal advice."

Cal chuckled. "Touché," he said. "But please know that I'm not asking for any other reason than I have a feeling these guys from Vegas are gonna come in here and basically scoff at you and your abilities in order to intimidate and discredit you. I'd just like to see for myself that you're the real deal."

I looked at Cal for a long moment, weighing my annoyance over the genuine need for the demonstration. I understood his barely veiled skepticism—I was faced with it every day—but at some point it just got wearisome. I mean, I wasn't asking him to prove his competence as an attorney.

With a sigh I said, "Normally I'd tell you to stuff it, Counselor, but under the circumstances, I suppose if it better helps you to advise me, then what choice do I have?"

Cal shrugged. "You always have a choice, Mrs. Rivers."

I stared hard at him. "Yeah, right. Whatever. I'll go along with it this one and only time, but you will need to credit me one hundred and fifty dollars in billable hours. Like you, my time is valuable."

"That's fair," Cal said, an amused look on his face.

"Good. So my impressions for you are this: I'm sensing a nasty divorce in your recent past that has made you really look at who you are as a person. I believe your ex-wife called into question the kind of man you are, and you've spent the better part of a year taking a long hard look at yourself and you've made a few improvements as a result."

Cal's eyes widened.

I continued. "The thing is that it wasn't really about

you. Your wife felt that she married too young and missed out on a lot from her youth. She wanted to be free not necessarily from you but from the shackles her life with you, her husband, created. You two never should have gotten married, and both of you had doubts prior to the wedding. Am I right?"

Cal's large eyes blinked. "Yes."

"She's getting ready to move. Did you know that?"

"I gave her the house in the divorce," Cal said. "She'd be stupid to sell it."

"Well, she's selling it. And she's moving west. I think to California because I feel it's still a warm climate and I can see the coast."

Cal's jaw fell open. "We spent some time in Santa Monica a few years ago. She loved that place and tried to talk me into moving out there when the kids were little."

"Once she moves, she won't be back," I told him. "I think you'll be okay, but it's going to be a long time before you start dating again. And even then there won't be anyone serious in your life for quite a while. You're going to focus on work, and that's probably a good thing because you still need time to figure out who *you* are. Still, I can see a vacation in the works. You're trying to decide between Paris and Spain. Go to Spain. You'll *love* Barcelona."

Cal made a noise that was sort of a choking laughing sound. Little did he know I was just getting warmed up. "On the work front," I continued, "there'll be a high-profile case in your near future that'll be quite difficult, but well worth getting involved in. It'll get national attention and the cause is worthy. There's a woman at the center. . . ." My voice trailed off as I stared hard into the ether. "It's not me, and it's not Candice, but it's weird; I feel like there could be a link back to one of us for some reason. I'm not sure why."

I shook my head because that thread felt a little too opaque to draw out any more information. "I also sense that you have both a son and a daughter in their late teens. They feel extremely close, but not in a bonding sort of way. . . . Hold on—are they twins?"

Cal appeared stunned. "They are."

"Yeah, I thought so. They live with you too, right?"

"They wanted to be with me after the divorce," Cal said.

"That was actually a good decision on their part. You're the more stable parent right now and your ex needs room to figure out what she wants in life. Anyway, your son is Mr. High Achiever. He's a great kid, studious, smart, applies himself, and he's a good athlete. Your daughter is the exact opposite, and what you don't understand is that she is incredibly talented in her own way. She has amazing artistic skills—she's a genius in that regard. You want her to go to school to become something analytical, like an accountant. She'd rather die. You need to let her be her, Cal. I know you're worried about her ability to support herself through the arts, but she'll do fine. Encourage her interests in the arts. She'll figure out how to earn a living and she'll thrive as a result."

There was a knock on the door then and Oppenheimer pushed his bullet face through the door again. "Can we get this show on the road?"

Cal cleared his throat and tugged at his tie. "We can," he said, and wrote something on his legal pad before turning it so I could read his words. He'd written, *"You're amazing!"* And I smiled.

Meanwhile Oppenheimer took his seat and behind him came another guy, tall and very skinny, with a face like a horse—he reminded me of Stan Laurel from Laurel and Hardy. He carried a briefcase that was beat-up and worn. "Mrs. Rivers," he said as he sat down. "I'm Agent Gould."

"Did you say Ghoul?" I asked (just to be snarky).

He eyed me snidely. "Goul*d*."

"Ah, my bad." I was now all smiles and solicitude.

Next to me Cal ducked his chin to hide a smile. I wanted to whisper, "This ain't my first rodeo," to him, but thought that might be pushing it.

Gould cleared his throat and began asking me all about Candice. How many years had I known her? How long had we worked together? Did we spend time together outside of work? Et cetera, et cetera, et cetera.

And then he pulled a file from his briefcase and opened it. "Have you ever been to Las Vegas?"

"Yes."

"When?"

"A few years ago."

"What took you there?"

"My husband's cousin went missing. We flew there to look for him."

Gould didn't look at me once while he asked the

questions. Instead he stared at the file as if skimming it for details. I knew what it contained—a detailed account of my rather harrowing adventures in Sin City.

"Looks like you got into some trouble while you were there," Gould said.

"No thanks to you guys." Cal put a hand on my arm. It was a warning that I needed to chill.

"So I gather," said Gould. He then folded up the file and leaned over to pull another one out of his briefcase. Opening it, he said, "Do you know this man?"

I sucked in a breath and turned my head away, sickened by the photo. "Oh, sorry," Gould said. "This is the wrong photo. The guy got shot in the face. Makes him nearly unrecognizable."

"Agent Gould," Cal said, his voice hard. "Can we please refrain from these theatrics?"

"No theatrics intended, Counselor. Here, Mrs. Rivers. Try this photo. Ever seen this guy before?"

I took a few deep breaths before risking another glance and when I did, my breath caught again, but I tried to hide it. "I'm not sure," I said. "He sort of looks familiar, but I can't say that I know him per se." The truth was that I did know him and my heart was racing with the implications.

Oppenheimer reached over and pushed the photo a little closer to me. "Take another look, Mrs. Rivers. He should look more than familiar to you."

I gulped. "I'm sorry," I said, wishing they'd take the photo away. "I know I've seen him before, but I can't place his face."

"Maybe you two have met before?" Gould said, like he was trying to be helpful.

"She's already answered your question, Agent Gould. Move on or ask a different question."

Gould stared intently at me. "According to the notes in the file on you from a few years ago, Mrs. Rivers, this man reported your whereabouts to the FBI. At that time you were a wanted fugitive of the law."

Out of the corner of my eye I saw Cal turn in surprise to me, but I kept my focus on Gould. "You know that whole thing was nothing but bullshit, Agent Gould, and I resent the implication that I was somehow on the wrong side of the law."

"I'm not implying that you were on the wrong side of the law, Mrs. Rivers. I'm implying that this man attempted to assist the FBI with your arrest, and now he's dead."

I knew they were holding back an even stronger connection, so I decided to call their bluff. "Oh, come off it! He's not dead because of me. You're fishing because of who he was once married to."

"So you do recognize him," Gould said.

"Only after you told me he was the guy who ratted me out."

"Right," Oppenheimer said with another roll of his eyes.

Cal cleared his throat. "Would anyone like to explain to me who this man is?"

"Lenny Fusco," Gould told him. "He was Candice Fusco's ex-husband. And, according to Lenny's wife, Candice once tried to kill him."

"She did not!" I yelled. They were twisting things, and it was really pissing me off. "I mean, sure, she was ticked off that he'd turned me in, but she didn't try to kill him, for God's sake!"

Cal put a hand on my arm to quiet me. "What does his death have to do with Mrs. Rivers?"

"We'd like to know her reaction to the fact that Lenny here took a bullet in the face about a month ago, when her BFF was in Vegas getting married for the second time."

My heart began to pound against my rib cage. "Wait . . . what?"

Oppenheimer leaned in. "That's right. Lenny was murdered in the exact same fashion as Dr. Robinowitz sometime between ten p.m. March sixth and six a.m. March seventh. According to our investigation, Candice Fusco was still in town on her honeymoon until the eighth. Ballistics show that Lenny and Robinowitz were each shot with the same caliber gun. We're just waiting on the lab to confirm the bullets were from the same weapon."

I shook my head slowly at first, then more vigorously. "*Why* would Candice shoot her ex?" I demanded.

Gould looked at Oppenheimer, who nodded, and Gould reached back into his briefcase to pull out yet another file. Opening it up, he said, "Maybe because Lenny Fusco had a contract out on him."

I blinked and then I got even angrier. They were accusing Candice of things I knew she hadn't done. "Listen," I said levelly, "Candice may have hated her ex because he was a con artist and a first-class douche bag, but she'd never put a contract out on his life. I mean, they've been divorced for what? Almost ten years? What did she possibly have to gain?"

Gould smirked at me. "We don't believe she put a contract out on Fusco. We believe she personally fulfilled the contract and collected the money."

I sat there stunned, and it was a moment before I was able to speak. "Wait . . . ," I said. "You think . . . you think *Candice* is some sort of hit man?!"

And then the image of my BFF shooting Dr. Robinowitz flashed in my mind and I physically winced because I knew that's exactly what they thought. And, no doubt, what a jury would think too. Texas and Nevada were both capital punishment states. If convicted of either crime, Candice would be lucky to avoid the needle.

Gould got my attention again by pulling out a grainy black-and-white photograph. I squinted at it suspiciously and he turned it around so that I could see that it was an aerial view of Candice huddled close to an elderly gentleman of considerable size. The pair appeared to be deep in conversation at a table and under the man's hand was an envelope. Gould placed another photo in front of me, which was the same scene except that the older gentleman appeared to be passing Candice the envelope. A third photo showed her tucking that envelope into her purse. In the bottom of the frame was a time/date stamp. The photo was taken March 6 at ten twenty-four a.m.

I didn't say anything; instead I waited for Gould or Oppenheimer to explain. Gould spoke first. "Know who that is?" he asked, pointing to the old man in the photos.

"No," I answered truthfully.

"That's Salazar Kato." My mind buzzed. I knew the name, but at that exact moment I couldn't place it. "He owns Lucky Lou's Casino. It's not on the Strip, but it does a hell of a business all the same. Sal's an old-timer who was around in the days when you couldn't swing a dead cat without hitting a mobster in Vegas. A lot of that element is gone now, but Sal barely avoided a racketeering and money-laundering conviction in the nineties. We've been running surveillance on him for years, waiting for a break."

"What does any of that have to do with Candice?" I asked, my mind still trying to place the name Salazar Kato.

Gould eyed me intently again. "Rumor is that Sal was the one who put the contract out on Lenny."

"Do you have proof of that?" Cal asked.

"Not yet," Oppenheimer said. "But we were hearing rumors that Lenny was caught making the moves on one of Sal's girls. He may be old, but the guy gets around, and he's got a jealous streak. He had one of his goons put a guy in the hospital a few years ago for giving one of his girlfriends a ride home from a club. We think Sal caught Lenny in the act, and took care of him. And now we've lost track of the girl too."

My eyes widened. Sal Kato sounded like no one I ever wanted to meet face-to-face. What had Candice been thinking to sit down with him and accept his money?

"Anyway," Oppenheimer continued, "right before Robinowitz came to Austin, he called our team and said that he had major dirt on a casino owner that'd help put him away for a long time. And we knew from our own long-term surveillance of Kato that he and Robinowitz were friends from way back. Robinowitz gave Kato's third wife a face-lift and a boob job a few years before Robinowitz retired. We have Kato on tape joking with Robinowitz that he thought the doc did too good of a job, because his wife dumped him a short time later to take up with a younger man. It doesn't take a rocket scientist to figure out that Robinowitz had dirt on his pal Kato and wanted to loop us in before Kato put a hit on him too."

"What was Robinowitz's motivation, though?" Cal asked. "If they've been friends for years, why'd the doc turn on his friend?"

Oppenheimer shrugged and said, "Robinowitz was in trouble with the IRS. He owed half a million in back taxes, and he had a drinking problem. He had his house in Palm Springs up for sale to cover the debt, but it'd been on the market for over a year and wasn't moving. We think he might've borrowed money from Kato, and as it wasn't looking like he'd be able to pay it back, Robinowitz must've thought that he could kill two birds with one stone: get rid of the debt he owed to the IRS, and have us take Kato out of the picture before he demanded his money back."

I looked again at the photo of Candice tucking that envelope into her purse and it felt like my heart was breaking. How could my best friend—someone I thought of as one of the very best people I'd ever known—do such a despicable thing? How could she be a killer for hire? And how had she fooled *me* for so long?

I felt dizzy with disbelief, and unable to take a full breath. This was all so overwhelming, and I wished very much that Dutch were here next to me. And then I heard Cal say, "So you have some pretty compelling evidence against Candice Fusco, but I fail to see what her dealings in Las Vegas have to do with Mrs. Rivers, here."

Gould laced his fingers together and leaned his elbows on the table. Looking directly at me, he said, "We need to find Candice. If we could offer her a deal, say . . . take the death penalty off the table and keep jurisdiction for both murders of Robinowitz and Lenny Fusco in Nevada, maybe she'd be willing to give up Kato."

"You think I know where she is," I guessed.

Gould and Oppenheimer nodded.

"I don't," I told them. They both looked skeptical. "Listen to me, guys—if I did know where she was, I'd be the first person to talk her into turning herself in. I swear. I don't want Candice to die. She's the best friend I've ever had, and I can't believe any of this is happening. I've known her for a long time, and never in my wildest dreams did I think she was capable of doing any of this." Pointing to the photos, I added, "This *isn't* the woman I know. And I just can't make sense of any of this."

Gould looked hard at me. "Well, you'd better come

to grips with it, Mrs. Rivers. It's the only way to save your friend."

Oppenheimer and Gould kept Cal and me for several more hours. They grilled me over and over again about where I thought Candice might be, and I stuck to the truth—I had no clue.

They asked me more than once if I thought Brice knew of his wife's dealings with Kato and I stuck to the truth on that one too. "Absolutely, positively *not*!" Then they asked about what I'd been hiding in the Witts' house. I told them the same story I'd given to Cal with one key difference: Instead of telling them that I'd received a voice mail from Candice, I merely said that she'd called me in the middle of the night and said that I had to go to her office and retrieve her computer. Next to me, Cal shifted in his seat, but he never corrected me and I hoped they didn't ask to see my phone. They didn't, but they were pretty interested in what I believed might be on Candice's computer—which I also informed them I hadn't seen when I'd gotten to the office. That part at least was true. I stuck to that story as they peppered me with questions and details, and after a while they let up on it because I think they probably believed me.

In turn, I learned a few things too. Things like that the Feds had been watching me and Dutch, but they'd started their surveillance the morning the police had been called to the Witts', so they hadn't seen anything suspicious other than me entering the garage and coming out with the file full of blank papers. I also learned that the Vegas bureau was very suspicious that Brice might have known about his wife's unlawful dealings and was perhaps a coconspirator and a dirty Fed.

I held back defending him to them, because I knew there was no point. Still it greatly alarmed me that they could so misjudge him, and I had a sneaking suspicion it wouldn't be long before Internal Affairs got involved and investigated Brice right out of his job. No wonder Gaston had been furious.

Finally, when my stomach was grumbling loudly and I was light-headed with hunger and thought I just couldn't take any more of their repetitive questions, I held up my hand and said, "Guys, if you're planning on arresting me, go for it. Just somebody feed me before I pass out, okay?"

"It's well past eight o'clock," Cal said. He looked just as hungry and annoyed. "My client hasn't eaten anything since . . ."

"Early this morning," I said.

Gould sat back and shared a look with Oppenheimer. Something unspoken passed between them, and then Oppenheimer nodded. Gould said, "You may go, Mrs. Rivers. But if you hear from Candice, we will need to be notified."

I got up and felt a little shaky and queasy. It'd been a very long day and I'd been running on nothing but adrenaline. Grabbing my purse and moving toward the door, I said, "I understand."

"We mean it," Oppenheimer said as I was about to exit. "You hear from her, you call us."

I stopped and looked back at him. My sixth sense

buzzed. He had something up his sleeve, and I didn't like it. Squaring my shoulders, I stared at him without blinking. "I understand, Agent Oppenheimer. If Candice calls me, my next phone call will be to you."

I could tell that no one in the room believed me, but I was too hungry and exhausted to care. Cal held the door open for me and we left.

I parted ways with my attorney at the sidewalk. He was headed home and I was headed two doors down for a couple of tacos. After getting my meal, I was on my way back to my car when my new phone pinged with an incoming text. I almost reached into my purse for it, but felt a hint of warning from my radar. Looking around surreptitiously, I saw a black SUV parked across the street and I swore there was someone in the car.

"Great," I muttered. "They're still watching me."

I quickened my step then and kept my chin down. No way was I going to pull out my phone anywhere but behind closed doors.

I drove home in a bit of a daze, nibbling on my taco and still reeling over all that I'd learned about my best friend.

And then I had a terrible thought: Were Candice and I even best friends anymore? Had I ever been her best friend? Or was our friendship some kind of ruse—a cover for her secret life as a Mafia hit man? Hit woman. Assassin.

I shook my head as I dwelled on those dark thoughts. "Who the hell *are* you, Candice Fusco?" I said to myself. "And how come *I* didn't know anything about who you really are?"

That was the thing I just couldn't get over. I prided myself on being a very good psychic. Sure, I'd been born with a talent for picking things out of the ether, but that talent had been honed over the years and fine-tuned. I'd come to believe that being a good psychic had less to do with talent and far more to do with honing a skill. Years of practice and self-examination had made me the gifted intuitive that I was, so how was it that in all the readings I'd ever given to Candice—and I gave her a reading at least once a year—I'd never picked up on this dark side of hers? How had she duped *me* of all people?

And Dutch?

And Brice?

And even Gaston?

All four of us were experts at detecting deception, so why hadn't *any* of us ever seen even a hint of falsehood in her?

It made no sense, either logically or intuitively. I just couldn't make what I'd been shown in those photographs sync up with what I felt in my heart—that Candice was still my very best friend, and I was still hers.

When I got home, I found Dutch sitting in the dark with a glass of scotch and both pups curled up beside him. "Hey there, beautiful," he said when I came through the door.

"Hey there, yourself, cowboy. You hungry?"

"I could eat."

I handed him the bag I'd carried in. "Fish tacos from Pueblo Viejo."

Dutch opened the bag and peered eagerly inside. I

figured he hadn't eaten much since breakfast either. "Best wife ever," he said, taking out one of the wrapped tacos.

I sat down next to him and lifted the scotch from his hand. After taking a sip, I rasped, "Smooth."

He chuckled. "There's beer in the fridge, dollface."

I got up and headed toward the kitchen and called over my shoulder, "How'd your interrogation go?"

"Brutal," he replied while I fished around in the icebox. "Cal called me a little while ago. He said you did great."

I came back and plopped down next to him, leaning my head on his shoulder. "He was good."

"He should be for a hundred fifty an hour."

I smiled. "One of those hours is free."

Dutch pulled his head back to look quizzically at me.

"I gave him a reading."

My hubby arched an eyebrow.

"He asked," I told him. "I think he didn't really believe I had any talent until I started fishing through his ether."

Dutch chuckled. "Oh, how hard those skeptics fall."

"Yeah, well, it was a good thing, I think. I'm going to work with him in the future on a case."

"What case?"

"Not sure yet. It hasn't happened. Or if it's happened, I haven't been pulled into it yet."

"I'm confused."

"It doesn't matter. Tell me about your session with the boys from Vegas."

Dutch kissed the top of my head and motioned to

the clock on the wall. "Later, doll. Brice should be here any minute and I promised to have his scotch ready."

I lifted my head off his shoulder so that Dutch could get up. "Brice is coming over?"

"Yeah," Dutch said, heading toward the kitchen for a glass and probably a refill of his own drink. "I called him right after I heard from Cal. He's in rough shape and I don't think it's a good idea for him to be alone right now. I told him to pack a bag and stay with us for a while."

I felt a rush of warmth for my husband. Ever since our wedding there were often moments when I was so filled with love for my marvelous man that it overwhelmed me. Dutch was the great love of my life, my complement in so many meaningful ways, and I could hardly believe that in a world with six billion people, we'd somehow managed to find each other. "That was really nice of you," I said once he returned to the couch.

He shrugged. "He'd do the same for us."

"He would indeed," I said, remembering a time not too long ago when I'd camped out on his couch for a week.

Just then there was a soft knock on the door. "Come on in, sir," Dutch called.

The door opened and Brice stood there with his phone pressed to his ear and his complexion white as a ghost. He looked stunned, and utterly heartbroken all at the same time. Dutch and I both stood up and went to him. I was worried he was about to faint.

"Brice?" I said gently as he continued to stand there,

his mouth slightly ajar and that phone still pressed to his ear.

Dutch reached out and put a supportive hand on his shoulder. "Hey," he said softly. "What's going on?"

Brice's eyes watered, and he stared straight ahead as if he couldn't hear us. I inched closer and put a hand on his phone. "Here," I said. "Let me."

He let me take the phone and I could hear a voice on the other end calling for him. "Hello? Sir? Are you there? *Sir?*"

"Hello?" I said into the phone. "This is Abby Cooper. Who's this?"

"Oh, man! Cooper, it's Rodriguez. Where's Harrison?"

"He's here with me and Dutch. Oscar, what's happened?" There was a slight pause and I became even more alarmed. Whatever had happened, it was bad. *Really* bad. "Oscar?"

"Let me talk to Rivers," Oscar said, but Dutch was easing Brice over to the couch. The second Brice sat down, he buried his head in his hands and began to weep.

"No," I told Oscar. "Tell me what's happened." Oscar sighed, and it was such a sad sound that my own eyes misted. "It's Candice," I whispered. "Isn't it?"

Dutch eyed me from the couch and he reached out his hand. "Let him tell me," he said. "Abs, give me the phone."

I shook my head and gripped the phone tightly. "Tell me!" I pleaded.

Oscar finally spoke, his voice wet with emotion. "Candice's car went off a bridge and into Lady Bird Lake. I just heard from one of the APD officers on scene. The fire department got her out, and they've been working on her, but she's unresponsive. She's gone, Abby. She's gone."

Chapter Seven

I sank to my knees and let the phone fall to the floor. Dutch was next to me in a second, but I was already curling myself into a ball. I heard a terrible noise, heart wrenching and awful—it filled the room and I realized it was the sound of my own grief as I cried out against the horrible news. *"Noooooooooooooooooooooo!"*

Dutch pulled me into his arms and hugged me tightly. I squeezed my eyes closed and struggled to take in a breath over the tightness in my chest. For a long time I couldn't do anything other than wail pitifully. I was only slightly aware of Dutch lifting me and carrying me over to the couch, where he rocked me back and forth and tried to console me. But it was no use. I was pulled down into a dark well of painful heartbreak, Oscar's words repeating over and over in my mind.

She's gone, Abby. She's gone.

Huge sobs rose out from my insides and I felt like I

was drowning in a sea of sorrow and regret. And then, after what felt like hours, I took a breath that didn't threaten to choke me and wiped at my eyes. Dutch laid a hand on the back of my head and kissed my forehead. "I'm so sorry, Abby," he whispered, and I realized he was crying too.

And then I thought of Brice and I lifted my chin away from his chest, looking around for Candice's husband. As deep as my grief was, Brice's had to be even worse. "Where's Brice?" I asked, my throat raw.

"Out back," Dutch said, motioning with his head toward our back porch.

"You left him alone?"

Dutch used his hands to wipe my cheeks. "I'll get to him just as soon as I know you're okay."

I dropped my chin and shook my head. How could I ever be okay again? A buzzing sound drew my attention toward the floor. Brice's phone was still there near the door where I'd dropped it.

"Should one of us get that?" I asked dully. I felt drained and functional only on the surface.

Dutch lifted me gently and set me back on the couch before getting up to retrieve Brice's phone. After swiping the display, he put the phone to his ear. "Rivers," he said crisply. He sounded so much more together than he looked, and I wanted him to come back to the couch and sit with me again so that I could comfort him like he'd comforted me.

But then something in his expression changed and he said, "Where?" Then he looked at his watch and added, "We'll be there in twenty."

Pocketing the phone, he walked toward me with his hand out. "Come on," he said. "We gotta get Brice."

I took his hand and let him pull me off the couch. "What is it?"

"They managed to get a pulse on Candice after all, and they've got her at St. David's."

I staggered as I followed behind Dutch. "She's . . . she's *alive*?"

"Yes," Dutch said, pausing as we got to the back door. Turning to me, he said, "It doesn't look good, though, Abs. She's got severe injuries from the crash, and she had no pulse for several minutes."

I felt my lip quiver. "So she could still die?"

Dutch cupped my cheeks. "Yes. And if she recovers, there's a good chance she may never be the same."

I got teary again. "Okay," I said hoarsely.

"We've got to be careful what we tell Brice," Dutch said, looking at me intently.

"What do you mean?"

My sweet husband stroked my cheek with his thumb. "He's going to look to you for hope, Edgar. And I'm worried that you're in no shape to tune in on anything right now. I don't want you to use that radar until you've had some rest and you're not in shock."

I gripped his wrists. "I'll be okay," I told him, but I knew he was right. I felt far too shaky to tune in on Candice's energy, even though I knew I should check the ether just to prepare myself in case her prognosis was for the worse.

Dutch pulled me close and kissed me on the forehead. "Whatever happens, I'm here, okay?"

I nodded because I got choked up again and couldn't speak. Dutch then opened the door and we went out to find Brice, sitting on the edge of the lawn chair with his face in his hands.

Dutch and I shared a look before we both sat down on either side of him. "Hey," Dutch began. I put my arm around Brice. He tensed, and I could feel him trying hard not to sob in front of us. "I just got a call from Oscar. He's on scene and they were able to get a pulse."

Brice lifted his face and stared hard at Dutch. "What?" he gasped. "You mean . . . she's alive?"

My husband nodded. "We need to go. I'll drive us over to St. David's."

Brice swallowed hard and wiped at his cheeks. It nearly undid me all over again to see him so overcome. I got up and held out my hand. He turned his attention to me and stared at my hand blankly. It seemed he was having a difficult time processing what was happening. "Come on, honey," I coaxed. "Take my hand and come with us. We'll bring you to her."

At last Brice reached up and took hold of my hand and I led him slowly back through the kitchen and out the front door. Dutch hurried on ahead of us to start the car and drive it closer to the front walk, where I led Brice around to put him in the passenger seat next to Dutch. I then got in the back and we were off.

It took about twenty minutes to reach the hospital, and no one uttered a word on the way over, each of us lost in our thoughts of what'd happened to Candice.

Dutch pulled up to the emergency room entrance

and I got out and took hold of Brice's hand again while Dutch went to park the car before meeting us inside.

We found Oscar at the nurses' station and he seemed surprised to see us there. Or maybe he was just surprised by Brice's blank stare as I led him along. "Sir," he said with a nod to Brice.

"How is she?" he replied hoarsely.

Oscar's gaze dropped. "Not good, sir. I'm sorry."

I felt my eyes water again, and I wanted so much for something to happen that would take me out of this nightmare and cause me to wake up in a different reality, one where Candice was alive, well, and not a murderer.

"I need to see her," Brice said so softly it was almost a whisper.

Oscar pointed toward the nurse at the desk. "I'll tell them you're here. They're working on her right now, but how about you go sit down and I'll come get you as soon as they come out to report on her condition?"

Brice turned toward a set of double doors that led to the trauma area and I felt him tense again. I figured he had to have thoughts about storming back there to be with his wife, so I gripped his hand tightly and tugged on his arm. "Come on," I coaxed. "We can't do anything back there and we'll only get in the way. Let's go sit down so the doctors and nurses can do their jobs without our interference."

Brice wavered another moment before letting me lead him over to a triple row of chairs. Dutch came in a few minutes later, looking winded, like he'd run from the parking lot. He sat down on the other side of Brice, who was simply staring at the floor, his hands clasped in front of him.

We waited like that for a long time—at least an hour—before Oscar came to find us. "The doc will be out in a minute," he informed us. And then he frowned and motioned over his shoulder. "The guys from Vegas are here, by the way."

Brice's head snapped up and he glared angrily in the direction Oscar had indicated. "You tell those sons of bitches to back the hell off," he growled.

Dutch rose to his feet. "Let me handle it, sir," he said, and I worried about the possible confrontation to come. Luckily, Candice's doctor came out of the back and over to us. "Are you the family?" he asked when he stopped in front of us. We both nodded.

"I'm her husband and this is her sister," Brice said, without missing a beat.

I wound my arm through his to let him know I was grateful for that. We both knew I wouldn't be allowed to see Candice unless I was family.

The doctor nodded. "I'm Dr. Reynolds. Sir, your wife's condition is, I'm afraid, most grave. She's sustained multiple injuries and she registered no pulse for several minutes. Normally I would suggest that the odds of her ever being more than a vegetable were very long; however, the fire department has informed us that the water temperature at the lake was barely above forty degrees, due to the unusually cold winter we've had. This put your wife in a rather immediate hypothermic state, which would have slowed down all of her metabolic functions. It is possible for patients who've experienced this particular condition to lose a pulse for several minutes and recover fully, but there are also other grievous injuries to consider."

Brice had gone pale again and I squeezed his arm. He seemed unable to speak, so I said, "What other injuries, Doctor?"

He took a deep breath before answering. I had no idea how he managed to hold it together enough to deliver news like this. "Candice has sustained fractures to three of her four limbs: her right arm and both legs. Both of her femurs were compound fractures. Six of her ribs are broken, her left lung was punctured, her spleen is swollen and may need to be removed, and every single bone in her face has been fractured. Right now she is comatose, and we don't know when, or if, she'll wake up. The next twelve hours are the most critical. We're going to try to manage her injuries symptomatically for now by attempting to control the swelling until she's stable enough for surgery. Her spleen is the most concerning right now; if it continues to swell and we have to go in to remove it, there's a very likely chance she won't survive the surgery."

The doctor finished his speech and it was a moment before I was able to inhale. "Sweet Jesus," I whispered.

Next to me Brice stood stiffly, his face pale but his eyes finally focused and intent. "Can we see her?"

Dutch came back to us at that moment and put his arm across my shoulders. I looked up at him and shook my head to indicate that Candice's condition was grave.

"Yes," the doctor told Brice. "I'll have a nurse come

out and take you to her, but, Mr. Harrison, please do not try to hug her or move her, other than to gently hold her hand, and I would encourage you to do that, in fact. Talk to her and let her know you're here. Remind her what to fight for."

"She can hear me?" Brice asked, his voice cracking with emotion.

"We don't know," Dr. Reynolds said. "Which is why you shouldn't hold back. Talk to her. Let her hear your voice. Convince her to fight, because that is the only thing keeping her alive right now."

I had to turn away at that moment and I let go of Brice's arm and buried my face in Dutch's chest. I tried so hard not to lose it, because I knew Brice needed some support right now, but I just couldn't. It seemed every time someone mentioned my best friend, the news that came with it was worse and worse.

Dutch wrapped me in his arms and squeezed me tight. "Hey," he whispered. "If you want to see Candice, now's the time, sweetie, and I think we should see her."

I nodded and tried to squash a fresh sob bubbling up inside of me.

"Hey," Dutch said again, holding me gently. "Abs. You can't go in there like this, okay? And she needs you."

I nodded again and swallowed hard. "I know," I said, taking a ragged breath. Then I looked up at Dutch, and found him staring at me intently.

"You can do this," he said.

I took another deep breath and stepped back to take up his hand. "Let's go."

We entered Candice's room amid a flurry of beeps and mechanical knocks. The room was dim, lit mostly by the machines surrounding Candice's bed and presumably pumping life back into her body.

She lay in the bed tangled in tubes, cords, and white sheets, but even as we edged closer to her still form, I was hard-pressed to recognize her.

Beneath all the bandages my best friend was little more than one giant bruise. Her face was unrecognizable—so swollen and bruised that it was hard to tell even that she was human.

And the rest of her wasn't much better. Her chest was wrapped in an Ace bandage, and three of her limbs were covered in casts. The only thing exposed that wasn't black-and-blue was Candice's left hand, and Brice moved to it to wrap it tenderly in his own. Tears leaked down his cheeks and it was perhaps the saddest sight I'd ever seen.

I felt my lower lip quiver as I watched him, not daring to breathe because I knew I couldn't lose it in here. Dutch was right, Candice needed us to be strong right now, but Brice needed it too.

I swallowed hard and felt Dutch squeeze my own hand and at last I felt I could inhale without exhaling out a sob. I moved to Candice's other side and had such an urge to touch her and let her know that we were there, but for a moment I was at a complete loss as to where I could gently place my hand so as not to hurt her. I finally settled for laying my palm at the very top of her head. Her hair felt so soft. Candice always had great hair. I felt a pang as I remembered that she'd had it cut just a few days before and I'd remarked on how beautiful she'd looked after her salon appointment. "Hey, girl," I said, my voice wavering a little. "We're here."

For the next minute or two no one spoke or moved; we simply gazed down at Candice's broken and battered form as if we were each trying to reconcile what we saw against the vibrant healthy woman we knew.

Our frozen stances were all broken when a nurse came in and smiled sympathetically at us. Brice let go of Candice's hand to let her check one of the many IVs snaking its way into Candice, and after making a note on her chart, the nurse smiled again at us and moved to leave. Brice spoke as she passed by him. "Her wedding ring?" he asked, and looked pointedly down at Candice's left hand. Brice had given her a whopper of a diamond when they'd gotten engaged, and had chosen a beautiful diamond-encrusted wedding band to join it and make it one ring.

"We always remove a patient's jewelry and personal property in the ER," the nurse said softly. "Check in with the nurse at the nursing station and we'll get you all of her personal belongings."

Brice nodded, wiping at his cheeks before turning back to take up the hand of his wife again.

I eyed Dutch meaningfully and he nodded in silent understanding. Brice should have a little time alone with Candice. "We'll be in the waiting room," he said, squeezing Brice's shoulder and holding his other hand out for me.

Before taking it, I leaned down and kissed the very

top of Candice's forehead. "We'll be back, sweetie. We love you. Please fight with everything you have, okay?"

Brice found us about forty-five minutes later. In his arms were Candice's wet clothes, her purse, and a clear plastic bag that held her wedding ring, earrings, a necklace, and her watch. He held the items tight to his chest, as if he were holding a part of Candice to his heart. I got up and led him over to a chair, sitting him down and cupping his cheek. "Hey," I said. "She'll make it, Brice."

He'd been staring distantly out into space, even when he'd come over to us, but his eyes focused on me now. "Are you sure?"

And there it was. The question I desperately wanted to avoid. My radar kicked in automatically—that's the thing about asking a psychic a question; we become so conditioned to tuning in that it's like a reflex. The answer came immediately and I felt a mix of information. Some good. Some terrible.

I owed it to Brice to tell him the truth. "She will," I said, holding his gaze. "But I don't know that she'll ever be the same." Motioning with my head toward Candice's room, I added, "She'll have a hell of a long road back, Brice. And at the end of that road . . . it's hard to say that she'll ever feel much like the old Candice again."

My words hung heavily in the space between us. Brice's expression wavered between relief and regret and finally settled to something that looked like reluctant acceptance. Bowing his head, he said, "Thank you."

I leaned over and kissed his cheek. "Hey," I said after straightening up. "Why don't you let me take those things from you. They're wet and getting you wet in the process."

Brice handed me Candice's clothes dully, including her purse and her jewelry while he was at it. "I'm gonna stay here awhile," he said. "I've gotta find out what the hell happened."

I blinked. The news of Candice's accident had been so shocking that I hadn't even thought to ask how Candice had ended up driving her car over a bridge into the river. And when I thought about it, I became even more shocked, because Candice had a secret fear of bridges, being that her sister had lost control of the car she was driving while crossing a bridge.

And Candice and I had been involved in two other bad car accidents, one involving a bridge and another involving a slick road and rushing water. It seemed crazy that she could've been involved in yet a similar fourth incident.

"Want some help?" Dutch asked Brice, and I was so glad that he had. Brice didn't look capable of ordering breakfast much less finding out what'd happened on that bridge.

Brice nodded and I got up with Candice's things. "I'll take these home," I said to Dutch. "Call me later and I'll come back to pick you two up."

He reached into his pocket and handed me the keys. Then he leaned in and gave me a kiss. "Drive safe, you hear?"

I knew then just how rattled seeing Candice in such a state had left him. But for a twist of fate it could've been me in that hospital bed.

I went out to Dutch's car and got a towel from the gym bag in his trunk to place on the passenger seat before setting Candice's clothes down. I then unzipped her purse and tucked the bag with her jewelry inside before I got in the car and drove home in a bit of a haze. As I pulled into the driveway, I realized I didn't even remember the trip. After parking Dutch's sedan in front of the garage, I leaned over and grabbed Candice's wet clothes and her purse, but as I was getting out of the car, the purse fell to the pavement, landing upside down and scattering the contents. "Dammit!" I swore, trying to juggle her clothes while I gathered up the items that'd fallen to the pavement. I scooped up Candice's jewelry, lipstick, her wallet, spare set of keys, and a ziplock bag with a folded piece of paper inside that I realized belatedly had my name on it.

I paused in the gathering of stuff to sit back on my heels and carefully unzip the bag and retrieve the paper from inside. Moving under the fog light atop the garage, I unfolded it and inspected the contents. It was a letter and it read,

Abby,
    What I've done is unforgivable. I can't go to jail. This was the only way. Help Brice. He wouldn't understand but I know you do. I hope you two can forgive me.
                                                            Candice

I gasped as I read the lines, then reread them several more times. "No!"

Standing up, I looked around, as if I could find

someone nearby who would help me make sense of the apparent suicide note Candice had left for me.

But there was no one about. And I suddenly felt extremely exposed—as if an unnamed person was watching me. Goose pimples lined my arms and I wasted no more time standing in the middle of my driveway, but hustled my butt inside.

Shutting the door, I made sure to secure the dead bolt. A seriously creepy feeling had come over me and I didn't like it. Shuffling into the living room with the letter and the rest of Candice's things, I was greeted by a sleepy Eggy, who'd come out of his bed to check on me. I bent down and dropped Candice's things before picking up my pup and holding him close. His warm little body did me a world of good. Of course the kiss he gave my cheek also helped. And after a minute Tuttle came out of her bed too, and with their help I shed the goose pimples and the creepy feeling.

Then I called Dutch. "Hi, dollface," he said when he answered. "You make it home okay?"

"Did you find out what happened?" I asked, not even bothering to answer his question; I was so anxious about the note.

There was a pause, then, "Yes and no. A couple of eyewitnesses told the police that they heard the roar of an engine, and Candice's car went straight at the guardrail of the bridge, crashing through it into the river. According to the initial report, Candice never hit the brakes. We don't know if she might've fallen asleep at the wheel, or something else happened to her, but the event seems to have more questions than answers right now."

My heart was racing. I couldn't believe that Candice, of all people, would choose to commit suicide. It just seemed unfathomable, and completely inconsistent with the woman I'd called my best friend for the past four years.

"Abs?" Dutch said. "You there?"

I blinked. "Yeah, honey. Sorry. I'm here."

"You okay?"

I stared down at the note still clutched in my hand. I was on the verge of telling him, but hesitated. I knew he'd tell Brice about it, and I just didn't think I could do that to Brice right now. "I'll be okay. I'm just really tired."

"Go to bed," he said. "I'll be home in an hour or two."

"But I have your car—"

"Oscar's here. I'll have him bring us home."

I sighed wearily. All the adrenaline of the evening was taking its toll, and I suddenly felt weary down to my DNA. "Okay, honey. I'll see you when you get home."

Before heading to bed, I threw Candice's clothes on the drying rack we had in the laundry room. Her fine clothes were always dry-clean only, and I vowed to take them to the cleaners the first chance I had. Her coat wasn't among her personal effects. I figured it'd gone down with the car. I set her purse on the dryer and got out everything still left inside. The purse was ruined, but I'd probably be able to salvage most of the contents. As I set out the contents, I realized that Candice's phone was missing. Not especially unusual, as she typically tucked it into the cup holder when she drove. I figured it'd probably gone down with the car, but then I eyed Candice's purse again and a weird thought occurred to me. "Why did they send your purse to the hospital, Candice?"

I closed my eyes, trying to picture the accident. I imagined Candice in the driver's seat, stomping down on the accelerator, and her purse would've been in the passenger seat. Unsecured.

Then, *crash*, Candice's Porsche hits the guardrail and the contents inside the car most certainly would've been jostled around, then a second *crash* as Candice's car hit the water, and the contents of the car would've been tossed around even more. . . . So how had her purse survived the plunge into the water? Wouldn't it have gone down with the car? I hardly thought the first responders would've been worried about retrieving her pocketbook.

I held up the purse, and noticed for the first time that the strap had been severed. I put the two ends together. The strap hadn't been torn; it'd been cut by something very sharp, like a pair of scissors.

With a furrowed brow I put the strap over my left shoulder across my body and realized that the strap had been cut right across the sternum. The only explanation I could come up with was that Candice had been wearing her purse when she went into the water—but that made little sense.

In all the time I'd known Candice, I'd never once seen her drive while wearing her purse. It got in the way of the seat belt after all. Then again, if Candice had really been trying to commit suicide, would she have bothered with the seat belt?

"Probably not," I muttered. "And you probably wore your purse so that when they pulled your body from the water, they'd find your identification. And the suicide note."

I reached for Candice's wallet again and flipped it open. There was her driver's license. I fished it out of the plastic casing, and studied it. On the license her eyes were hazel and her height was five feet seven inches.

Feeling a ping from my radar, I hurried to the bedroom and into the closet, using the step stool to retrieve the folder I'd tucked away for safekeeping.

Comparing the license in Candice's wallet with the one in the file, I saw that she'd purposely changed those two details, maybe to conceal her identity in Vegas, or maybe to honor her sister, but then I noticed something else that puzzled me. The address on the Nevada license was the same as the apartment listed on the lease agreement.

But why?

Had she been planning on disappearing from our lives altogether and setting up a new life in Vegas under her sister's name? And if so, then why change that plan and drive her car over the side of a bridge? Candice was incredibly resourceful—if she'd wanted to make it out of town and set herself up in Vegas, she definitely could've done that—so why had she done something so desperate as to drive her car into the lake?

As I stood there pondering, I realized where I knew the name Salazar Kato from. It was one of the names on the DNA test results. But why did Candice have his DNA results, and who was Olive Wintergarden? And, further, what was so important about the contents of this file that Candice needed to keep it out of the hands of the law?

I stepped down and sat on the stool, trying to put the puzzle together, but the more I thought about it, the more questions I had. None of the scenarios I came up with made any kind of sense and after twenty minutes of simply sitting there and thinking, I gave up and replaced the folder, adding to it the suicide note. I didn't want Brice to find it. At least not yet. I'd tell him about it all later. Maybe.

At last I changed and called to the pups, lifting them into our massive bed because I couldn't bear the thought of falling asleep alone. Curling myself around Eggy and Tuttle, I fell into an exhausted sleep within seconds.

Chapter Eight

I woke up to the soft snores of my husband. Blinking my eyes against the light filtering in from the windows, I saw that Dutch was now the one curled around Eggy and Tuttle, while I was left a small section at the edge of the bed. "Traitors," I whispered to the pups as I eased quietly out of the bed and tiptoed from the room.

I found Brice sitting alone at the kitchen table, half of a cup of coffee in front of him as he stared blankly off into space. He didn't even seem to notice me.

When I put my hand on his shoulder, he jerked. "Sorry!" I said softly. "Didn't mean to startle you."

"I couldn't sleep," he said, rubbing his eyes.

"Can I fix you something to eat?"

Brice shook his head. "Not hungry."

I sat down across from him and waited for him to lift his gaze to mine. "She's alive," I said. "And that's something, Brice. We have to hold on to that. While she's breathing, there's hope."

Brice's gaze fell back to the tabletop. "That's just it, Cooper. Even if she made some kind of miraculous recovery, she's wanted for murder. Either way we'll never get Candice back. Either she'll be a vegetable, or she'll end up in jail for the rest of her life, and I've been sitting here for hours wondering which of the lesser evils to wish for."

I had no answer to that, so we simply sat in silence for several moments before Brice said, "I still can't believe this is happening. I mean, last weekend Candice and I were looking at lots for sale. We even interviewed a couple of builders." Brice looked up at me again. "How did we go from there to here, Abby?"

I reached out and squeezed his hand. "I don't know," I said honestly. "But the one thing I do know is that there is more to this story. There has to be. I refuse to believe that Candice isn't the loyal best friend to me, and devoted wife to you, she seemed to be."

Brice's eyes watered and he turned his gaze to the ceiling. "I don't know," he said. "I mean, all of this . . ." He waved his hand to indicate the magnitude of recent events. "If *any* of it's true, then I've been living with a total stranger for the past two years. It's like she's not even the same person."

Something clicked in my mind; maybe it was my intuition, maybe it was all my history with Candice, a woman who had never, ever let me down, but something made me get up then and say, "Brice, I'm gonna find out. I'm gonna get the other half of this story and put all this together so that it makes sense. Okay?"

But Brice was back to staring at his coffee cup, and he nodded absently. "Yeah, okay, Cooper."

I squeezed his shoulder and headed back to the bedroom. Dutch had rolled over and slung an arm across my pillow, but otherwise he was still sleeping soundly. Gathering some jeans, a light sweater, my boots, and my purse, I headed to the bathroom to change. Once I was dressed, I checked my purse to make sure I had everything I'd need, and that's when I retrieved my phone. Clicking the home button to check the time, I was startled to see a text from "Cassidy." Candice had sent me a text.

My heart pounded as I swiped the screen, my mind filling with questions: Had Candice woken up? Had she texted me from the hospital? How had she made such a dramatic recovery in mere hours?

I read the text. It said, *What game?*

I blinked. "What game?" I said aloud. And then I remembered. I'd sent Candice a text the day before when I'd spotted her car following me and I'd accused her of playing games, and I'd deleted it when I hadn't heard back from her. She must've been replying to that text. According to the time stamp, she'd sent her response about an hour before she'd driven her car over the side of the bridge.

Which made absolutely no sense. If Candice had truly attempted to commit suicide, why would her one text to me simply say, *What game?*

Why wouldn't it contain a confession? Or an apology? Or an explanation?

I sat down on the side of the bathtub and stared at the phone for a long time, my mind awhirl with questions without answers. And then I got up, grabbed my purse, and opened the bathroom door.

Dutch was standing on the other side looking very sleepy but oh-so-doable if only I was in the mood. "Hey there," he said. "Did you get any sleep?"

I moved in close to him and gave him a quick hug and a peck on the cheek. "I gotta go, babe. Sorry, can't talk right now."

Dutch grabbed my arm as I turned away. "Whoa, hold on there, speedy. It's five thirty in the morning. *Where* is it that you have to go?"

"The hospital."

Dutch grimaced and let go of my arm. "Sorry, doll-face. Of course. If you want to wait five minutes, I can go with you."

I shook my head. "Brice needs you more than I do right now. I'll call you later, though."

Dutch eyed the door of the bedroom warily. I knew he was really worried about Brice.

"He's doing okay, all things considered," I assured him. "But if you could get him to eat something, that might be good."

"On it," Dutch promised, leaning sideways to kiss me before turning back toward the bathroom. "Drive safe, Edgar," were his parting words, and I was free.

After pulling into the parking lot of the hospital, I parked and sat for a moment to collect my thoughts and gather my courage. And then I switched on my radar and approached the hospital with determination.

I was allowed in to see Candice even though visiting hours didn't start for a few more hours, because she was an ICU patient and they make allowances for those family members of critically ill patients.

I found my way to my best friend's room and entered as quietly as possible, not wanting to disturb her should she be even slightly aware of her surroundings. I approached her bed and stood there, pointing my radar directly at the still form in the bed.

Right away I sensed how deeply injured Candice was. Her energy was barely more than a feeble pulse, so weak and broken that it was a miracle she was still alive at all. There was pain there too, and that made me wince because I didn't want her to be in any pain. I wanted her to be blissfully unaware of her condition, but the throbbing of every limb, every joint, and especially those shattered bones in her face radiated pain.

My gaze traveled to the IVs hanging all around the bed. I didn't know how much pain meds the hospital staff could safely give Candice, but it didn't feel like enough and I planned on telling Brice to call Candice's doctor and have them see what they could do about it.

And then I began to search through Candice's energy looking for clues as to what'd led her here.

I could feel a strong connection to Las Vegas, but what was odd was that the connection felt much stronger than it should have. Candice had lived in Vegas for much of her youth and early adulthood, but she hadn't spent any significant time there for several years. And yet, when I dove into her ether, symbols for Sin City overshadowed any other location I was able to pick up.

It was almost as if she'd spent many years there—recently.

Puzzled, I moved on to other topics, and was shocked to see a triangle enter my thoughts.

Cheating partners are always symbolized in my mind's eye by a triangle. Candice had been cheating on Brice. "No way!" I mouthed. I checked the ether again to make sure, and the truth of it was there, attached to the woman in the bed.

I could tell that the other man was older than Candice, and apparently he'd had a *lot* of money to lavish expensive gifts on her. I could see all of that clear as day in the ether and it greatly upset me.

For a moment I had to turn away. I felt a rush of anger and betrayal. Brice was a great guy; *how* could Candice do this to him?

I paced the floor for a few moments trying to rein in my anger, but it was impossible. Candice hadn't just cheated on Brice; she'd cheated on everyone who'd ever trusted her.

I glared at the figure in the bed. "How could you?" I whispered, wanting to quit the room and head back home. With a heavy sigh I realized that being angry at her wasn't helping the situation, so I moved over to Candice's side and pulled up a chair to sit closer to her. I had to forgive her and I couldn't take my time about it, because Brice needed answers, and frankly so did I. So I laid my hand gently across her open palm and took a deep breath.

Early in my relationship with Dutch we'd taken a break from each other, and I'd found solace in the arms of another man, so I understood a little what it was like to love one man and find another man attractive. Maybe that's what it'd been with Candice.

Closing my eyes again, I tried to accept that as the truth, because I could sense that love had been a part of the equation, so maybe this other man had simply been a tryst. But the more I focused on him, the more I didn't like what I was sensing in the ether.

The man felt powerful and not like the kind of man you'd ever want to cross. He seemed to enjoy getting his way in business and in his personal life. He didn't seem at all the type to share a woman with anyone, and I couldn't understand how Candice would ever take up with such a man.

There was also a thread of betrayal in the ether that felt so sinister and filled with repercussions that I didn't quite know what to make of it.

And then I felt an even deeper and perhaps even more dangerous thread snaking its way through the ether. Whatever Candice had gotten mixed up in, the other man didn't seem to be her only threat. Not that she needed any help to do harm to herself.

"So many secrets, Cassidy," I sighed. "How did you keep all of it straight?"

I looked down at my hand resting on hers and realized for the first time how cold she felt. I pressed both my palms around her hand to warm it and gently lifted it, thinking of what Brice had said, how we'd essentially already lost Candice and even if she somehow managed to come back from all her grievous injuries, she'd never be my sidekick or fully his wife again.

With tears misting my eyes, I held her palm close to my cheek, and cried a few tears before easing her hand back to the bedsheet. It was then that something about Candice's palm caught my eye.

I squinted in the dim light the machines were giving off, and lowered my head to take a closer look.

When I'd first started exercising my intuition, I'd played around with palm reading, as it's a very easy thing to pick up, and my little impromptu readings were so accurate that the experience had given me some much-needed confidence. I'd given Candice a palm reading once years ago when we were first getting to know each other. She'd been a bit of an experiment, as the accuracy of reading someone's palm is tied to which hand is dominant, and as Candice is left-handed, I'd been excited to put the theory to the test.

Palms for our right and left hands aren't mirror images of each other, and if you were to read the right palm of a left-handed person, the accuracy wouldn't be nearly as good. Back then I'd read both of Candice's palms, her right first, then her left, and the left had been spot-on, while the right had provided some information, but much of the rest hadn't fit.

In the reading of Candice's left palm I'd seen a long life and good health—sort of a given as Candice is a health nut—and it had also indicated that she'd have no children, but two marriages with the second marriage being the one that lasted till death-do-them-part.

As I gazed down at Candice's left palm in the hospital room, however, I saw no marriage line and a shortened Lifeline. "What the . . . ?" I whispered before bending down to retrieve my purse from the floor where I'd set it when I sat down.

Lifting out my phone, I clicked it on for the light and pointed it at Candice's palm, letting out a gasp as the surface of her left hand lit up and told me everything her broken body couldn't.

"Ohmigod!" I whispered, clicking off the phone and putting her palm down. For several seconds I simply sat there and blinked, not knowing what to do. And then I looked again at the swollen, bruised face, which hid every defining feature I knew so well.

Getting up, I fished around in my purse again and retrieved my compact mirror. Wiping it clean with the bedsheet first, I lifted her thumb, then the four fingers of her left hand, and pressed them gently but firmly onto the compact. Then, using the bedsheet again, I carefully put the compact back into a side pocket of my purse and bolted toward the door, barely reining in the urge to run through the hallways and out of the hospital. Once in my car I raced home, and as traffic was still light, I made it there in no time.

Dutch's car wasn't in the driveway, and I breathed a sigh of relief. I found Brice in exactly the same place I'd left him. "You're back?" he asked as I rushed to sit down next to him.

Taking his hand, I squeezed it tight and said, "I have something to tell you, but you have to *promise* me that you won't tell Dutch until we talk it through."

Brice blinked and then his face drained of color. "What's happened?" he asked. "Is it Candice? Is she . . . ? Did she . . . die?"

I realized that rushing in like I'd done had been a mistake. "No, no!" I said quickly. "She's fine. I mean, the woman in the hospital is still alive. As for Candice, I'm not sure."

He blinked and shook his head slightly. "What?"

"Brice," I said. "When you were in with Candice, was there any part of you that maybe thought it might not be your wife?"

His brow furrowed. "Well, yeah, Cooper. I mean, you saw her. She didn't even look human."

It was my turn to shake my head. "No, not that. What I'm talking about is that the woman in that hospital bed might not actually *be* Candice."

Brice stared intently at me. "Tell me what you know."

I bit my lip. If I was wrong, I'd cause Brice undue harm by offering him the hope that Candice wasn't the woman who'd crashed in her car. "I don't know that the woman in that bed is my BFF. I think she might be somebody else. Another person entirely, wearing Candice's clothes, driving Candice's car, and with all of Candice's personal belongings."

Brice didn't say anything for a long moment. Then, "You think she's an impostor?"

I nodded. "It's her hands, Brice. They're different."

Brice stood up and I let go of his hand. He started pacing back and forth and I couldn't imagine what he was going through. "Who is it?" he asked.

"I don't know. I only know how to prove that it's not her." Using a paper napkin, I fished out the compact from my purse and placed it on the table. "The prints from her left hand are on there. Candice's prints are already in the system. We just need to run these and see if they match."

Brice frowned. "I've been suspended, Cooper, remember? I couldn't run anybody's prints right now."

"Right, but Oscar would if I asked him."

Brice's frown got even grumpier. "I don't want to involve anyone on the squad," he said. "It's bad enough your husband and I are both under the scrutiny of Internal Affairs. Oscar's a good agent. He doesn't need this on his record."

I rolled my eyes. Brice was so by the book it drove me crazy. "Listen, I get it—really, I do—but I'm calling him and I'm asking him and you can protest all you want, but I'm doing it."

With that, I took out my phone and pulled up my contacts list. Brice eyed me with a mixture of uncertainty and hope while I dialed Agent Rodriguez, who picked up on the third ring. "Oscar? Hey, it's Abby. Listen, I need a favor. . . ."

Two hours later, after I'd dropped off the compact to Oscar at the coffee shop around the corner from the bureau and had gotten back home, my phone rang. "The prints belong to a Saline Hamon," Oscar said. "She's in the system on a solicitation conviction from thirteen years ago in New York. She's been clean since then, though."

"New York?" I said, trying to ignore Brice's impatient hand waving.

"Yeah, she moved to Vegas right after her probation ended. Her current address looks like it's just west of the Strip. She's also got a Realtor's license, and is the owner of a title company also right off the Strip."

I scribbled a note to Brice with all the information Oscar was feeding me. "Anything else you can tell me about her?" I asked hopefully.

"Only if you let me know why I'm breaking every rule in the book to run her prints without probable cause," Oscar replied.

I bit my lip. "I can't. At least not right now, Oscar, and I'm so sorry, but the less you know, the better."

"So this has something to do with the mess Candice created, right?"

I was silent.

"Yeah, okay, Cooper. But if I get canned for this, you'll owe me big-time."

"Oscar?"

"Yeah?"

"Can you at least tell me what Saline's address in Vegas is?"

"Yeah, okay. But like I said, you owe me big."

I jotted down the address Oscar gave me, thanked him profusely, and hung up. Brice started asking questions before I even lowered the phone. "Who the hell is she?"

"I don't know."

"Why was she wearing Candice's clothes and driving her car?"

I shrugged.

"And she had all her jewelry. She even had Candice's wedding ring, for God's sake!"

I shrugged again, but a theory was starting to form

that I didn't like. "Brice, there's something else I haven't shown you yet."

"What?" he demanded. I could tell the stress and lack of sleep of the past few days were really starting to wear on him.

"Wait here." Heading into the bedroom, I pulled down the file and retrieved the suicide note I'd found in Candice's purse.

"What's this?" Brice asked when I returned and handed it to him.

"It's a note I found tucked into a ziplock bag in Candice's purse."

Brice's mouth fell open as he read the suicide letter. "What the . . . ?"

"I can't tell, but I think it's Candice's writing, right?"

Brice ignored me for a moment, his eyes roving back and forth across the page as he read and reread the letter. "It sure looks like her writing," he said. Then he crumpled the letter in his fist and threw it across the room angrily.

I had a feeling that I knew what he was thinking. "Maybe there's more to it than meets the eye," I said.

Brice shook his head, his anger building and causing his face to flush. "She tried to fake her own death," he growled. "Somehow she talked this poor girl into impersonating her, and sent her over that bridge in the Porsche, thinking we'd find a drowned woman with multiple injuries which would render her unrecognizable, along with a suicide note. And given that this woman was also wearing Candice's clothing and jewelry, I'd identify her in the morgue as my wife. Nobody would need to run dental records or prints if I said it was Candice, and given what a wreck all this has made me, of course I would've said it was her!"

I got up from the kitchen table and moved over to the fridge to grab a bottled water. My stomach grumbled, but I didn't feel much like eating. I didn't feel like doing much of anything but going back to bed and pulling the comforter over my head. I figured I'd stay there for the next few weeks until I could handle all this.

But then I had another thought.

If our situations were switched, Candice wouldn't have gone under the blankets to hide. She would've figured out *exactly* what was going on. She would've looked at all the unanswered questions still lingering, and she wouldn't have stopped investigating until she had every single answer.

Eyeing Brice, who was now sitting hunched over at the table with his head in his hands, I knew I owed it to him, and to me, and even to Candice, to find out what the hell was going on.

If my best friend wasn't the person I'd always thought she was, then I needed to find out exactly who Candice Fusco was.

I left Brice in the kitchen, giving him a sympathetic squeeze on the shoulder as I passed, and headed to the bedroom. I packed my suitcase quickly and efficiently, then made a flight reservation on my iPad.

Brice had moved to the living room. I found him sitting dully in front of the TV watching basketball highlights. I parked my suitcase next to the couch and took a seat. He didn't seem to notice either me or the luggage, so I cleared my throat to get his attention. "What's with the suitcase?"

"I'm leaving for a few days."

"Leaving?"

"Yes."

Brice sat up, a little of the dullness leaving his eyes, but he still looked so tired. "Where?" he asked.

"Vegas."

"What? Why, Cooper?"

"Because I need answers. And I know you need answers too."

"She's there, isn't she?" he asked me.

"I don't know," I told him honestly. "I only know that Vegas is the place where all of this started, so that's where I'm going."

Brice started to get up. "I'll go with you—"

"Like hell," I said, putting a hand on his arm and pushing him back down. "What you need to do is to sleep. And then eat. And then get some more sleep. Also, I doubt IA is going to let you go off to Vegas without either firing you or bringing you up on obstruction charges. Wait—knowing them, they'll probably do both."

"I'll send in a letter of resignation," Brice offered.

I rolled my eyes. "Really, Brice? For what purpose? So that the Feds in Vegas can get the heads-up that you're coming and bring both of us up on obstruction? No way. I'm going alone."

"It's too dangerous," he argued.

I rolled my eyes again. "Luckily, this ain't my first

rodeo. Listen, I've been Candice's PI sidekick for a few years now. I know what I'm doing. I'll investigate so subtly nobody will even know I'm there. And I'll be using the old radar at every turn. No way will my crew let me get into trouble."

"But—," Brice protested.

I cut him off. "Listen to me, will you? You can't come, Brice. You have to stay and focus on playing the role of the good FBI agent in charge that didn't have a clue his wife was a criminal. You've got to be seen as the distraught husband and keep everybody here interested in this case in Austin and focused on believing that Candice is in ICU. The *second* the Vegas bureau gets wind that Candice isn't in that hospital bed, they'll start looking for her in earnest, and my guess is that they'll figure she's fled back to Vegas to pick up her paycheck for killing Robinowitz. We're the only two people that know that Candice is alive and well, and if she's in Vegas, I'll find her—"

Brice gripped my hand. "She could hurt you, Cooper. If she really did all of this, then you can't trust her. If you find out where she is, call me, and I'll have her brought in."

I knew it must've killed Brice to say that, so, simply to appease him, I said, "Yeah, okay. If I find her, I won't try to approach her."

"You'll call me, right?"

I held up my pinkie. "Pinkie swear."

Brice frowned. He didn't trust me. I couldn't blame him, because I was totally lying through my teeth.

"This girl, Saline," he said. "When you're out in Vegas, try to find her next of kin, okay?"

I nodded. "I will. And while I'm gone, you stick to her bedside and help her get better. We owe her that at the very least for using her this way for a few days."

"We do," Brice said. I could tell none of this sat well with him.

"I gotta go," I said before Brice's conscience got the better of him. "My flight's at eleven."

"Wait," Brice said, getting up with me. "What am I gonna tell Rivers?"

Oh, crap. I'd forgotten about Dutch. "Er . . . ," I said. "I'll text him from the airport."

Brice frowned again. "You're going to lie to him about where you're going, aren't you?"

"Yes. But only because he would expect nothing less from me."

"Cooper . . ."

I waved my hand. "It's no big deal, Brice. I'll just tell him that I needed to get away from all this Candice stuff and I'm headed to my sister's for a visit."

"He'll buy that?"

"Probably not. But as long as you play dumb about where I really am, I think I can prevent him from coming after me for at least a few days."

Brice did something very unexpected then. He stepped forward and gave me a big hug. "As your boss, I shouldn't let you go off and do something so stupid."

"Good thing you're not my boss anymore, huh?"

Brice stepped back but held me by the shoulders.

"No. I'm your friend, and I *really* shouldn't let you go off and do something so stupid."

I smiled at him. Already I could see a little bit of hope coming back into his eyes. He wanted me to get to the bottom of all this and find Candice as much as I did. "I'll be careful," I promised.

"If something happens to you, you know Dutch is going to kill me for letting you go."

"Nothing's going to happen to me." I was kind of . . . almost . . . *fairly* certain of that.

"Call me every day and report in," he said.

I held up another pinkie. "Pinkie swear."

Brice hugged me again and then I was off.

Chapter Nine

Before I got to the airport, I had a quick stop to make, which was on the way. I'd plugged in the mysterious street address of the piece of paper I'd found in the file, and it'd come back with a hit in Austin, which, coincidentally, wasn't far from the airport.

I pulled up alongside the address and double-checked my GPS to make sure I was in the right spot. I was. Pulling into the empty parking lot, I got out of the car and headed to the small brown brick office building. It was locked up tight and dark inside. The plaque on the side of the building read DR. S. GLENHURST, DDS.

I peered through the glass. The lobby looked dusty and unused for quite some time. I moved over to one of the side windows and peered into another window. A dental chair and a big surgical light were all that was left in the room. A sign on the window said the place was for lease.

I grumbled as I went back to the car. When I'd

punched in the address, I'd gotten a half dozen hits, none of which were in Nevada, and the only other one I'd recognized from the list was here in Austin. But why would Candice be interested in an abandoned dental office? Like so much of this case, nothing seemed to make any kind of sense.

As I got back on the road to the airport, I made sure to call my sister, which was risky in its own right, because my sister, Cat, does two things extremely well: make money and drive me bat shih tzu crazy. "Oooo, you're coming here for a visit? Wonderful!" she exclaimed. "What time does your plane get in?" Cat said all this immediately after I'd given her the short version of why I needed her to cover for me. The short version had still taken at least five minutes of explanation, but Cat had only heard me say, ". . . coming to visit you."

Taking a (deep) breath, I tried again. This time it took three minutes.

"Right," Cat said. "So, did you want me to send a car to the airport to pick you up?"

By now I was circling the parking lot of ABIA—Austin's airport. "No, Cat. For the third time, I'm not coming to visit. I'm just telling Dutch that I'm going to Boston to hang out with you for a few days so that I can work on a case out west. If Dutch calls, you have to cover for me and tell him that I'm in the shower, or napping, or something else, then call me and let me know he's looking for me. I don't really think he'll call you, but then again, it's Dutch and he doesn't always take me at my word." (Smart man.)

"Uh-huh," Cat said. "So no driver, but you'll take a cab?"

I pulled into a vacant slot and palmed my forehead. Maybe if I spoke Tarzan. "Cat. Me no visit you. Me go west. You lie to Dutch if he call. Say me napping."

"Oh!" Cat said. "So you need me to pretend you're here if Dutch calls."

"Yes!" (And don't think I wasn't making a mental note to myself to speak Tarzan the next time I needed Cat to listen to something important.)

"Okay, but after you're done with your case, you'll come for a visit."

I stifled a groan. Cat said that like it wasn't really an option. Like, if I wanted her to cover for me, then I had to promise to hang out in Boston for a few days. "Uh . . . sure, honey. Of course. I can't wait to see you," I said flatly.

"Gee," Cat said, "could you maybe muster a little enthusiasm?"

"I can't *wait* to see you!"

"Better, but maybe you'll work on it before you come. When can we expect you?"

I got out of the car and grabbed my luggage. I was gonna have to boogie if I wanted to clear security and get something to drink before my flight. "I don't know yet, honey, probably in a few days. Maybe next week."

"Okay!" Cat said, and *she* sounded enthused. "It's been a long time since you've been out here, Abs. Wait until you see what we've done with the house!"

"I'm looking forward to it," I vowed, and there was a part of me that actually was. Cat was right—I hadn't been out to see her in a while. And truth be told, I knew that if I discovered Candice had been a psychopath all these years, I was definitely going to need the comfort of my sister's company. And maybe some professional therapy. At the very least some retail therapy.

I didn't call Dutch until I was seated at the gate waiting to board. "Wait, you're going where?" he asked once I'd told him I was at the airport on my way to see Cat.

"To Boston. I gotta get outta here for a few days, cowboy. This whole Candice thing is just too much for me to process and Cat suggested a few days with her might do me a world of good, so I took her up on it."

"So, you're just *leaving*? Right *now*?"

"Yes."

"Without letting me know?"

"Isn't that what I'm doing with this call?"

"Not a lot of heads-up there, Edgar."

"I know, and I'm sorry, but . . . I need to do this."

Dutch was quiet for a long time. I knew he was disappointed that I was simply leaving town, sticking him with Brice and the Candice mess to deal with on his own, but if I told him I was actually headed to Vegas, there'd be nothing I could say or do to stop him from either (a) trying to stop me from going or (b) insisting on coming with me.

Both scenarios were problematic because I was definitely going, and if he came with me, he'd lose his job. I wasn't going to be responsible for my husband getting fired.

"Yeah, okay," he said at last. "Call me when you land and say hi to Cat from me."

I breathed a huge sigh of relief. He'd bought the story. "Thanks, honey. You're the best."

"By the way," he said. "What's your flight number?"

"Delta flight thirty-four sixteen. It leaves at one and gets into Logan at five." I'd researched the flight to Boston right before calling him, even down to the departure gate number.

"Got it," he said. "Have a safe flight, dollface."

We hung up and I wiped my brow. I knew Dutch would look my flight up online to see if I was feeding him a line of shih tzu, but I hoped he'd stop short of checking the passenger list. He did have access to all sorts of cool tools at the bureau, but maybe because he was under the scrutiny of Internal Affairs, he wouldn't risk a bend of the rules. I had to hope so, because if he discovered I wasn't on the Boston flight, he wouldn't stop until he'd discovered what other flight I'd taken.

I relaxed a little more when we boarded, and even fell asleep on the plane. When I woke up, we were circling the airport waiting for our turn to land. An hour later I had my bag and was making my way out of the rental car parking lot in a silver Honda Accord. Plugging in the first address I wanted to check out, I drove across town to a well-kept, slightly upscale apartment complex with a red clay roof and white stucco walls.

The apartment I was looking for was all the way around the back of the complex, an end unit with a small deck and a sliding glass door. I drove past it slowly, trying to peer inside the glass door, but the blinds were drawn and there was no way to tell if someone was inside. I parked the car a little bit down from the front door, then fished around inside my purse for the set of keys taped to the back of the file Candice had left in the safe.

Heading to the door, I stepped close and pressed my ear to the wood before inserting the key. I didn't hear anything from inside, so I crossed my fingers and unlocked the door.

Inside it was cool—the air had been left on, and it was also dim. I shut the door quietly, and moved into the apartment.

The furniture was tasteful and expensive, lots of plush creams with small pops of color. Tangerine throw pillows and a matching cashmere throw blanket adorned the overstuffed velour white couch and ottoman.

There was some expensive-looking art on the walls—Abstract Expressionist–era stuff that I could never make sense of—and a vase on the dining room table that held a wilted bouquet of flowers.

Moving over to the kitchen, I saw that it was neat—no dirty dishes in the sink—and the fridge had a few staples but not much in the way of supplies. Then I headed to the bedroom, which was large and spacious with a luxurious white silk coverlet topping a queen-sized bed adorned with dusky-rose-colored pillows. The room was decidedly feminine, and I went straight to the closet.

I'd been trying to deny something since first stepping into the apartment, but as I took in the furnishings of the bedroom, it was hard to overlook. The whole place was decorated in the style and taste of my BFF. If

Candice lived alone, I could totally imagine her living here, but it wasn't until I pulled open the bedroom closet that I was convinced.

An array of business suits hung neatly to the left, and to the right were more casual outfits, all in a size six. Candice was a size six. The clothes weren't things I'd ever seen her wear, but most of them looked new and a few had the tags still on them.

The shoes were another clincher for me. Candice wore a size eight—the same size as me. I knew this because sometimes she'd let me borrow a pair of her shoes. Candice has awesome taste, especially in footwear, and after picking up one of the sandals in the shoe rack, I knew that this was Candice's hideaway.

The whole place had her energy all over it. With a sigh, I put the sandal back and closed the door. Turning around, I surveyed the room again. "If this is your new pad, then where are you?" I asked aloud.

I then had an idea and went back to the kitchen to begin rummaging around in the drawers. "Aha!" I said, pulling up the small key I found in the third drawer I opened. The key was even marked "Mail Key."

I headed out of the apartment and it took me a bit to find the mailboxes, but within a few moments I had Candice's box open and was pulling out an assortment of flyers, coupon inserts, and what looked like bills. There was also a large manila envelope in the mix, and like all the other nongeneral mail, it was addressed to Samantha Dubois.

Hurrying back to the apartment, I sat down at the dining room table and opened up the manila envelope first. The contents shouldn't have surprised me, but they did.

Inside was a photo of Dr. Robinowitz along with his flight information and the hotel he would've stayed in had he lived through his first night in Austin. There was also a note clipped to the photo. It read "Make it clean."

I set down the contents of the manila folder and had myself a really good pity party. I'd been trying to convince myself that all of this was just one big mix-up, and all I had to do was to figure out what was really going on and my best friend would emerge glimmering with goodness, her reputation and her intentions intact.

But the photo of Robinowitz along with the note and his hotel reservation felt like the clincher in a badly plotted whodunit. *All* roads led to Candice as a mob hit man. Woman. Person. (I was really going to have to figure out the politically correct way to say that.)

"So you're guilty," I said to Candice's electric bill. "You killed Robinowitz and you tried to kill Saline. You pulled the wool over my eyes, Dutch's, and your husband's. For *years*."

I got up from the table and began to pace as my anger mounted. "We trusted you!" I yelled to the empty apartment. "You were my best friend! Jesus, Candice! How *could* you?"

I went on like that for a little while and finally settled down. I knew I needed to call Brice and tell him the bad news, but I simply couldn't bring myself to do it yet.

It would crush him.

Brice was someone I respected. Someone I liked. Someone I trusted. He was as good, honest, and decent a man as my husband, and that was saying a lot because my hubby is one of the very best people I've ever known.

All of this was so unfair! And there was a part of me . . . a very *angry* part of me that didn't want to let Candice get away with it.

I eyed the stack of mail on the table. It was thick. She hadn't been here in at least a few days. I didn't think she was still in Austin. No way would she wait around after sending Saline over the bridge. She would've gotten out of town fast. Granted, it was only a day later, but still, if Candice were coming back here, she would've by now, and nothing in the apartment indicated she'd been here recently.

And I thought I knew the reason: She'd pointed me to the file in her safe knowing I'd come here and find out that she'd been using her sister's ID to set up a fake identity and . . . wait a minute. "*Why* would you have told me about the file in the first place?" I asked aloud.

I sat back down and tapped my fingers on the table, thinking. If Candice had really wanted this place to be her hideout, why would she set it up in Samantha Dubois' name when she knew that Brice, Dutch, and I all knew about her fake ID? Additionally, why would she have told me about the file in her safe in the first place? I mean, either the police or whoever trashed our offices would've found it eventually, but . . .

Wait another minute. . . .

I'd forgotten all about the break-in at our offices and the additional break-in at the Witts'. That certainly wasn't Candice's doing. So who was after that file and *why* had Candice entrusted it to me?

She knew once she sent Saline over the bridge, I was probably going to turn it over to Brice, which I hadn't, but only because I'd reasoned that he was mentally and physically drained—no way did I want to heap one more worry onto his already overburdened shoulders.

So why had she given me the file? I reached for my purse and pulled it close, digging out the file. I opened it again and sorted through the contents. The DNA test was what was throwing me. It was the part of the story that made absolutely no sense.

I set the DNA test down and rubbed my temple. Then again, not much about this case made any sense either.

Frustrated, I closed my eyes and flipped on my radar. Sometimes, when the mood is right, I can use my intuition a bit like a Magic 8 Ball. It comes in handy when I need a simple yes or no to a question, but I can't overuse the technique because things start to get cloudy and if I ask more than just a few simple questions, I'll start to feel that "Ask later" sensation.

"Is Candice my friend?" I asked aloud for my first question.

I felt a light, airy sensation in my solar plexus. My sign for yes.

"Is she guilty of murder?"

The light airy feeling turned to a heavy, weighed-down sensation. My symbol for no.

I thought about my next question carefully. "Is she working for the mob?"

The light, airy feeling returned, but it wasn't nearly as strong as when I'd asked if Candice was my friend.

I knew I was likely good for only one more question, so I said, "Will I find her?"

My solar plexus lit up with such a light feeling that it was undeniable. I'd find Candice. What would happen next was anybody's guess. I could only hope she wouldn't shoot me.

A bit later, after thoroughly searching the rest of the apartment for any sign of where Candice might be, I put everything back exactly as I'd found it. Before locking up, I returned to the mailboxes and put all the mail back except for the large manila envelope—I decided to keep that for now. Once I was done, I put the mail key back, locked the door, then went over to sit in my car for a good hour watching the apartment, hoping Candice would make it easy on me and simply show up, but no one even drove past.

Finally I headed out and, using my phone's GPS, looked up the next address on my list.

It took almost an hour to make it across town in the opposite direction, but eventually I arrived at a set of upscale condos overlooking a beautifully well-groomed golf course. The complex was gated, but there wasn't a guard posted, so I simply drove up and down the street a few times until I saw someone pull in and insert their card. They didn't even notice when I tucked in behind them after the gate had opened.

Making my way around the complex, I drove slowly,

looking for the right address, and finally found it. There was an elderly man watering some potted plants on a deck jutting out from a condo two down from the one I was interested in. "Good," I muttered, pulling into an empty space. Getting out of the car, I went around to the trunk and took out my luggage, then strolled toward the condo in front of me, making sure to smile up at the man watering his plants. He nodded and returned my smile, but I could tell he was interested in what I was doing there. When I got to the door, I knocked loudly, so that the old man on the porch could hear. Of course there was no answer, so I knocked again, making a good show of it.

"Excuse me," the man on the deck called.

I leaned back from the door and put a hand up to shield my eyes from the sun. "Yes?"

"You looking for Dr. Robinowitz?"

"Yes," I said, pushing up a big old smile onto my lips. "I'm his niece, Kara. Uncle Dave was supposed to pick me up from the airport this morning, but I think he forgot. I finally got a rental car and came here. Do you know if he's maybe out golfing?"

The man on the balcony blanched. "Oh, my, young lady," he said. "Didn't the police call you?"

I put a hand to my chest, feigning surprise. "The *police*? No. Why? What's happened?"

The elderly gentleman set down his hose and held up a finger. "Wait there, miss. I'll be right over."

He disappeared inside his condo and appeared just a minute later looking like he couldn't wait to share the terrible, tragic news with me. He was exactly the kind of neighbor I'd been hoping to run into. "I'm sorry to have to tell you this," he said. "But your uncle is dead."

"What?" I cried. "No! No, no, no! That can't be!"

The old guy nodded. "I'm really sorry."

I buried my face in my hands and began making sobbing sounds. I even managed to make my eyes water too, something I was a little proud of. I felt the old guy pat me on the back a couple of times, and after what seemed like a good amount of time, I lifted my chin and said, "How? When? Ohmigod, was it his heart? Uncle Dave never did eat right. I should've insisted that he take better care of himself! Oh, *why* didn't I push him to eat right? Why? *Why?*" I buried my face in my hands again. "It's all my fault!" I wailed. "He's dead and it's because I didn't push him to take care of himself!"

I made a few more sobbing sounds and the old guy continued to pat me on the back and say, "Hey, please don't cry, miss. It wasn't your fault, okay? It wasn't."

I sniffled and lifted my chin again. "Did it . . . did it happen here? Were you with him when it happened? Please don't tell me he died alone!"

The old guy was looking increasingly uncomfortable. I could tell that he knew exactly what'd happened to Robinowitz, and I was hoping he'd also be my ticket inside the condo. He was just the type of neighbor you'd leave your key with in case you got locked out.

"I wasn't with him," the man said. "And it wasn't his heart. Say, maybe you should call the police, miss. They can tell you what happened."

I scrunched up my face again and made my lip

quiver. "Was it . . . was it a car accident? Was Uncle Dave drinking and driving again?"

Finally the old guy sighed and said, "Your uncle was murdered, honey."

"Wha . . . *what*?!" I gasped, then pretended to let my knees buckle.

The old guy caught my arm and helped me stand up. "Let's get you inside where you can sit down," he said. Still holding on to my arm, he bent over to reach for a potted plant on Robinowitz's balcony and moved it aside. There was a key there and he took that and moved to the door to unlock it. Behind his back I smiled in triumph.

He led me inside and as we entered a tile-covered foyer, I allowed the kind gentleman to lead me to the living room just off the foyer. "Here," he said. "Take a seat and I'll get you a glass of water."

I sat there trying to look stunned and when he came back with the water and a box of tissues, I made another big show of covering my face and crying. "I can't believe it!" I said. "Uncle Dave was the nicest man on the planet! He heard I was coming back from Europe after losing my job at the art museum, and he told me I could stay with him for as long as I wanted. Until I got back on my feet. I mean, you knew him. He wouldn't hurt a fly! Who would want to kill him?"

Robinowitz's neighbor ran a hand through his feathery white hair. "I don't know, miss. But you're right. Dave was a good guy. I only knew him for a few months, but he was always very nice to me and the other owners around here."

I dabbed at my eyes. "I'm Kara," I repeated, holding out my free hand.

"Bill. Bill Cox."

"You're very kind, Mr. Cox."

"Call me Bill," he said, offering me the tissue box again. I was doing a great job at getting my eyes to water. Of course, I'd had a lot of practice at it lately.

After wiping my cheeks with a tissue, I looked around the condo. It was nice but predictable. Lots of tans and olive greens and not much in the way of personal touches. "It didn't happen here, did it?" I whispered.

"No, Kara. The police said it happened in Texas. Austin, I think."

I furrowed my brow. "Austin? What the heck was Uncle Dave doing in Austin?"

Bill shrugged. "He told me a few days ago that he had to go out of town to help a friend. He asked me to look after the place while he was gone."

I put a hand on his arm. "You're a good neighbor."

He blushed and smiled. "I'm retired and home a lot. Everybody asks me to watch their place when they're out of town."

"What did the police say?" I asked next.

Bill grimaced. "They said that Dave had been murdered in a parking garage in Texas. They thought they knew who did it, and they showed me a picture of some woman, asked if I'd ever seen her before."

Alarm bells went off in my head like crazy. "A woman?" I asked carefully. "A woman killed my uncle?"

Bill nodded. "That's what the cops said. Your uncle didn't tell you about his girlfriend?"

I blinked. "His what, now?"

"His lady friend," Bill said. "She was the one in the picture the cops showed me."

"Uncle Dave was dating a woman who killed him in Texas?" I said. What the heck was this old man talking about? Candice wouldn't have . . . She couldn't have . . . *Could* she have been having an affair with Robinowitz?

Bill was still nodding. "Your uncle took up with this really pretty blonde," he said. "She was young too, maybe your age. I only saw her a few times, but she's not someone you forget, you know? Anyway, when the cops showed me her picture, I told them that she'd been here a couple of times and then I didn't see her again."

A sudden thought came to me and I wondered if perhaps Bill could be talking about Saline. She was blond, and she came from Vegas—maybe there was a connection? And then another thought occurred to me: I had seen Saline only after the accident, when she was unrecognizable. What if she and Candice looked similar enough for Saline to have posed as Candice and she was the one who shot Robinowitz? My heart leaped a little at the idea. I had to find out whose photo they'd shown Bill. "Hold on, Bill," I said. "You're saying they showed you this woman's photo? How'd they get her picture?"

"Well," he explained, "first they showed me a still of her they said came from surveillance video of a parking garage right before she shot your uncle, and then they showed me her mug shot."

"Her mug shot?" Candice had never been arrested in Las Vegas to my knowledge.

"Okay, so maybe not her mug shot, just a blowup of her driver's license. They said her name was Cathy Frisco, or something like that."

My heart sank. They'd shown Bill a photo of Candice's driver's license. He seemed quite certain that he recognized her. I knew it hadn't been Saline who'd come here and befriended Robinowitz, and then later posed as Candice in the parking garage. My hopeful theory of an alternative scenario went out the window.

I couldn't deny it any longer; Candice knew Robinowitz. That smile he'd worn in the parking garage as he approached her *had* been one of recognition.

But then, why had Candice needed the contents of the manila envelope in my car? If she'd already known the doctor, why would she need a picture of him to identify him? And if they'd been friendly, why wouldn't she just ask him for his flight information? Why would someone send her his itinerary and photo if she already knew it? Also, Robinowitz was hardly the kind of guy Candice would go for. I couldn't imagine her cuddling up next to some retired doctor with a paunch and liver spots.

"You're sure Uncle Dave was dating this woman?" I asked Bill. "As in, they were really having a physical relationship?" He seemed surprised by my question, and I realized it wasn't exactly the type of question Robinowitz's niece would ask. "Uncle Dave didn't seem interested in anybody since my aunt died," I added quickly.

Cox shrugged. "I only saw them together twice. They didn't make out in front of me, but they seemed to like each other okay."

"Got it," I said, my mind filling with even more unanswered questions about Candice and her secret life. An awkward silence followed and I felt like I should probably try to get Bill out of the house so that I could snoop around. I didn't know if he completely bought my story about being Robinowitz's niece, so I knew I'd need to act fast before he started to ask me questions.

Standing up, I extended my hand and said, "Thank you so much for telling me about Uncle Dave. I think I'm going to have a good cry now. Then I'll call the police and my family. I don't even know if any of them have been contacted yet."

Bill stood and handed me the key to the condo before putting his hand in mine. "You take care, now, Kara. And if you need anything, I'm right over in number three-C."

After Bill left, I made sure all the blinds were closed and began searching out the place. Robinowitz was a neat and organized man. He had files for his utility bills, mortgage payments, and bank statements, but nothing for anything else that might be of interest. I looked all through the filing cabinet in his den, hunting for anything that might mark him as a bad guy, but there was nothing.

Even his bank statements weren't very interesting. I scrolled through the printouts and saw that he only kept about fifteen grand in checking, but got regular monthly checks from his retirement account. Considering his expenses, they weren't for much, a total of about fifteen thousand a month, and after payments for his credit cards, utilities, two mortgages, and a hefty five-thousand-dollar payment to the IRS each month, he just about broke even.

There was nothing to suggest that the good doctor had been anything but a regular guy, trying to live out his golden years in a Vegas condo. It was actually sad when I thought about it.

As I was putting things back together, there was a knock at the door. I stiffened before creeping to the front door and peering through the peephole. I saw that Bill was standing there expectantly.

"Crap," I whispered. I figured he wanted to nose around a little more. "Who is it?" I asked, trying to sound sad. I was supposed to be in mourning after all.

"Kara, it's Bill. I've got your uncle's mail here. He asked me to collect it for him while he was out of town, and I forgot about it until just now."

I opened the door a crack. "Oh," I said, getting my eyes to tear up again. "Thank you so much, Bill. You're so kind. Uncle Dave was lucky to have you for a neighbor."

Bill nodded, and seemed to get choked up himself; then without another word he handed me the mail and left.

"That was easy," I said after shutting the door.

I sorted through Robinowitz's mail. There wasn't much in the way of excitement: a cable bill, a bank statement, two credit card statements, an electric bill, and a coupon for a free car wash.

With a sigh I put the mail on the credenza in the foyer and moved to gather up my purse and carry-on bag. I had another address to check out and I wanted to go there before it got too dark, and I certainly wasn't going to leave my luggage behind.

As I was passing through the foyer on my way out the door, however, my radar pinged and my attention was drawn back to the credenza. Moving to it, I looked down at the small stack of mail. "What is it?" I muttered, picking up the envelopes while I tried to find out what my radar was working to pinpoint.

I sorted through the stack, reading them off one by one. "AT&T, Nevada Energy, Discover, AmEx, Chase Bank, Oasis Car Wash. What's here other than bills?"

As if on cue one of the envelopes slipped out of my hands and fell to the floor. Bending over, I picked it up and read, "Chase Bank. Hmmm."

Opening someone else's mail is a federal offense, but that didn't stop me or even give me pause. Tugging open the envelope, I pulled out Robinowitz's bank statement and studied it curiously. My eyes bugged at the available balance listed on the first page. "One hundred and twenty-two thousand dollars? What the hell?"

Holding tight to the bank statement, I went back to the filing cabinet in the den and pulled open the drawers, digging out the previous month's statement. That ending balance had been a little over twenty thousand. "How'd you come up with a hundred grand, Dr. Dave?" I asked myself.

I sat down at the desk and studied the statement,

finding a series of deposits all during the previous four weeks. Each deposit was made in cash and none of them totaled more than $9,900. I knew after working with law enforcement all these years that any deposit of $10,000 or more would immediately be reported to the IRS, which would've raised a red flag with them and the Feds.

I traced my finger up and down the page, looking at the dates of the deposits. "Every Wednesday at four forty, like clockwork, then on Thursday, Friday, and Saturday, all at random times." I tapped my lip, thinking. "So whoever gave you this cash probably gave it to you between four and four thirty p.m. on Wednesday, because you never missed that four forty deposit, and had to wait a few days to put in the rest and spread it out. But, Dave, where'd the money come from?"

I searched the statement again for clues and discovered that on a few of those Wednesdays, there was a charge at a place called Lucky Lou's and that charge was almost always at three thirty in the afternoon. The charges from Lucky Lou's were never more than fifty dollars, and sometimes considerably less; one charge was only for ten dollars and ninety-five cents.

I knew from my public records search that Robinowitz had once had a drinking problem, and because the charges were fairly small, I doubted that he was drinking again. Lucky Lou's sounded familiar for some reason, but my mind was a little muddled with events and facts, and I couldn't place it. I suspected Lou's might be a casino, but I didn't think Robinowitz was a gambler. If he'd been sober the past few years, he knew how tempting any compulsive hobby could be. I doubted he'd risk his sobriety by taking up gambling. "No," I muttered, "these look like small meals. A late lunch, or a midafternoon snack." That led me to think that he probably frequented a restaurant or diner called Lucky Lou's, and because of the time stamp of the charges and the time stamp of the subsequent deposits every Wednesday, I concluded that whoever was giving Robinowitz the money, he or she probably met him at Lou's, shared a snack with him, and left him with the cash.

Scrutinizing the statement again, I saw that the last deposit was two days before Robinowitz died. It was the largest one at $9,999, just under the wire for the bank to report the deposit to the IRS.

I stood up and began to pace the room, trying to work out what the heck was going on. And then I had it. Oppenheimer and Gould had suggested that Robinowitz was borrowing money from his buddy Kato, and if I wasn't mistaken, they'd said that Kato owned a casino named Lucky Lou's. And here in Robinowitz's bank records was the apparent proof of that money changing hands. But what I couldn't quite figure out was why Kato would agree to give Robinowitz the payments in such small doses. I could see Robinowitz wanting to avoid the detection of the IRS, but wouldn't the small payments flag Kato's accountants? It seemed an odd risk to take for a casino operator who had to know he was being watched by the Feds.

Then I had to wonder if Kato had loaned his friend the entire lump sum to pay his back taxes, and Robinowitz was then just regular about making those deposits every Wednesday at four forty in the afternoon, but my radar kept discarding that idea. I felt strongly that Robinowitz was accepting small lump-sum payments of about twenty-five grand every Wednesday between three and four p.m., then heading to the bank to deposit the first part of that payment, and metering out the next payments when he had time over the weekend.

"So why go to Austin?" I said as I continued to pace the floor. "What was in Austin, Dave? Candice? You two were seen together here in Vegas. If Candice had wanted to lure you there to kill you, why would she be so sloppy as to show up here in full view of your neighbors?"

It seemed like a whole lot of work for Candice to put such a charade together when it would've been far easier for her to simply sneak over to the doc's condo one night, kill him while he slept, then slip away unseen.

None of what'd happened fit with the Candice Fusco I knew. If Candice really was a psychopath who'd somehow managed to fool all of us, who were trained and adept in the art of detecting deception, why would she be so sloppy about killing Robinowitz in plain view of surveillance cameras and attempting to kill Saline? She had to know we would've figured out the truth eventually. This just wasn't Candice's careful, methodical, well-planned style, and so many of her recent actions were so sloppy and out of character that I just couldn't understand what the heck she was thinking.

"And what did Saline have to do with all this?" I

asked myself next. "What did a Realtor from Vegas have to do with any of this? Why would Candice lure her to Austin and set her up to take her place in the Porsche when it went over the bridge? Wouldn't it be easier to find someone in Austin to set up?"

I moved back over to the chair at the desk and with a sigh I sat down and went over the bank statement again, comparing it to the month before. What struck me as odd was that Robinowitz was taking in a lot of cash, but he hadn't changed the monthly allotment to the IRS he paid regularly. The guy had had over a hundred grand in the bank, and yet, his most recent payment to them had been for that same five thousand dollars. Why hadn't he sent in a larger payment when he had the cash on hand?

I sat back in the chair to think over my next move. Today was Tuesday. I wondered whether if I went to Lou's the next day, I might snoop around and find out a little more about those regular Wednesday meetings.

"It's risky," I admitted aloud. "But worth a shot." My mind made up, I stood and put all the old bank statements back, but took the new one with me, as I wanted to keep the evidence of my federal mail-opening crime out of sight.

Grabbing my purse and my luggage again, I left the condo in search of yet another address.

Chapter Ten

"Well, this can't be right," I said, pulling into the large parking lot of Big G's, a midsized hotel casino just west of the Strip. I looked down at my phone, then up at the large brass numbers on the side of the white slab building. Still puzzled, I rummaged around in my purse and pulled out the bit of scrap paper I'd written Saline's address on. The street address was a match.

Frustrated, because clearly Oscar had given me the wrong address, I pulled farther into the lot and parked in the nearest space. I then called Oscar, but it went to voice mail. "Hey," I said. "It's Abby. Call me when you can, but be discreet. Don't let IA know you're calling me."

Hanging up the phone, I leaned back in the seat and waited impatiently. After ten minutes of staring at the phone, willing it to ring (if only my psychic sense could control minds!), I gave up and looked around.

I felt a little exposed as I sat and waited for Oscar's call, and thought several times about giving up and just heading back to the apartment Candice had rented, but something was keeping me there. So I stuck it out another half hour until my stomach gave a loud rumble.

"Well, I gotta eat," I reasoned. Starting the car, I backed out of the space and drove down the aisle toward the exit, but at the juncture I suddenly had the urge to turn left instead of right. Listening to that whisper of intuition (hoping it would lead me to a good cheeseburger or pizza joint), I turned left and followed the drive around the building to the other side, where there was an additional exit for the street around the corner from the one I'd come down, and right across that street was Lucky Lou's.

I stopped the car and stared. Lucky Lou's was a casino of about the same size as the one I was about to exit. And right then I knew there was some kind of connection between Robinowitz and Saline, because it had to be more than a coincidence that the address that Oscar had given me for Saline and the casino that Robinowitz had frequented every Wednesday, where he collected payments from his buddy Kato, were directly across the street from each other. There had to be something more to it.

I made a U-turn just in front of the exit and went back to park the car. The sun had nearly set, and business at Big G's was starting to pick up. Once I'd found a space for the car, I grabbed my luggage to use as a prop and headed inside.

The casino was fairly predictable: big interior with a low ceiling, filled with the echoing sounds of bells, whistles, and jingles as old folks sat in front of electronic gambling machines and played poker, blackjack, and whatnot.

I took a whiff. The place smelled of cigarette smoke, spilled liquor, and desperation. It looked about as good as it smelled. The walls were a dark wood paneling, which hid the nicotine pretty well. A few waitresses walked around in formfitting miniskirts and low-cut blouses. They all seemed a bit annoyed, as if they'd been groped one too many times by the patrons, and you could see the dark glint in their eyes, like if one more dirty old man grabbed for their butt, they'd go waitress-postal on his ass.

I moved through the first row of beeping, buzzing machines to the center of the main floor, which was outfitted with an oval bar. There was a big sign on the counter that read SMILE! IT'S HAPPY HOUR! A few people sat there, but no one looked happy. Least of all the bartender. Still, when he saw me with my suitcase, he pointed to his left. "Check-in is up the escalator."

"Thanks," I told him, heading in the direction he'd pointed.

I rode the escalator to the second floor and found this much more refined. The walls were painted an aqua green, offset by gold leaf crown molding and lots of white marble. For a minute I didn't quite know what to do. I wasn't about to "check in," as I didn't have a reservation, and no way did I want to stay at a noisy casino, but something on my radar had tugged me in here. Feeling a bit discouraged, I looked at Saline's address again, and realized that she'd added what I'd thought was an apartment number.

But the number listed didn't make much sense, because it was room number 46E. A hotel of this size wouldn't have rooms numbered like an apartment, would it?

Wondering if maybe the concierge could help me, I took the bit of paper with Saline's address on it over to him and he smiled as I approached. "Hi, there," I said. "I'm wondering if you might help me out. My cousin gave me this address when she told me to come see her, and I think there's a digit missing, or maybe that *E* should be . . . I don't know, a three?"

I showed the paper to the concierge, and he said, "No, she got it right, ma'am. There are fifty condos in the hotel, and it looks like hers is on the top floor." The helpful man then pointed across from us to a dimly lit corridor and said, "If you take that hallway all the way down to the other side of the casino, you'll see a set of elevators dedicated to the condos. Just put in your code, and it will take you all the way up."

"My code?"

The concierge cocked his head. "Yes, the security code. Didn't your cousin give that to you?"

"Uh, no," I said, trying to look helpless and overwhelmed. "This is my first time in Vegas and Seely has never been great with the details, or answering her phone." For good measure I held up my cell and wiggled it, like I was totally frustrated with her. "I mean, come on, cuz! Get it together for your favorite relative's birthday visit!"

"It's your birthday?" the concierge asked.

"Tomorrow," I lied. Man, I was a lying *savant* today.

The concierge seemed to take pity on me. "Punch in six-two-four when you get into the elevator, then hit the button marked *E*, and it'll take you to your cousin's floor."

I reached over and squeezed the kindly man's arm, gushing with thanks, and then hurried off to find the elevator.

About five minutes later I stepped out onto the top floor and looked around. The place was elegantly appointed with an off-white Berber carpet, cocoa-colored walls, and a deep espresso-colored chair molding. Along the walls were vintage photos of Vegas from the fifties and sixties, beautifully framed. And not a speck of dust anywhere.

I went left from the elevator, down the corridor watching the numbers next to each door. At last I got to door number 46E and not knowing what else to do, I knocked. Of course there was no answer, but I'd been sort of hoping that maybe Saline had a roommate. Thinking this was a giant waste of time, I was about to turn away when my radar pinged and the memory of Bill reaching under Robinowitz's flowerpot for the spare key floated to my mind. Curious, I dropped my gaze to the little welcome mat in front of Saline's door. Could it really be that easy?

I cast a glance up and down the corridor before bending down and lifting up the mat. There, shining up at me, was a silver key. "Wow," I whispered, a little amazed at my good fortune. Inserting the key into the lock, I crossed my fingers and turned the lock. It gave way and the door clicked open.

"It's not really breaking and entering if there's a key under the mat," I told myself as I slipped inside.

Flipping the switch next to the door, I sucked in a breath as the condo came to light. It was gorgeous. Lightly stained hardwood floors spread out underneath my feet, offset by an array of plush white lambskin rugs, and a seating area that was arranged like something right out of *Architectural Digest*. A plush, oversized white sofa and love seat dominated the space, with indigo blue pillows lining the backrest, and a lovely plum-colored throw over one arm of the sofa. The walls were painted a plum so light and soft it was almost translucent, and a tall tropical plant butted up next to a set of nearly floor-to-ceiling windows with an amazing view of the distant mountains to the right and a view of the Strip to the left. A galley kitchen was off the entryway, and I turned to admire its white windowed cabinets, stainless steel counters, and matching appliances. The energy felt feminine and so easy and carefree that I thought, if I'd never met Dutch, I could've lived in a place exactly like this.

I moved through the condo to the bedroom, and was awed again. The walls were just a blush of color, tinted a shade of apricot. The bedspread was silk, pearly and white; it begged to be sat on. I indulged with a contented sigh. "I want to marry this bed," I said, lying back to get the full experience. Closing my eyes, I thought, *I'll just lie here for a quick sec and then I'll snoop around and head out.*

I'm not sure what time it was when I woke up. I only know that I was in the middle of a crazy dream where

Candice pointed a gun at me and said, "It's not how it looks," right before she pulled the trigger. The second I jerked awake, I knew I wasn't alone.

For a solid minute I simply lay there, frozen in fright. The room was dark, so I couldn't see much, and I didn't want to make any moves that might indicate I wasn't still asleep. Adrenaline flooded my system, and I felt the thud of my heart against my rib cage. For many seconds I tried to figure out where I was and who was in the room with me. My brain hit on the where first, and I wanted to slap myself for the stupidity of falling asleep in Saline's condo. I knew I was tired when I sat down on the bed—I never should've laid back and closed my eyes.

Still, all that regret wasn't going to help me now—I had to figure out who was in the room with me and how the heck to get away without being thrown in jail, or out the window.

Just as I had that thought, a light flicked on. I put a hand up to shield my eyes. I couldn't pretend to be asleep any longer.

"Who the hell are you?" a male voice demanded.

I took a steadying breath and sat up. In the chair next to the bureau sat a man I thought was likely in his mid-to-late thirties, with slicked-back black hair, a gorgeous square face, and eyes so dark they were ebony. He looked a lot like Don Draper from *Mad Men*. "Kara," I said, thinking I might as well stick to the fake name I'd used with Bill Cox.

One of the man's brooding brows arched skeptically. "That's not what your driver's license says."

Belatedly I realized he held my purse in his lap. "If you already know who I am, then why'd you ask?"

The eyebrow dipped down again and I regretted my flippant reply. "What're you doing here?" he said next.

I scooted back on the bed a little. It was a stall tactic. The guy was giving off a dangerous vibe, and I was sorta hoping that he actually would call the police and have me thrown in jail, versus tossing me out that window. "I'm a friend of Saline's," I said, deciding there was nothing in my purse to indicate otherwise. "We met in real estate school a few years ago, before I moved to Texas."

"I've never heard her talk about you, Abigail Cooper from Austin," he said.

I cocked my head. "Oh yeah? And you've known Saline how long?"

"Two years."

I shrugged. "Then you've known her long enough to also know that she's pretty tight-lipped about her personal life." I hoped I'd guessed her personality correctly, or at least given this guy pause before he decided to have me arrested.

He pursed his lips, and I could tell I'd hit on the truth. "Okay, Abigail Cooper, friend of Saline's, how'd you get in here?"

"She gave me a key," I said, and motioned to my purse, where I'd put the key from under the mat.

Don Draper dug through my purse again and I had to fight against the urge to jump off the bed and grab my purse back. He came up with the key and his frown deepened. "When did she give you this?"

"You ask a lot of questions for a guy who hasn't even introduced himself yet."

He set my purse aside and withdrew a gun from under his jacket. "Sorry. The name's Smith."

I rolled my eyes. "Smith, as in Smith and Wesson?"

"So you've heard of me."

"You're a popular guy."

"How'd you get the key?"

"Like I said, Saline sent it to me."

"When?"

I shrugged. "Maybe a week or two ago."

"Why?"

"I was having a hard time getting over a breakup, and she suggested that I come out to Vegas for a couple of days to take my mind off it."

Draper pointed to the large emerald-and-diamond-encrusted wedding band on my left hand. "A breakup? You and the hubby split?"

I smiled wickedly. "No. But don't tell my husband about my ex-boyfriend."

For the first time Draper's hard expression softened, and he even gave in to a chuckle. "Yeah, okay. You're just the kind of friend Saline would have."

"So where is she, anyway?" I asked, wondering if this guy, who seemed to know Saline intimately, would also know what'd happened to her.

Draper's expression became hard again, except for his eyes; they betrayed his worry. "Don't know," he said. "I was hoping you could tell me."

I pretended to look surprised. "What do you mean you don't know? Aren't you her boyfriend?"

"Fiancé."

I waved a hand. "Whatever, Don Draper. I just want to know where she is."

"Don Draper?"

"Saline told me you looked like the guy from *Mad Men*." I was hoping to convince this guy that Saline and I were buds by dropping a few personal details that would be hard to refute.

Draper rubbed his chin thoughtfully. "Frank," he said, pointing to himself. "But most people call me G."

I blinked. "As in 'Big G'?"

"Yeah."

"Ah. So you own the place."

"Didn't Saline tell you that?"

"Nope. She said you were rich, but she didn't say you owned a casino."

"When was the last time you talked to her?"

I tucked a strand of hair behind my ear. "Hmm, I think it was right after my boyfriend and I split up, so, maybe last week sometime."

"And that's when she sent you the key?"

"Yeah. I got it a few days ago wrapped in a note with her address on it."

Frank tucked his gun away, and inwardly I relaxed a little. "Did you call her to tell her you were coming?"

"No. I wanted it to be a surprise. I found out how dumb that idea was when I got here and nobody was home."

Frank nodded, but I could practically see the wheels turning in his mind.

"So, did she hit some party last night?" I asked, still pretending like I had no idea where Saline was.

"Don't know," Frank said. "She cut out on me a few days ago, and I haven't seen or heard from her since."

I feigned surprise. "Hold on—she *cut out* on you? As in, you two broke up?"

Frank stood and put his hands on his hips. "I don't know. Like you said, Saline doesn't share a lot about what's going on with her, not even with me. It's what attracted me to her in the first place. Well, besides that rockin' bod of hers. She didn't come with a lot of baggage. She never talked about her past, and I always knew where I stood with her, except that last Saturday she just disappeared. She wouldn't return my phone calls, and I came up here looking for her and found some of her stuff was gone. She took a Louis Vuitton suitcase I gave her last Christmas, along with some of her clothes, but there was no trace of where she'd gone, or why."

"Well," I said, pretending to look confused, "I haven't heard from her, and she didn't return the voice mail I left her last night either."

Frank shook his head and walked back and forth in front of the bed. "I always knew that girl carried something crazy inside of her." Tapping his head, he said, "And I knew I shouldn't have gotten mixed up with her, but she's like this drug, you know? Once you get to know her, you're hooked."

I nodded like I fully understood. "Was she acting weird before she left?" I asked, hoping there was a clue that would explain how Candice had met Saline.

Frank sat down in the chair, putting his fingertips together in a steeple under his chin. "She was acting weird," he said. "I thought maybe it was 'cause I was pushing her to set a date for the wedding, but a few weeks ago she disappeared on me like this for a few days, and when she came back, she wouldn't tell me where she'd gone or what she'd done."

"Weird," I said. "She never mentioned anything like that to me. Of course, I was kind of full of my own drama when we talked."

"I had her followed," Frank suddenly confessed, and I held very still, hoping he had something interesting to share. "My associate said she met a girlfriend for lunch across the street, and I told her I knew about it. I couldn't believe she'd betray me like that. We had a big fight. The next day she was gone."

I cocked my head. "Betray you like what? Having lunch with a girlfriend is a betrayal?"

Frank shook his head. "No. It's *where* she had lunch. She met the other girl at Lucky Lou's."

My radar pinged like a pinball machine. "What's wrong with having lunch at Lucky Lou's?"

Frank's eyes narrowed and he pointed in the direction of the other casino across the street. "That scumsucking son of a bitch is my archenemy."

"Whoa," I said, trying to hold in a laugh. "Your *arch*enemy?"

"Don't joke," Frank warned in a way that made me really regret making light of it.

"Okay, okay," I told him. "Sorry. So Saline ate at Lou's with a girlfriend. Maybe the friend wanted to eat there and talked her into it."

"Saline knows how I feel about Lou's. She shouldn't have set foot in that place, no matter who asked her to."

My radar practically pulsed with energy. I needed to know a little more about the incident that inspired the fight. "Who was the friend that Saline went to meet?"

"Don't know," Frank said. "But I've been trying to find her, because I'll bet she knows where Saline is."

"Maybe I can help," I suggested. "I used to live here and Saline and I floated in some of the same circles. Maybe I can tell you who this friend is if you tell me what she looked like."

Frank pulled out his phone and tapped at it a few times; then he came over to the bed and sat down next to me to show me the image on the phone. "My associate took a few pictures," he said. "This was them having lunch."

I squinted at the scene and had to work very hard at not visibly reacting to the image. Candice and a lovely-looking girl with long dark hair sat together at a table, leaning in toward each other as if they were deep in conversation. I stared first at Candice to confirm it was her, and then the profile view of Saline, who wasn't blond in the photo, so obviously at some point after this photo was taken she'd had her hair done and styled to look like Candice's. But why?

"Recognize her?" Frank asked, pulling me from my thoughts.

"No. Sorry."

Frank sighed and tucked his phone away. "Yeah, okay," he said. Then he got up again and moved to my purse. Fishing through it, he took out the key I'd taken from under Saline's mat, and pocketed it, then moved toward the door. "You can stay here till morning, but then you gotta go. I don't care if Saline invited you here or not. I don't want anybody in her place with her gone."

"Got it," I said.

Frank left and I held my breath until I heard the front door click shut. Then I shot up off the bed to retrieve my purse, thanking God that I'd made it out of that encounter in one piece. Gathering up my luggage, I hustled to the door. No way was I staying here one more second now that I knew Frank could get in.

I made my way down to the second floor and retraced my steps out to the car. When I started the engine, the clock on the dash read two a.m. Now that the adrenaline of my encounter with Big G was over, fatigue was settling in again. I sat in the car weighing my options. My head lifted and the neon lights from Lucky Lou's seemed to beckon. Whatever was going on, I knew that many of the answers could likely be found there. Still, it was a risky endeavor because I didn't know where Candice was. If she was hanging out across the street, and she saw me, well, who knew what would happen next? Then again, the opportunity to draw her out felt a little too tempting to ignore. Putting the car into reverse, I backed out and aimed toward Lucky Lou's.

Six hours later I woke up in a room overlooking the parking lot. I'd slept well, knowing that by throwing the latch at the top of the door I was at least fairly safe from waking to a stranger in the room, but the second my eyes opened, I felt beyond famished. I hadn't eaten since the previous morning at the airport, and I'd been skipping more than my fair share of meals lately.

I changed quickly into jeans and a light sweater, then headed downstairs to find a place to eat.

Lou's was very much like Big G's, with a main floor dedicated to electronic gaming machines, and a second-floor hotel lobby.

By studying a map in the hotel lobby, I also discovered that Lucky Lou's had three restaurants: a diner called Louissa's, a sports bar called Lucky Lou's Tavern, and a fine-dining eatery called Mabel's on the Green. I figured Robinowitz must've met Kato at the Tavern, but I wasn't quite sure which restaurant Candice and Saline had eaten in.

Making my way to Louissa's, I was shown to a little two-top and ordered a plate of eggs Benedict—a favorite of mine. The meal came promptly and I dug in, eating with gusto. I may have been so involved in my meal that I didn't realize I was being watched until a large man sat down across from me. The second he sat down, I froze, midchew. For several moments no one said a word. "Abigail Cooper?" he asked.

An intuitive whisper entered my mind. *Ruh-roh.*

I set my fork down, picked up my napkin, finished chewing, and cleared my throat. "Who wants to know?" I asked, finally looking up to take him in.

He was a big guy, built to be genetically intimidating with lots of mass around the shoulders and torso, and a neck as thick as a sequoia. His eyes were small and squinty, but his other features were lost in a doughy face and rounded jawline. "I'm Arlo Valente," he said casually, twisting the saltshaker like a top. "My employer would like to have a word with you."

I waved casually to my half-eaten meal. "I'm a little busy at the present. Maybe another day."

Arlo smiled in that way that suggested he thought I was cute, about the same way a cat might be amused by a cornered mouse right before you have to avert your eyes. "It looks like you're almost done," he said. "And my employer doesn't like to be kept waiting."

My eyes darted to the right and left. Would anybody here help me if I started screaming? "Don't," Arlo warned, and I knew he'd shut me down quickly if I tried to make a scene.

I had an inkling about who Arlo's boss was, and I was quite certain that even if I was wrong, whomever he worked for wasn't anybody I was chomping at the bit to meet. At that exact moment, my cell phone rang and almost reflexively, I picked it up and answered it. "Hi, honey!" I said, while holding up a "one sec" finger to Arlo. He eyed me like the Grumpy Cat. He wasn't amused.

"Hey, doll," Dutch said. "I hadn't heard from you, so I wanted to make sure your plane got in okay."

I slapped my forehead. "Oh, crap, Dutch, I'm so sorry! I forgot to text you when I landed. Yes, the plane got in safe and sound."

"Having fun with your sister?"

"I am!" I said, all smiles and good cheer, while Arlo

grumped harder at me. "You know Cat. Always fun when we get together."

"How're the boys?" Dutch asked next.

"Oh, they're great! Growing like weeds and so smart!"

"And Tim?" my hubby asked of my brother-in-law.

"He's ducky, babe. But he wants to know when you'll come out to visit and take in a round of golf now that spring's here."

"How about now?" my sweet husband asked as Arlo made a sign with his hand that I should wrap it up.

"Now what?"

"How about I catch a plane tonight and hang out with you guys for a couple of days?"

"Uh . . . er . . . ," I said, trying to think fast. "You know, this week *would* have been great, but Tim's got a thing and he won't be in town."

"Oh, that's too bad," Dutch said, and I was almost able to breathe a sigh of relief until he added, "Hey, Abs?"

"Yeah?"

"How come your phone is pinging off a cell tower located in the Greater Las Vegas area right now?"

Aw, shih tzu. I'd underestimated the suspicious nature of my husband, who had at his disposal all the investigative tools of the FBI at his fingertips. I decided to stick to the story, no matter how insane that strategy was. "What? That's crazy! I'm sitting with Cat right now, honey. In Boston. Seriously. There must be something wrong with your equipment."

"Really?" Dutch said. "That's weird. Because I just

called your sister and after telling me she didn't know where you were, she then abruptly changed her story and said that she'd just dropped you at the hair salon."

I forced a laugh. "Oh, that Cat! Such a prankster. Listen, I'd love to chat longer, but the stylist is ready for me now, so I gotta go."

"Abby," Dutch growled. "Don't you dare hang up on me before telling me where the hell you are."

I knew I was caught and with a heavy sigh I did the only thing I could given the circumstances; I hung up. "That was my husband," I said to Arlo. "He works for the FBI and he knows where I am."

Arlo arched an eyebrow. "Yeah, you're in Boston. With a cat."

"Oh, please. I've been with him for four years now. He knows better than to trust me. He was actually calling to tell me that he knows I'm in Vegas, at this very hotel. So if you're thinking of doing anything to me, you'll have the FBI on your heels faster than you can say Lucky Lou's."

Arlo sat there and stared hard at me. I didn't know what he was thinking, but it was clear he wasn't in the mood for my games. "Come on," he said, standing up and moving close to my chair to grab my arm and "help" me up.

"Hey!" I protested. "What about my breakfast?"

Arlo squeezed my arm tighter and pulled me in close to him. "I would calm down if I were you," he said icily, before pulling out some cash and casually tossing it on the table to cover the tab.

I shut up quick. Well, mostly I shut up. There may

have been a small squeak that leaked out, but can you blame me?

My escort continued to hold tight to me as we exited the diner and made our way over to the elevators. We moved to the double doors on the far left, and I saw that there was a keyhole built into the wall. Arlo inserted a key from his pocket, turned the lock, and the doors opened. We went in, and when another couple began to come in behind us, my captor gave them a look that stopped them in their tracks. "This is a private elevator," he snapped, before pressing a button and shutting the doors in their faces.

The second I was alone with him, I started in. "I don't appreciate being manhandled!" I snapped, yanking my arm out of his grasp. "And what the hell is going on, anyway?"

Arlo ignored me and kept his focus on the digital display above the doors, which showed our steady progress upward.

"Who is this boss of yours, anyway?" I tried.

Arlo blinked dully and continued to stare at the digital readout.

"Hey!" I yelled. "This is kidnapping, you know!"

Arlo's eyes narrowed and he cut me a look. "You should know all about kidnapping," he said. "You and your partner sure pulled that off good."

I blinked at him. "Me and my partner sure . . . ? *What the hell are you even talking about?*" (Swearing doesn't count when you're being kidnapped by a big goon.)

Just then the elevator pinged and the double doors opened. Arlo abruptly gripped my elbow again and led me into a very large open room with enough white marble and gold leaf to make the gods of Olympus envious.

I attempted to pull out of his grasp, but this time he held tight, and tugged me along with him across the room to a section that was partially screened by bookcases.

As we rounded the corner, I found myself staring at an elegantly dressed man I'd put in his early-to-mid seventies, with a well-trimmed mustache, sleek silver hair, and eyes that assessed me the moment I came into view. "Is this the girl?" he said to the big man pulling me. I detected a slight British accent, which made him even more mysterious.

"Yes, sir," Arlo answered, then nodded with his chin toward another figure standing near the floor-to-ceiling window, whom I only just noticed. "Thanks, Michelle."

The woman he'd indicated was tall and thin, with short, spiky jet-black hair and horn-rimmed glasses that dominated her otherwise delicate features. "She was easy to spot," Michelle said with a shrug.

The bossman indicated a seat across from him. "Sit," he said, as if I were a disobedient dog.

"Think I'll stand," I said.

Arlo wasn't having any of my insolence. He pushed me rather indelicately forward, then clamped his meaty hand on my shoulder to basically shove me into the chair. "Okay," I said as my bum hit the seat. "Here's also good."

Arlo kept that hand on my shoulder, his fingers digging into me a little. I eyed him angrily. "You'll get more out of me if you're nice," I told him. He squeezed harder.

I turned my head to the bossman and smiled casually before slapping my hand up to cover Arlo's; then, quick as I could, I gripped his pinkie and pulled up as hard as I could. Arlo growled low in his throat and let go of my shoulder, but then he wound his hand back ready to hit me.

"Arlo!" the bossman barked. His goon's hand remained high, while he looked to his employer. "That will do," the bossman said. Arlo slowly lowered his hand and moved to stand just a pace or two behind me. I rolled my eyes and focused on the big kahuna who'd ordered this little get-together.

"I don't believe we've met," I said, crossing my legs like I was a proper young lass.

"No," he said, eyeing me critically. He didn't seem impressed.

"I'm assuming you're Salazar Kato," I said, just to move things along.

"I am," he said. "And you are Abigail Cooper. Self-proclaimed psychic and business partner to Candice Fusco."

I didn't much care for that "self-proclaimed" bit, but I held my tongue. "Is she here?" I asked him.

Kato's brow furrowed, as did Michelle's. I wondered if Arlo's brow mirrored theirs. "Is who here?" Kato asked me, his words distinctly pronounced as if he wanted to make a point of turning the question back on me.

"Candice," I said, and I could feel a bit of anger rise as I said her name to the man who'd hired her to kill Robinowitz and maybe even Lenny Fusco.

Kato reacted unexpectedly. He stood up abruptly and his face flushed with fury. "You think to joke with me?!" he shouted.

My jaw dropped and I pushed back into the chair. "Joke?" I said when I found my vocal cords. "Nothing about this is a joke, Mr. Kato!" And then my eyes misted and I couldn't control the quiver to my lip. A bubble of emotion rose up from my chest and I felt powerless against it. "You think finding out my best friend is a hired hit man for you is something I want to joke about? Do you know how many lives you've ruined? I *love* Candice like she's my own sister, okay? Until a week ago, I thought she was the best person I've ever known! She's saved my life countless times! *Countless!* And because of you, she's now a monster, and she'll be lucky to avoid the death penalty!"

Salazar's face lost its flush and he sat back down to stare at me curiously. I continued to dribble there in my seat, seething with anger of my own. Also, I was scared shitless because I'd just yelled at a mobster. (Swearing doesn't count when you're scared shitless.)

"Where is Saline?" Salazar asked me.

I wiped at my cheeks and tried to swallow a sob. "Who?" I asked, trying my best not to appear as if I knew the name.

"Saline," Salazar repeated levelly.

I thought I should probably go with a bit of the truth here, because he seemed to know that I was lying.

"She's in the hospital in Austin," I said to him. "She was pulled from Candice's car when it went over a bridge two nights ago."

Salazar's face drained of color. Michelle leaned forward and put a hand on his shoulder, as if to comfort him, and he raised his palm to cover it, as if he needed the lifeline to take in the news. "What is her condition?"

"Not good," I told him.

"Which hospital?" Michelle asked, lifting her cell phone.

"St. David's," I said. "But you won't get any information on her. She's listed as Candice Fusco, and if I were you, I wouldn't alert the authorities to the error, or you're going to have the FBI down here asking you a whole lotta questions, Mr. Kato."

Kato and Michelle exchanged a look. "I'll be discreet," she said, getting up to walk around the bookcase and out of sight.

"What questions would the FBI want to ask me?" Kato said as Michelle's murmurs echoed from the other side of the room.

"Well," I said, hoping that mentioning the FBI would keep me alive, "I know they want to ask you why you hired Candice to shoot Dr. Robinowitz."

Kato's brow furrowed again. "Why would I hire Candice to shoot my good friend?"

I shrugged. "Maybe because the Feds think you loaned him some money and he couldn't pay it back. Or maybe it's because he had dirt on you and was willing to share it with the Feds."

Kato's gaze shot over to Arlo. I wanted to turn around to see the silent exchange, but decided to keep my eyes on Kato. "That's absurd," Kato said. "David was *my* best friend, Ms. Cooper. He would never betray me. And as for the money, it was I who owed him. A great deal, in fact. I would have given my own life for him if it came to it, and now he's dead because of *your* best friend."

I sat there for a moment considering the fact that my lie detector hadn't gone off even once since I'd sat down. Was Kato telling me the truth? "Well, then who hired Candice to kill Dr. Robinowitz?" I asked.

"That's what I was hoping you could tell me," he said, leaning forward to study me again.

Just then Michelle came back around the bookcase, wearing a grim frown. "She's stable," she said softly, taking up her chair right behind him again. Placing a hand on his arm, she said, "Her prognosis is guarded, though, Sal. She's sustained some head trauma and they don't yet know how her recovery will go. I'm so sorry. I can head to Austin immediately if you want."

Sal covered her hand again. "Thank you, Michelle," he said. "I've asked quite a lot of you in recent weeks when you were having so many of your own difficulties, haven't I?" She smiled fondly at him, as if it were no trouble.

"You were there for me. I want to be there for you," she said.

He took her hand and kissed it. "Yes, please go, *bella*.

Be with her and report back to me if there's any change."

Michelle got up and kissed Sal's cheek. "I'll book the first flight out and call you as soon as I get an update on her condition." Then she nodded to Arlo. "Watch over him while I'm gone," she practically ordered. "I'll tell Andy to cover security."

And then she moved off toward the elevator, walking with a grace and confidence that was hard not to envy.

When she was gone, Kato turned once again to me. "Why do you think Candice was hired by me to kill my friend?" he asked.

"Because the Feds showed me a photo of you giving her money."

Kato pursed his lips. "Ah, that," he said, but didn't elaborate. "And you think Candice has returned to Vegas because . . . ?" he asked next.

"Because I thought she'd come here to collect her payment for killing Robinowitz."

Kato tapped his fingers on the desk. "You came looking for her here, at my casino?" He said that as if he couldn't fathom someone doing something so stupid.

"In hindsight it might not have been the smartest idea," I admitted. "But I need to find her, Mr. Kato, and get her to explain. This isn't Candice."

"Oh, I beg to differ with you, Ms. Cooper. I've known Candice since she was still wet behind the ears. She's quite capable of something like this. What I can't reconcile, however, is why she would betray me so cruelly. To kill David and hurt Saline . . . Candice knows what I'm capable of. To cross me in this way isn't just suicidal—it's setting herself up for the most hideous death imaginable."

I gulped. Kato said that casually, as if he were commenting on the weather. "Listen," I said to him. "I know you're going to want to get your revenge, but I'm telling you, Mr. Kato, that there's more to this than meets the eye. I know you might not believe in psychics, but I swear, I'm legit, and I'm good. Really good. If anyone can find Candice, it's me. So, please, I'm begging the part of you that's known her since she was wet behind the ears, if you ever cared about her at all, let me try to find her and tell her side of the story before you do anything . . . er . . . drastic."

Kato inhaled deeply and let out a sigh. "Very well, Ms. Cooper," he said. "You have seventy-two hours to find Candice and bring her to me to explain herself. If, at the end of those seventy-two hours, you either fail to find her or you don't bring her to me, I will hunt both of you down and make her punishment yours."

My mouth went dry, because Kato looked at me and I could tell he wasn't kidding or even exaggerating. He'd find a way to kill me if I didn't get to Candice and bring her to him.

The best I could hope for if I didn't find Candice was to seek the protection of the FBI, but would they protect me when they discovered I'd come to Vegas knowing full well that the woman in the hospital wasn't my BFF?

"I understand," I told Kato, simply because I knew I had no other choice at the moment but to accept his terms and hope I could get the hello Dolly out of there.

The corners of Kato's mouth quirked in the slightest of smiles. "Arlo," he said, waving to his goon. "You may escort Ms. Cooper to the lobby."

Chapter Eleven

I got out of the casino as fast as I could. Luckily, I hadn't unpacked much of my suitcase from the night before, so it was mostly a grab and go. As I exited the lobby, I could sense lots of eyes on me, and I looked around nervously, feeling very exposed. My gaze landed on a camera mounted to the ceiling, and I just *knew* that security was watching my hasty exit.

I hustled through the parking lot, glancing over my shoulder as I went. No way was Kato going to let me go without putting a tail on me; of that I was certain. And I doubted that he'd let me bring Candice back to him for a chitchat when I found her. He definitely felt like the kind of guy who would sic his goons on us the second he knew I'd discovered her whereabouts. As I trotted down the asphalt, I didn't see anybody in the parking lot who looked like they were keeping tabs on me, but that did little to settle my nerves.

After throwing my stuff in the car, I pulled out of

the lot and sure enough, my radar pinged and I spotted a dark brown SUV in my rearview mirror, tucked just a few cars back. I made a right turn the first chance I got. Like I knew it would, the SUV turned right too.

"Amateurs," I muttered. Well, Candice had taught me several ways to lose a tail, and I drove until I found an opportunity at a Burger King about two blocks down. I entered into the lot and made like I was about to pull into a parking space, and just as I'd hoped, the SUV followed suit and began to pull into a parking space a few down from me. I kept the engine idle, however, and as a maroon minivan was about to enter the drive-through, I gunned the engine and zipped ahead of it, pulling up to the order window first. I saw in the rearview mirror that the mother driving the car was pretty furious at me, but better her than a mobster goon.

Behind her the SUV began to pull out of the space, but now there was the minivan between us, and because of the close proximity of the building next door, if they wanted to continue to tail me, they had to get into the drive-through line. What's more, by the time the two guys in the SUV figured out that they'd been tripped up, another two cars had pulled in behind them. They were trapped and I couldn't help but laugh.

At the order window I ordered a ton of food: burgers, fries, Cokes, shakes, and even a few goodies for dessert. When I got to the payment window, I handed over two twenties, took one of the fries and a Coke, and told the girl that the entire rest of the order was for the minivan behind me, with my compliments. Then I simply drove out of the exit and back onto the street.

For the next twenty minutes I put some serious distance between me and the Burger King. I figured I had at least a five-minute head start on the goon squad, but I wanted to make sure they couldn't possibly catch up with me.

An hour and a half later I had pulled in to the apartment Candice had rented, tucking myself neatly into the parking space I'd taken up before. I wasn't exactly happy about being back here, but I had a feeling that Candice had kept this place on the down low, and it was as good a place to hide as any other.

After looking around for a few minutes to make sure no one suspicious came into view, I got out, grabbed my luggage and my purse, and headed to the door. After working the key and getting inside, I came up short.

During the time I was away, someone else had been inside the apartment.

It wasn't any one thing that alerted me—it was a shift in the energy of the place that I noticed immediately. For several seconds I stood stock-still, hoping that whoever had come into the apartment wasn't still hanging out. I strained my ears to listen, but I heard nothing. "Hello?" I called, keeping one hand firmly on the door handle should I need to heave it open and bolt the hell out of there. (Swearing doesn't count when you're getting ready to make a run for your life.)

There was no reply, which didn't necessarily mean I

was alone. "Candice?" I called again. Straining my ears to pick up even the slightest sound, I continued to hover in the entryway, until I sort of convinced myself that no one was in the apartment besides me.

Still, I kept my purse slung over my shoulder and the bag by the door while I moved farther inside to investigate.

Peering around the living room, I saw that all the mail I'd tucked back into the mailbox had been taken out and opened up to be organized on the dining room table.

Looking toward the kitchen, I saw a set of pots drying on a cloth on the counter, and the place had the scent of roasted garlic about it. Someone had cooked a meal.

I then moved into the bedroom, and although I couldn't be certain, I felt the bed looked different than it had the day before—as if someone had slept in it and made it back up again, but rearranged the pillows in a different order.

There was no telltale half-packed suitcase lying about, but still, I knew someone had come here, cooked themselves dinner, and slept in the bed the night before. And the only person I could think of who might've done that would be Candice. Perhaps most telling of all was what I found in the bathroom. A wet towel hung over the rod, and there were several small, brown rusty stains, about the size of a quarter, in one patch that definitely looked like dried blood. I shivered a little as I inspected the towel.

In the wastebasket were some discarded cotton

balls, also stained with blood. A tube of antibiotic ointment was set to the side of the sink next to a bottle of painkillers. I wondered if Candice had cut herself on a knife while preparing dinner or something. Still, the towels and the cotton balls made me a little queasy, so I moved out of the bathroom and searched out the rest of the apartment, finding no further trace of Candice.

When I'd finished my search, I put my back against the wall of the living room and tried to think of what to do.

I reached for my phone and started to call Dutch, then thought better of it and dialed Brice instead. "Where have you been?" he demanded the moment he picked up.

"Vegas. Just like I told you," I snapped back. After the day I'd had, I was in no mood for the third degree.

"Abby, you've been gone for over twenty-four hours without checking in. Your husband has been threatening to quit the bureau and go chasing after you, you know."

"Well, talk him out of that!" I yelled. God, why was everybody always so ticked off at *me*?

Brice took a deep breath and tried again. "Listen, I'm sorry. I've just been worried, and now that Dutch knows you're not in Boston and in Vegas, he's getting more worked up by the second."

"Is he there?" I asked.

"No. There was a death threat against the governor this morning, and he's been rerouted from San Antonio back here to help with the investigation."

"A death threat against the governor?"

"Yeah. We get them every once in a while. They're usually nothing, but this one had enough markers in the threat to take it seriously. Rivers should be tied up most of the day, that is, if he doesn't quit midshift and catch the first plane to Vegas."

"Does he know you know where I am?"

Brice sighed. "Not yet. But when I tell him I knew you were going, he'll probably punch me in the face."

I smirked. "I've seen your face. It looks like it could take the punch."

Brice actually laughed. "Ouch," he said. "Talk about coming out swinging. What do you have for me on the Vegas front, Rocky?"

"Nothing good, I'm afraid." I then proceeded to tell him everything. I felt like I was in way over my head and I knew it was time to come clean to Brice. I told him all about the file Candice had left in her safe and what I'd found in it. Then I told him everything that'd happened since I'd landed in Vegas, including my little tête-à-tête with Kato.

He surprised me by yelling only a little. Once he'd calmed down, he said, "You need to get on a plane and come home right now."

"Brice, listen to me. I can't. Candice is here—I *know* it. I can feel that she was here, in this apartment, just a few hours ago."

"Which is why you need to leave there right now, Cooper!" Brice said, his voice strained with urgency. "It kills me to say this to you, but you can't trust that she won't hurt you if she finds you there. She's already murdered one person, possibly two. And two days ago she tried to kill an innocent woman to fake her own death. How many more signs do we need to realize Candice isn't who we thought she was?"

His words hit me like a punch in the gut. "Are you giving up on her too, Brice?"

He was silent so long I thought he'd hung up. When I called out to him, he said, "I'm here. Listen, I still love her, okay? And I can't believe I still love her through all of this, but I do and I probably always will. What I can't allow is for you to take the chance of confronting her, and having her turn on you. So get the hell out of that apartment and give me the address so that I can call the Feds in Vegas to tell them where to pick her up."

I eyed the door on the other side of the room. It'd be so easy to do what Brice suggested, but when I checked in with my own intuition, I had the opposite feeling. I needed to stick with it and find Candice. "It's not how it looks," she'd said. I closed my eyes to remember exactly the way she'd said it and I realized my lie detector had never gone off while I'd listened to her words.

Candice had spoken the truth. There was more to this than met the eye. I had to see it through.

"Brice," I said levelly. "I know you don't trust Candice right now, so I'm not going to ask you to do that. I'm going to ask you to trust me. Trust me, because more than I still believe in your wife, I believe in me. She couldn't have fooled me and my crew all these years. She just couldn't."

Brice sighed again. "Then why, Abby? Why has she done all this?"

"I don't know. The only person who does know is

Candice. So I'm going to find her, and I'm going to ask her. And then I'll call you and we can decide what to do after that."

"I don't like that you're out there on your own," he said. "Setting Candice aside, Kato isn't a guy to fuck around with, Abby."

"I'll be okay. For the moment, Kato doesn't know where I am, and I'm careful."

"Still . . ."

"Is there anything new on Saline's condition?" I asked, hoping to change the subject.

Brice took the bait. "She's stable, but still in a coma. I'm playing the part of concerned husband, and at least she has someone to hold her hand a couple of hours a day. Poor girl."

"Yeah, on that note, if you see some woman with black hair and horn-rimmed glasses hanging around the hospital, it's one of Kato's people. Her name is Michelle, and I'm thinking she's going to want to stick pretty close to Saline."

Brice was silent for a moment and I figured he was processing that. "What's Kato's connection to Saline?"

"I have no idea. Like I told you, I learned that she was the fiancée of another casino owner, but when I read her energy at the hospital, I did get the feeling she was fooling around with someone else. Maybe she and Kato were lovers."

"That would explain why Lenny Fusco was killed," Brice said, and I remembered Oppenheimer and Gould's theory about Lenny's getting friendly with Kato's girlfriend and that's why he was offed. I realized that I'd never asked Kato about Lenny. Then again, by the way he and Michelle were practically purring at each other, I'd figured the two of them were a couple.

"How is the investigation into the crash going?" I asked next. It was probably only a matter of time before the Feds figured out Candice had staged it.

"It's just like the rest of this case, more questions than answers. They found a fair amount of blood on a blanket near the crash site and they think it came out of the Porsche when it went over the bridge. CSI has already tested the blood on the blanket, and they know it doesn't belong to the woman they pulled out of the car. They're going to analyze the DNA before running it through the database to see if they can get a match to someone who could be in the system."

My radar pinged and I said, "Is the blood male or female?"

"Funny you should ask—it's female."

"Blood type?"

"AB negative."

Candice and I had been in more than a few scrapes together, and at the hospital after one of those scrapes I'd learned that she had AB negative blood. I remembered from my freshman biology class in college that AB negative was the rarest type of blood, which was why the odd fact about my BFF stuck in my head.

"Brice?"

"Yeah?"

"Candice has AB negative blood."

He paused before saying, "Well, if she were going to fake her own death, she'd probably put something like that in the car to make us believe it was really her."

"But that makes no sense," I said. "Candice knows full well that water corrupts blood evidence. Why would she waste her own blood on something that would likely be useless to the investigation? And, what's more, you said that they already checked the proteins against Saline's blood type, right?"

"Maybe she planted it at the crash site," Brice said reasonably.

"Yeah, but that makes no sense either," I told him. "Candice knows she has a rare blood type. Less than one percent of the population has AB negative blood. Why would she put a blanket covered in her own blood at the scene when she should also know there is a ninety-nine percent chance of it not matching Saline's blood type? And with something like that at the scene, CSI would definitely test it against Saline's DNA if she came up dead, just to make sure it matched the victim."

And then I remembered the bloodstain on the towel in the bathroom and I felt a small shudder travel down my spine. "I don't think she left that blanket there on purpose, Brice. I think Candice is hurt. Bad."

"Tell me what you're thinking," he said, his voice tight as if he couldn't bear the thought of his wife somewhere out there, injured.

I told him what I'd found in the bathroom and he and I talked for several more minutes, going over the facts as we knew them and trying to put the pieces together to form a coherent picture. I think by the end of the conversation we were more confused than when we started, and I knew I'd rattled him by telling him about the bloody towel. I finally hung up with him and moved over to the dining room table to take a seat. I'd made up my mind while talking to Brice and my plan going forward was simple. I was going to stay put until Candice came back and then I was going to confront her and hope like hell she didn't kill me.

So I sat there for an hour, drumming my fingers on the tabletop, watching the door, basically waiting for something to happen.

Nothing did.

After two hours, when I was good and bored, I went to my suitcase and pulled out my laptop, thinking I might as well try to work on the case while I waited. Using my phone as a hot spot, I logged on and began to write out everything I knew about what was going on. That took nearly forty-five minutes.

At the end of it I sat back and studied the screen. It was so much information that it felt overwhelming. Getting up from the table, I rooted around in my suitcase again, coming up with a set of blank three-by-five cards.

This was a trick I'd learned from Candice, who taught me to write out the most basic facts about a case, lay them on a flat surface, and wait to see what dots I could connect. The method had worked well for us in the past, and it seemed like this case could also benefit from the technique.

Before writing down the facts, I decided to follow a timeline; I'd start with what I believed was the first relevant fact. "Candice goes to Vegas to get married," I said as I wrote that out on a card. Eyeing the calendar on my phone, I added the date almost exactly six weeks before and set that on the dining room table.

"Next, she meets with Kato. . . ." I put that card on the table and moved on. "Next she meets with Saline." I paused then and realized I didn't know when Candice had met with Saline. It could have been either before or after she met with Kato. Still, I knew she'd met with her, so I jotted that down; then I got another card and said, "She hangs out with Robinowitz at some point too." As I didn't know what specific date she'd met with the good doctor, I wrote it out and put it next to the Saline and Kato cards.

I tapped my lip while I thought about what might've come next and realized I did know at least one date. "March sixth, Lenny Fusco is murdered," I mumbled. As I was writing that out, however, my radar pinged, and not just a little ping—it was more of a PING!

"Hmmm," I mused. "Lenny Fusco. The domino that set this whole thing in motion?"

I knew very little about Candice's ex-husband, other than he'd been the one to train Candice in the art of private detecting, but he was such a sleazeball that he'd eventually lost his license and had operated under Candice's license for the duration of their short marriage.

I also knew that the last time we'd encountered Lenny, Candice had been mad enough to kill him.

Still, that was over two years ago, and it wasn't like Candice to carry a grudge. Or was it? I sat down at the table and pulled my laptop close. My fingers flew over the keyboard as I did a search on Lenny Fusco.

The first hit was the story of his body being discovered, and the police indicating that he'd been shot in the face, execution-style and at point-blank range. One week earlier, he'd been reported missing by his wife, who said that she'd seen him off to work, only to learn later that Lenny had never arrived at his job at the Bellagio. His abandoned car was found in the parking lot of the hotel, but no one remembered seeing him enter the casino/hotel.

And then I read a quote that made me suck in a breath. It was taken from the detective assigned to the case, Detective Robert Brosseau, who said, "We are investigating possible links between the victim and organized crime, but at this time, I cannot state definitively that this was a mob hit."

Feeling almost too excited to type, I switched away from that window over to my personal list of contacts and scrolled through the *B*s. A few seconds later I had the detective on the phone. "Robert!" I sang. "It's Abby Cooper calling."

"Abby!" my old friend replied. "Long time no talk to, lady. How's that husband of yours? You two enjoying married life?"

"We are, we are," I said. Then I got down to business. "Listen, Robert, I'm doing a little digging into one of your cases, and I'm hoping you can give me some background on it."

"I'm guessing you want to know about Lenny Fusco. Am I right?"

"You are."

"Abby, don't you think this is one case you shouldn't get involved in?"

"You mean because Candice is my best friend and the prime suspect for the murder?"

"Exactly because of that."

I sighed. "Robert, I know that Candice is looking pretty guilty right now, but until I hear a confession come out of her mouth, my money is still on her."

"How's she doing, by the way?" Robert asked. "I heard she's in a coma."

"She's . . . hanging in there. Anyway, about Lenny Fusco. I'm assuming you put it together that Lenny and Candice were once married?"

"I did, and I was the one who brought it up to the Feds when they came knocking."

I felt my temper flare, and even thought Robert and I were old friends, I couldn't help snapping at him. "Why would you *do* that? Candice was your friend too, Rob!"

"Hey, hey, take it easy on me, would ya?" he said. "Listen, I wasn't going to mention it to them until I found out that Lenny met with Candice the same day he was murdered."

"Wait, *what*?"

"I found all this out when I started digging into Lenny's job at the Bellagio," he explained. "I remembered Candice calling me right after she and Brice arrived in town; she wanted to have dinner with me and Nora, but I was on my last week of working the night shift, and Nora's mom had knee surgery and needed some extra attention, so we couldn't make it work.

"Anyway, Candice had mentioned that she and Brice were staying at the Bellagio, and I didn't even make the connection to the two of them until I heard from one of Lenny's coworkers that in the days leading up to his disappearance, he'd been overly interested in one of the female guests at the hotel. Lenny had a pretty good gig going, monitoring the surveillance cameras for any security issues. They pay those guys top dollar to catch and report people trying to cheat the system, or who look like they're about to cause trouble. When I started poking through Lenny's workplace hunting for clues, the coworker pointed me to Lenny's computer logs, and that's when I discovered that he'd had Candice under surveillance almost from the moment she walked into the hotel. His computer log shows him tracking her from camera to camera throughout the hotel, restaurants, and casino. Then the tracking stopped sometime around noon on the fourth day she's there, and that happens to be the same time Candice fails to show up at a massage she'd scheduled in the hotel spa, but going back through the surveillance tapes, we were able to see her leaving the hotel with Lenny hot on her heels. We're not sure where they went or what they talked about, but they both came back to the hotel about an hour and a half later. A couple of days after that, the exact same scenario occurs: Candice schedules a spa appointment, cancels at the last minute, and she and Lenny leave the Bellagio within ten minutes of each other, both of them returning an hour or so later. A while after that, Lenny agrees to cover the night shift for a sick coworker, and his boss lets him head home early to catch some z's.

"Lenny's wife confirms that she found him sleeping on the couch when she got home from work. She woke him up for dinner; then he went back to sleep for a few, then took a shower and told her he'd see her in the morning. He left their place at eleven and that's the last anyone saw or heard from old Lenny."

"But where was Candice at that time?" She had to have been with Brice, and therefore had a solid alibi. The security cameras at the Bellagio would no doubt show that.

"We fished around for more footage and found Candice leaving the hotel at around eleven. She returned fifty minutes later with a plastic bag with the CVS logo on it. According to the statement her husband gave the Feds, Candice said she had a headache, and went out for some pain meds."

"Did you follow up with footage from CVS?"

"We did," Brosseau admitted. "And we see her there for about a half hour, lingering in the magazine section."

"Okay, so at least she has an alibi for Lenny's murder."

"There're still twenty minutes that are unaccounted for, Abby."

I rolled my eyes. "You really think Candice murdered her ex-husband and disposed of his body in twenty minutes?"

"I'm not saying it wouldn't have been a challenge, but it's physically possible if Candice really wanted to pull it off."

I put my elbows on the table and rubbed my forehead. Why was absolutely everything pointing back at Candice? She had to have known she was under video surveillance at the Bellagio. If Lenny went missing and was later found dead, of course they'd look at her, especially since the pair had such a volatile past.

Desperate and grasping at straws, I said, "Robert, is there anyone else you looked at for Lenny's murder?"

"Well, sure," he said. "Lenny still worked the occasional case out of an office on the south side. We found a file that he'd worked up on a woman named Saline Hamon."

My breath caught. "You're kidding."

"You know her?"

"No," I lied. "But keep talking. What was in the file?"

"According to Lenny's research, she arrived in Vegas about ten years ago at the ripe old age of nineteen. She worked the strip joints for a while and moved up to the escort service. Eventually, she started hanging around old men with heart conditions."

"You're serious?"

"Yep. She dated three guys old enough to be her grandfather, and they all died within a year of meeting her—of natural causes according to the coroners' reports—trust me, I checked. Anyway, after each one bit the dust, he left Saline a little money, which she used to go to real estate school, and then parlayed that knowledge into some property investments that made her some pretty good coin. Of course, the real estate bubble popped in 'oh seven, and Saline was up to her eyeballs in debt. Then she starts hanging around with this guy, Frank Garafolo, who owns Big G's Hotel and Casino, and suddenly she's the owner of a swanky new condo and she opens up a title company that handles all of the condo sales for Big G's. But in one or two of the surveillance photos in the file, Saline is seen on the arm of Salazar Kato, and shortly after that, she's shopping at all the best stores in town. It doesn't take a genius to figure out that she was playing both men for their money, and they're known rivals—definitely not the kind of guys you want to cross, especially against each other."

"Why is she a person of interest in Lenny's homicide?"

"It's a couple of things," Robert said. "Mostly it's the way Lenny conducted his investigation. It starts out pretty normal—some photos, some background checks, some credit reports—but then he's tracking her across town on his days off from the Bellagio. And the photos go from faraway shots of her in a shop, to close-ups of her face, her chest, her legs, and her rear. I saw the photos and I can't really blame the guy—Saline is a looker— but it's pretty obvious he became obsessed with her."

"You think she found out about the surveillance?"

"I do. Mostly because the file is an inch thick and it appears it was never delivered to whoever ordered him to dig up dirt on her. Well, that and now she's disappeared. There's no trace of her since last week."

I knew exactly where she was, but I wasn't about to

divulge that to Robert. "Did you share any of this with the Feds?" I asked next.

"Of course, but they didn't want to hear it. They like Candice for the murder, Abby."

"Yeah, well, I don't."

"Do they know you're rooting around in this?"

"Not yet."

"Then I'll keep my mouth shut, but I really think you should butt out. Candice got herself into this mess. There's no reason you should go down with her."

"Noted," I said stiffly. "Thanks, Detective. Please give my best to Nora."

I hung up with Brosseau and tapped my finger on the card marked "Lenny Fusco." All of this started with him. He ran surveillance on Saline and then he monitored Candice and then he got killed. By either Candice or Saline.

"What if they were working together?" I said aloud, and I felt a lightness in my stomach. I sat up straighter. "Saline and Candice were working together?" Again I felt that familiar lightness that indicated I'd hit on something that was true. And yet, somehow it didn't quite fit.

I stood up and began to pace, trying to talk it out. "So, Saline finds out that Lenny Fusco is running surveillance on her, and she and Candice team up to kill him?" That felt way too far-fetched given the leaden heavy feeling in the pit of my stomach.

"Okay, then maybe Lenny mentions Saline to Candice and . . ." I paused. My whole middle had lit up like the Fourth of July. "Lenny told Candice about Saline!"

Finally I had a piece of the puzzle that felt solid, like the corner piece I could work everything else off of.

I just knew that was the beginning of the timeline too. I began to talk it out. "Lenny sees Candice at the Bellagio and recruits her for something having to do with Saline. Like, maybe he's concerned about her habits with older men, or . . . Oh! Wait! Saline is engaging in dicey activity by leading on two dangerous men: Kato and Big G. Maybe Lenny tries to warn Saline off, but she won't listen, so he asks Candice to intervene. Candice and Saline meet and have a talk, which is where Frank gets that photo he showed me, and between the two of them they come up with a plan to end it with Kato, so Candice then goes to Kato on Saline's behalf, and at the meeting she tells him it's over and he gives Candice a big wad of cash for . . . for . . . Saline's expenses? As a farewell gesture? For old times' sake?" I threw my hands up in the air. "I have no idea."

Moodily I sat down in the chair again. Just when I'd been making progress, I came to a point in the story that made little sense.

Kato, Candice, Saline, and Lenny. These were the four players with multiple connections to one another, but how they all lined up I still wasn't sure.

I then had another thought, and that was to do a spread of three-by-five cards with all the characters involved in the case. Maybe if I created a cast, I might be able to follow the play.

It took me only a few minutes, but I wrote out every person I thought was involved, and laid them on the table, thinking I'd be able to visualize a possible hidden connection.

During the time I was writing out the cards, I allowed my intuition to guide me and I set the characters on the table almost without thinking, allowing my radar to choose the spot on the table. When I was done, I realized two things right away. The way I'd arranged the cast was roughly in a circle, and the middle space, where everyone else revolved around, was empty.

"I'm missing someone," I whispered, feeling my senses tingle. I looked long and hard at the cast, and ticked them off as I read their names out loud. "Candice, Saline, Dr. Robinowitz, Salazar Kato, Frank Garafolo, Lenny Fusco. Who could I be missing?"

I tapped my finger impatiently on the tabletop. The answer felt right in front of me, but I couldn't for the life of me figure out whom I'd left out. What's more, that mysterious person was at the center of all of this; I felt that deep in my gut. So I wrote out a note card with a question mark and the name "Mystery Person," put the card in the center of all the other names, and shifted farther down the table, where I went back to the timeline and tried to work it through from there, writing out even more cards as I went.

"Lenny runs surveillance on Saline. He discovers Candice at the Bellagio. He makes contact with her. They meet. She then meets Saline. Next she meets with Kato. Kato gives her money. Somewhere in there Candice also hangs out with Dr. Robinowitz. She rents this place under an assumed name and has it furnished and fully stocked. She and Lenny meet again, and that night he's murdered. Candice flies home. Robinowitz flies to Austin. Candice shoots him in the parking garage. She calls me and tells me about the file in her safe; then she disappears, but tails me from time to time. Someone breaks into our offices and then the Witts', searching for the file. Somewhere in there Saline flies to Austin, and meets up with Candice. Candice renders her unconscious and sends her over the bridge in the Porsche. Candice comes back to Vegas, bleeding from a mysterious injury. I sit here rambling on and on about facts that don't add up or make any kind of sense."

With a heavy sigh I got up from the table and headed to the kitchen. I had a headache and I was hungry and hoped there was something edible in the pantry.

Luckily, the place had a few supplies, and I even found some herbal tea that promised to relax me. Setting the pasta and sauce I'd recovered from the pantry aside, I fished around in the cabinets for cookware, coming up with pots, pans, and even a gorgeous ceramic blue teakettle.

"It's a shame to put this away when it's so lovely," I mused, moving to the faucet to fill it with water. As I lifted the lid, however, I realized why the teakettle had been tucked into a cabinet. There was a piece of paper jammed inside. I lifted it out carefully, so as not to tear it, and unfolded it with a racing heart. I just knew it was big.

I wasn't wrong. The paper was actually two pieces of paper, stapled together. The top piece was a copy of something I'd seen before. Something I had with me, in fact, and I raced to my suitcase to dig it out from the inside pocket.

I held the original DNA report in my hands, comparing it to the copy before flipping the page to the one stapled behind, which, I quickly discovered, was a legal name change for Olive Wintergarden. A judge in the state of New York had granted her the new name of Saline Hamon. "No *way*!" I whispered, just as my cell pinged with an incoming text.

Distractedly I picked up my cell and glanced at the display. The text was from "Cassidy," and it read:

Get the hell out of that apartment!

Chapter Twelve

I was so stunned that for long seconds I simply stood there, staring at the screen. It went dark and I swiped at the display to light it up again. I thought of a dozen replies to text back, but what could I say that would make Candice reveal where she was?

Finally, I simply texted back, *No.*

If Candice wanted me out of here so bad, she could damn well come in and get me. (Swearing doesn't count when your BFF—an accused murderer and possible psychopath—orders you around.)

Not even three seconds later there was a knock on the door. I clutched my phone. Maybe being obstinate wasn't such a great idea.

The knocks came again—this time they seemed impatient. Creeping to the door, I peeked through the peephole. All I saw was black. Leave it to Candice to be difficult. Marshaling my courage and plastering what

I hoped was an annoyed look on my face, I swung the door open and nearly kissed the muzzle of a gun.

I reacted by stumbling backward, and the gun followed me into the apartment. I didn't even know who was holding it, so focused was I on that giant muzzle, poised to take my head off.

As my back hit a wall, I began to lift my gaze, and in a flash there was a flurry of movement along with the buzz of electricity, and all of a sudden the person holding the gun crumpled to the ground, taking me down with him.

I screeched and pushed and shoved away from him, but the foyer was tightly cramped and there wasn't much room to maneuver. "Ah! Ah! Ah!" I cried, frantic to get away.

My right arm was grabbed roughly, and I was yanked away from the still form puddled around me. "Stop fighting!" I heard a familiar voice say.

My gaze flew up to the new figure in the doorway, and I realized Candice was standing there with a grimace on her face, attempting to free me from the tangle of the heaped figure at my feet.

Somehow I found my footing and pushed my way to a standing position before backing away from the door. I watched Candice bend low and take his gun away. A gun she then turned on me.

"Candice, don't!" I cried, my hands flying up in surrender.

She looked at me like I was an idiot, before pocketing a Taser, then sliding back the muzzle on the gun to release the clip. It dropped into her palm and she pocketed it before popping out the bullet in the chamber and tossing the gun across the room to the couch. "Grab your stuff," she commanded.

I felt slow to react. I couldn't quite figure out what was happening. I kept blinking at her, wondering if she was real. She looked terrible—bone thin, pale, with a swollen black eye, and her hair was matted with a bit of dried blood on the back right side of her head. "Abby!" she yelled angrily, while she pulled free an electrical cord from a nearby lamp. "Get your stuff!"

I jumped and that got me moving. I ran to the kitchen table and scooped up my laptop and my purse. Leaving the note cards where they were, I simply shoved what I could into my suitcase and turned to Candice, hoping she hadn't strangled the gunman while I was gathering my things.

To my relief I saw that she'd only tied his hands, and was attempting to drag him inside. "A little help here?" she said when she saw me standing there, gaping at her.

I rushed over to help heave the man, who I realized belatedly was Arlo, into the apartment. "Come on," she said, reaching for my arm once we'd dragged him all the way inside. "We have to go."

Frail as she looked, her grip on my arm was still quite strong. I barely had time to nab my suitcase and purse before she was shoving me out the door and locking it behind her. "Move," she ordered, motioning with her head toward my car.

I didn't argue. Candice had just saved my life (again), so the least I could do was follow instructions. When we got to my car, she put her hand out for the keys. I dug in my purse and handed them over. A moment later we were speeding out of the apartment complex and heading toward the highway.

We were both silent for much of the initial part of the drive, mostly because I was still a little too stunned by what'd just happened. But then I turned to Candice and looked at her—really *looked* at her—and what I saw alarmed me even more.

Candice's clothes hung on her, and in addition to the black eye, I saw a fading bruise on her cheekbone; at her temple was a cut that looked like it should've gotten stitches. There was another cut on the back of her head that looked mean and matted the short blond locks that were normally kept so perfectly coiffed.

Defensive bruises lined her arms where the sleeves slipped back and her knuckles were also bruised and swollen. "What the *hell* happened to you?" I asked, and I meant much more than just the obvious beating Candice had received.

"I can't get into that with you," she told me curtly.

My own temper flared. "Really, why? Because if you told me, you'd have to kill me?"

Candice cut me a look and in her eyes I could see anger, sure, but also a sadness and fear that I was unprepared for. "You shouldn't have come here, Abby."

"Candice, please tell me what the hell is going on," I begged. (Swearing doesn't count when you find your BFF in such condition.)

But Candice shifted her gaze back to the road and ignored me.

"Brice is out of his mind with worry," I said, hoping that'd make her crack.

Her shoulders shifted, but she remained stubbornly silent.

I sighed and turned away to stare out the window. "I *can* help, you know."

"By getting yourself killed?"

I knew she was referring to the incident back at the apartment. "Maybe I wouldn't have been in jeopardy if you'd leveled with me."

Candice pulled over to exit the highway. At the stop sign at the bottom of the exit she turned to me and said, "I have leveled with you, Sundance. I've never once lied to you."

"Omitting the fact that you're a hit man . . . hit woman . . . hit *person* for the mob is still a lie, Candice!"

"So even *you* believe that bullshit?" she asked, hurt evident in her eyes.

My jaw dropped. "Bullshit? Candice, how the hell could I believe otherwise?! Saline Hamon is lying in a hospital bed fighting for her life as we speak, and she came in wearing *your* clothes, *your* wedding ring, and driving *your* car! Your ex-husband was *murdered* a few hours after meeting with you! And if that weren't enough, there's *video* of you *executing* Dr. Robinowitz in a parking garage and look what I found in that mailbox at the apartment you were using!" I held up the envelope I'd taken containing Robinowitz's photo and his flight info, and waved it in her face.

Candice took it from me and pulled out the contents, her shoulders slumped as she looked it over.

"Tell me that's not someone trying to supply you the information about your target!" I yelled. I was really getting worked up now that I was sitting next to her. "I mean . . . *come on!*"

Candice's reaction shocked me. She looked up and stared at me with wide eyes for a long moment before her eyes misted and a tear leaked down her cheek. I felt my heart soften. Even though she'd done terrible things, Candice was *still* my very best friend. "This is a plant," she said softly, tossing the envelope on the floor. "It was sent to make me look guilty."

I bit my lip, torn between hugging her fiercely and shaking her. "If you want me to believe you, you're gonna have to do better than that."

Candice sighed wearily. "How many times have you looked at the video?" she asked me, her voice barely above a whisper.

Her question shocked me. "Once. It was enough."

She nodded and wiped at her tears. Turning her focus back to the road, she turned left and headed down the road to a motel with a blinking neon sign. She parked at the office and said, "Did you happen to take the cash from the safe?"

"Yes," I said, hugging my purse to show her that I had it with me.

She held out her hand and I dug into my handbag to retrieve the wad of cash stuffed into my makeup case and give it to her.

Candice peeled off about a thousand dollars and held it out to me. "Here," she said. "Use this to pay for the room tonight, and tomorrow get a cab to take you to the airport. Use the remaining cash for the first flight home you can catch, Abby."

I stared at her. "I don't understand—"

"I'm going to take your rental. Don't worry—I'll drop it off tomorrow at the rental agency. I just need to borrow it for a few hours."

"Candice—"

She took my hand and slapped the money into my palm while looking at me earnestly. "Don't argue with me, Sundance. Please just grant me this one favor and do what I tell you to. You can't be here. As long as you're in town, you can be used against me, which is way too dangerous for both of us."

I could tell it'd be useless to argue, so I took the money and got out of the car. After grabbing my luggage from the backseat, I stood there, waiting to see if maybe she'd change her mind. Instead she rolled down the window and said, "You need to look at that video again. Really *look* at it before you decide who I am and what I'm capable of."

With that cryptic message, she was gone.

I spent much of the night at the motel wearing a track in the carpet of my room, the image of Candice's earnest face imploring me to leave town burning a hole in my brain. Around two a.m. I sat on the edge of the bed and cried. I'd never felt so helpless in my entire life. Candice needed me. Intuitively I *knew* that. But I also realized that her warning to me was also true. If I stayed, I was endangering both of us, simply because I didn't know the full story, and by investigating and trying to help, I could absolutely do more harm than good.

It was like being caught between the frying pan and the fire. There was no move that didn't come with serious consequences. If I left to save my own ass, I was leaving Candice vulnerable to capture by either the FBI or Kato. And it looked like he'd already gone back on his word to give me seventy-two hours. Arlo hadn't shown up at the apartment to welcome me to the neighborhood.

But how could I help Candice by staying? What could I possibly do that I hadn't already done? My radar hummed and that's when I remembered her cryptic message to me. "You need to look at that video again. Really *look* at it before you decide who I am and what I'm capable of."

I got up from the bed and dug out my laptop. I'd left all the three-by-five cards at the apartment, which was a bummer, but I could always map it out on the computer. Using my cell as a hot spot again, I logged on to the Internet and Googled the video of Robinowitz's murder. I knew the story was juicy enough for there to be at least one posting of the video.

I was wrong about that. There were ten sites dedicated to the "Shocking!" video. I logged onto the first and took a deep breath before hitting the play button. It's an awful thing to watch your best friend commit murder.

The video began playing and I forced myself not to blink or look away. I saw Candice's Porsche pull up and park. Then she got out of the car and stood next to the open door. From the left side of the screen Dr. Robinowitz appeared, pulling his luggage behind him. He waved slightly to Candice and he seemed to smile. His body relaxed at the sight of her, but then it stiffened suddenly and his step faltered. Candice pulled out her gun, took two steps forward, and fired. I jerked even though I'd seen the video before and knew it was coming.

Robinowitz crumpled backward, his luggage falling back with him. Candice turned back to the car, got in, and put the Porsche in reverse. A moment later she was gone.

I took in a deep breath and let it out slowly, trying to calm myself. The header was right; it was shocking.

So why had Candice wanted me to look at it? And not just look at it—*really* look at it.

I hovered my finger over the touch pad, debating whether I could stomach another viewing. I figured that in order to make my decision to stay or go, I pretty much had to look at the video at least once more. Candice wanted me to see something that I'd clearly missed, so just because I loved her, I played it again. And then again. And then six more times and every time it was as ghastly as the first.

"What is it that you want me to see, Cassidy?" I said, replaying the video for the seventh time. I talked it out aloud as the video played. "Candice arrives in the Porsche. Parks. Gets out. Robinowitz appears. He's happy to see her. Then he's not. He stiffens. She draws the gun. Takes two steps. Pow . . . wait," I said. "Hold on!" Using the touch pad, I backed the video up to the moment Robinowitz appeared. He smiled and waved at her, and then he paused, his posture stiffening, but Candice hadn't yet drawn her gun. It was subtle, but it was as if Robinowitz had seen something about Candice that had immediately caused him to become startled, or afraid, or both.

I replayed that part of the footage three more times. I wasn't wrong. Robinowitz had been alerted to danger prior to Candice drawing a gun on him. I switched my focus over to Candice. What had she done to alert Robinowitz? Her face was only in profile, partially hidden by her hair, but her lips never seemed to move. She hadn't spoken to him, so what was it?

And then I focused on her coat. Had he seen the bulge in her coat from where she drew her gun? It came out of her coat from her left side, but the way her jacket draped her body I couldn't really make out the bulge of the gun. I squinted hard at the screen and replayed that section frame by frame. On the final frame before Candice withdrew the gun, I nearly fell off the bed.

"Oh . . . my . . . GOD!" I gasped. Finally seeing exactly what Candice had wanted me to pick out from the video.

Reaching for my phone, I dialed as fast as my fingers could slide across the screen. "Pick up, pick up, *pick up*!" I pleaded.

"Harrison," said a gruff voice, foggy with sleep.

"Brice! It wasn't Candice! It wasn't her! She didn't shoot him! She's innocent!"

"Abby?" Brice said.

"Listen to me!" I demanded. "Candice is left-handed.

The woman in the video shot Robinowitz with her *right* hand! It's not Candice! It's someone made to look like Candice!"

There was a pause and I knew Brice was trying to wake up enough to keep up with me. I kept talking, hoping something I said would click for him. "You need to go online right now and look up the video of the shooting in the parking garage. Watch her pull out her gun, Brice. She uses her right hand. And then watch Robinowitz's reaction as he gets close to the woman posing as Candice. He thinks it's her, but as he gets close, he can see that it's an impostor. He stiffens even before she pulls out the gun!"

"Where are you?"

I grunted impatiently. "It doesn't matter where I am, Brice! Get your damn ass out of bed and go online!" (Swearing doesn't count when you've just learned your BFF is innocent of murdering a man in cold blood.)

Brice cleared his throat. "Yeah, okay—hang on." I heard him shuffle around in the background, and I imagined he was setting up his laptop.

"Are you ready for the link?" I asked impatiently.

"No, Cooper. I've still got the copy APD gave me."

I waited for several more seconds through the silence that followed and couldn't help but ask, "Are you watching?"

"I am," he said. A moment later he added, "Holy shit! How did I miss that?"

"We all did!"

"It's not her," he said, his voice now choked with emotion. "Jesus, Abby, it's not her!"

"I know!" My own eyes misted again. I felt a well of relief so intense it was euphoric. "She's innocent. All this time, Candice was innocent. But somebody's gone to great lengths to frame her, and set her up to take the fall for multiple murders."

"Who?"

"I wish I knew, Brice. And there's more, but you're not going to like any of it."

"Tell me."

For the next twenty minutes I explained everything that'd happened since I'd spoken to him earlier. He interrupted a few times after I told him Candice had saved my life and that I'd noticed what rough shape she was in. And I ended with her telling me that I needed to leave town at once.

"I know that Candice is in big trouble here, Brice. Someone is out to frame her but good, and it seems that they're one step ahead of her at this point. I can't just leave her to try to figure this out on her own. But I don't think she was exaggerating when she said my being here makes both of us vulnerable. She needs me, but I also put her in danger the longer I stay."

"She's right, Abby," Brice said, and I could hear him moving around. "You can't stay there. At least not on your own. Do like she said. Head to the airport."

My heart sank. "You think I should come home," I said.

"No," Brice replied. "I think you should go to the airport and pick me up. I'll get the first flight out and be there in a few hours."

* * *

I used Candice's cash to pay for the cab to the airport and waited anxiously for Brice. In spite of the fact that I hadn't slept a wink, I still felt wide-awake and ready for action. I didn't just want to help clear Candice's name—I wanted to slay dragons for her. Underlying that was the grinding guilt for ever having doubted her; even though I'd been ready to forgive her for anything she might've done, I still should've kept the faith from the beginning. If I had, maybe I would've been a little more objective about the video, and I would've picked up on the right-handed shooter more quickly.

From the looks of Brice as he came down the escalator, I knew he had to be feeling much the same guilt for ever doubting his wife and the love of his life. "Let's grab my bag and then get a car," he said after giving me another of those out-of-character hugs. I think we both needed the reassurance.

"What'd you say to Dutch?" I asked after he'd gotten his luggage and we were on our way to the rental car kiosk.

"I told him I was going to Vegas to bring you back."

I smiled. "And he bought that?"

Brice grinned sideways at me. "Hook, line, and sinker."

"You'd think by now he'd know better."

"You would," Brice agreed. "But he's probably gonna hold a grudge for a while."

"Hmmm. We should stop by the store on our way home once we clear Candice. I've learned that a well-cooked steak and a fresh supply of beer go a long way to melting my hubby's cold shoulder."

"A well-cooked steak, huh? So, I'm gonna have to stick around and grill it for him?"

"Duh," I said. The only thing I knew how to operate around the outdoor grill was the fire extinguisher.

Brice and I got a rental under his name and before getting inside, I watched him pull out his Glock from his bag, tucking it into the back of his belt. I felt so much more secure having him here with me.

"Where do you want to start?"

I'd had the last several hours to think about that very question, and my radar kept pinging back to Lenny Fusco's murder. For some reason I thought that was the key. "We need to go see a friend of mine," I told Brice. "Detective Robert Brosseau. I've already called and told him we're on our way."

Brice glanced over at me. "Can we trust him? I mean, at this moment I still have a job, but if the Vegas bureau finds out I'm here, snooping around, my suspension is going to turn into a discharge."

"Yes. I already told him that if he rats us out to the Feds, I'd tell his wife on him. Trust me—he'll keep our secret."

I directed Brice to Robert's Vegas PD substation, and he was waiting for us in the lobby. He greeted us warmly, and I was grateful to have made such a good friend a few years back. "In here," he said, leading us into a conference room. He carried a police file with him, and I suspected it was Lenny Fusco's.

"So, Abby, you said on the phone you have proof

that Candice isn't guilty of the murder of Dr. Robinowitz. What do you have to show me?"

I opened up my laptop and swiveled it around so that Robert could see, playing the video for him and pointing out the inconsistencies. At the end of it, I could tell Robert remained skeptical. "Couldn't she have used her right hand just to create reasonable doubt later?"

"It's not her, Robert," I said firmly. "The more I look at how she stands, how she holds her weapon, and Robinowitz's reaction to her—I just know it's not her."

Brice said nothing while Robert and I discussed the video, but I could tell that he was biting his tongue. He was itching to defend his wife, no doubt about it.

"Okay, so it's not Candice. Who do you think it might be?"

I had a hunch, not a good one, or even one that made any of the puzzle pieces fit together easily, and it was one I had briefly considered while at Robinowitz's condo. I was thinking that, as Saline had been found in Candice's car, wearing her clothes and her jewelry, maybe it could be her posing as Candice in the video. Pointing to Lenny Fusco's file, I added, "I know you probably have the file Lenny collected on Saline Hamon. Can I see it?"

"I turned that over to the Feds," Robert said. "I've got a copy on my computer, but it's pretty thick and it'd take me a while to print it out, Abby. Is there something in it you're looking for in particular?"

"Well, for starters, I'd really like to see a photo of her if you have one on file."

Robert smiled. "I've got one of her right here, actually," he said, sorting through Lenny's file. "I was looking at her as a possible suspect, so I dug up some stuff on her." After a moment he said, "Here it is." He then placed a DMV photo on the table, turning it so that both Brice and I could take a look.

Saline was strikingly pretty. She had long brown hair, beautiful brilliantly green eyes, a straight delicate nose, and the kind of full lips women would kill for. Her only flaw seemed to be a rather square jaw that made her appear perhaps a bit too serious. "Wow," I said, thinking how sad it was that Saline would never look like this again. "She's gorgeous."

"She's a looker," Robert agreed.

I then compared Saline's picture to the woman in the video on the screen of my computer. It was impossible to tell whether it was her because the woman in the video was captured only in profile and much of her jawline was hidden by her hair. But then I read something on the DMV copy that gave me pause. "Hold on," I said. "This says that Saline is five-four. Is that true?"

Robert pulled up his laptop and began to type something into it. "Seems to be," he said. "She lists the same height for each of her driver's licenses."

I looked at Brice. He read my silent question perfectly. "After we figured out it wasn't Candice, I went back to the hospital. She's definitely smaller."

I dug into my purse and pulled up the file Candice had asked me to hide for her. Taking out the fake ID Candice had created, I looked again at the information at the bottom, listing Samantha Dubois as five-four with green eyes. My eyes flickered back to Saline's photo, those green eyes popping in the light from the flash. A few more puzzle pieces were starting to come together, including what Dr. Robinowitz might've been doing in Austin, and suddenly I knew why Candice had written down the address of an abandoned dentist's office.

Still, just to be absolutely sure, I went back to the frozen image on the video. I advanced it a few frames to the last step she took before drawing her gun. "Do we know how tall Dr. Robinowitz was?"

Brosseau turned again to his computer. "His driver's license lists him as six-two."

"No way is that Saline," I said pointing to the woman in the video. "Look, Brice, I know she's wearing heels, but still, she's at least five-eleven in them. I've seen those boots up close, and they'd never add seven inches. I'd say that in bare feet this woman is at least five-seven to five-nine."

"So, whoever she is, she's Candice's height or maybe a little taller," Brice said.

"Yes." Then I thought of another angle to try to identify who she could be. "Brice, did Candice ever mention any woman who had a serious grudge against her? Someone who lived here who might be capable of doing something like this?"

Brice shook his head. "You know Candice," he said. "She's pretty tight-lipped about her past."

I frowned. "Yeah. She's like that with me too. Maybe the wife of one of her clients heard she was back in town? I know Candice used to specialize in catching cheating spouses in the act. Maybe Candice caused some woman to lose a lot of money as a result?"

Brice scratched his head. "That's a little far-fetched, though, don't you think?"

"All of this is a little far-fetched," I countered. "I mean, this took some *serious* planning."

At that moment Robert's cell phone rang. Lifting it from his belt, he looked at the display and said, "Excuse me. I gotta take this."

He left the room and I continued. "You can't put something like this together on a whim. Someone had to have been keeping tabs on Candice, and still has that capability. I mean, it's almost like Candice is up against an evil Candice." And just like that, a clue so huge I couldn't believe I'd missed it bulleted its way into my brain and I actually gasped. "Ohmigod!"

"What?" Brice asked.

Instead of answering him, I pulled Lenny Fusco's file toward me and began to sift through it in earnest. "Lenny *is* the key!" I said, frantic to find the piece of paper that would prove my theory. "But not in the way we thought!"

"Abby, what is it?" Brice demanded.

At last I found the witness statement I was looking for. Holding it up, I felt a tremor of excitement go through me. "Lenny found Candice when she was young and naive. He trained her and groomed her to be an amazing PI. Then he took advantage of her and used her license to get away with all sorts of questionable stuff. At least, that's the story Candice told me when she talked about Lenny, which was only once while we were out here and he nearly caused us to get killed. Lenny was a scum, but he was a pretty smooth-talking scum. He had this ability to get women to trust him. And after Candice, he moved on to someone who was a whole lot like her."

I turned the witness statement around so that Brice could read it. "Lenny's wife?"

"Michelle Fusco," I said. "I remember an especially tense encounter we'd had with her a couple of years ago. I don't remember her face, but I do remember that she was Candice's equal physically: tall, lean, and so strong she put your wife in a headlock. That bitch was cunning and quick."

Abruptly, the door opened and Robert came back into the room. "Sorry, guys, I've got a possible homicide I have to get to. I'm not sure when I'll be back, but I'd appreciate it if you two would stay put here until then. No going off to investigate on your own, or you'll get me in hot water."

I smiled brightly at him, hoping I looked especially trustworthy. "Go. Do your thing. We'll wait right here."

The second the door was closed, I reached for his laptop and pulled it close. "How does this work?" I pointed urgently to the screen, which showed the DMV database search for David Robinowitz.

"Here," Brice said, moving closer and reaching for the laptop. He typed in the query for Michelle Fusco and I watched the screen populate with a face I was stunned to recognize. "Oh. My. God!" I said, pointing to the screen again and thinking myself an idiot for not putting it all together sooner. "I *know* her!"

"You said you met her the last time you were out here, right?" Brice said.

I shook my head. "No. We didn't exactly 'meet.' It was more like I saw her at a distance, but I've actually been introduced to her again while I've been here in Vegas, and *everything* now makes sense!"

Brice stood up, grabbing the file and my hand. "Tell me on the way," he said.

Chapter Thirteen

Brice drove while I slowly wound my way through what I thought Michelle had done to kill two birds with one stone.

"Lenny cheated on Candice with Michelle back when they were married," I told Brice. "When we found Lenny after he tried to turn us in two years ago, they were living in a trailer park. It must've galled Michelle that Candice had done so well for herself over the years, while she got stuck with a scum for a husband. Then, and this is just a working theory, Lenny gets hired to run a background on Saline Hamon, who he learns is Olive Wintergarden. And Olive's birth certificate from England reveals something startling—it lists her father as Salazar Kato. He wonders if this is the same powerful casino owner who runs Lucky Lou's, so somehow he obtains a DNA sample from both, sends it off, and sure enough, the results come back a match.

"Knowing Lenny, he probably tried to work an angle, but here's the tricky part that I don't quite understand yet. Somehow Candice gets roped into a plot to change Saline's identity."

"How do you know that?" Brice asked me.

"It's the only thing that makes sense," I said. "Candice updated her Nevada driver's license with the same height and eye color as Saline. In Saline's photo, she has long brunette hair, and yet when she's pulled from Candice's car, she's got short blond hair, cut and colored to perfectly match Candice. In the file Candice told me to hide was an address for an abandoned dental office in Austin, which still had a lot of the medical equipment in it when I went to check it out. Robinowitz was a plastic surgeon. Maybe he was hired to alter Saline's appearance to make her look enough like Candice to take on the fake ID."

"But why?" Brice said, and I could tell the theory was a little hard for him to accept.

I shrugged. "Maybe Lenny was worried for Saline's safety, or maybe there was some money in it for him if he kept his mouth shut, but when he sees you and Candice at the Bellagio, where he worked, he knew it was his one chance to ask her for help."

"But Candice hated Lenny," Brice interjected. "She barely talked about him to me, but even I knew she never wanted to set eyes on him again."

I frowned. "I know. That's the part of the scenario that's not really working for me either, and yet, there's this surveillance footage from the Bellagio that suggests they met at least twice during the time she was here on your honeymoon."

It was Brice's turn to frown. "All that effort to hide Saline's identity," he said. "I still don't understand why."

"She had to have known something. Something big," I said. "And Lenny knew about it, and because he was obsessed with her, he wanted to protect her."

"But why would Candice meet with Kato and accept the cash from him? I've studied that photo, Abs. That is *definitely* my wife in the photo."

"I don't know, Brice. As much as I really think we're onto something, I know we don't yet have the whole story. But my working theory is that Kato approved of the plan to alter Saline's appearance. She was his daughter, and maybe he was worried about any resemblance she might pose."

"That's just creepy," Brice said.

"Yeah, I know. So maybe that part still needs to be revealed. Suffice it to say, Candice was recruited to help Saline alter her appearance. She set up the ID, an apartment here in Vegas, and arranged to meet Robinowitz at the airport until Saline could arrive. Somewhere between when I last saw her and the time Robinowitz landed at ABIA, Candice gets jumped by Michelle, beaten to a pulp, and her clothes, personal belongings, and her car are stolen. Michelle then drives to the airport where Candice had agreed to meet the doctor, and in plain view of the parking garage cameras—and Michelle is an expert at surveillance cameras—she poses as Candice and shoots Robinowitz. Then, she lets Candice go, knowing that the entire city of Austin will be searching for her, and Candice can't make a move without being brought in on a murder charge. After that, Michelle makes sure to tail me a couple of times so that I can think it's Candice, and then, she renders poor Saline unconscious and sends her over the bridge, planting the blanket with Candice's blood at the scene so that even if we believe it's Candice at first who's been pulled from the lake, at some point we'll know it was all staged, and Candice committed another murder."

"Holy shit," Brice said. "This Michelle is one evil bitch!"

"Right?" I said, rubbing my hands together. I kinda couldn't wait to get my hands on her.

"She did all this because . . . why?" Brice said next.

"I don't know," I admitted. "I mean, it seems a little crazy to think that she'd be *that* mad at Candice to do all this, right? I think there was something else motivating her. Clearly she was after the file in Candice's office—I'm convinced she was the one who broke in and wrecked the joint—but why that was so important to her, I couldn't say."

"This all sounds so insane," Brice said, rubbing his face with his hand. "I wish Candice had trusted me enough to come forward the second she got away from Michelle."

"I think she wanted to protect you at all costs, Brice," I told him, knowing my best friend well. "She was probably afraid for both your safety and your job. If she came to you, you would have talked her into turning herself in, which would have left you vulnerable. I'm sure Michelle expected Candice to go to you and do just that. She probably even counted on it, and Candice probably thought that as long as Michelle could keep guessing about her whereabouts, she'd have to keep her focus on Candice, and not on you."

Just then Brice pulled into a subdivision of small row houses, pulling up to the curb just down from a brown stucco home with a red tile roof and a FOR SALE sign in the front yard.

Turning to me, Brice said, "How do you feel about confronting Michelle and getting some clear answers?"

"You still have your Glock?"

Brice nodded.

"Then I feel pretty good. Let's do this!" As we got out of the car and began to approach the house, I said, "What's the plan?"

Brice reached behind him and pulled out his gun. Checking the clip, he tucked it into his waistband and covered it with his jacket. "We go to the door and knock, and hope she opens up and talks to us."

I made a face. "That doesn't sound like a great plan."

"Do you have something better?"

I looked to the house. "Not really."

"Okay, then," Brice said, continuing toward the house.

I followed him up to the sidewalk and over to the driveway. "Stay behind me," he said softly, and I knew he meant that if there was trouble, he'd be on point.

We went to the door and Brice knocked. No one answered, but we could hear the TV playing inside. "Think she's home?" he asked me.

I used my radar, which at times can be better than

X-ray vision. "Hmm," I said, a bit confused. "I'm sensing her energy, but it's faint. Maybe she's in the backyard."

Brice motioned with his head to follow him, and I did around the side of the house to the privacy fence. He tried the gate and I was relieved to find it open. "Hello?" he called, his hand sliding under his jacket, and I knew he'd have a loose grip on his gun until he could assess the situation. "Michelle Fusco?"

No one replied, and yet, I still felt that faint sensation that Michelle was close by.

As we rounded the yard and looked around, I saw that the back door was open. A fluffy white cat sat perched on a lawn chair, licking its paws. I stopped in my tracks and grabbed Brice's arm. "What?" he whispered.

"The cat!" I whispered back. "On its paws. That's blood!"

Brice stiffened, and reached back to tuck me behind him before withdrawing his gun and handing me the keys to the rental. "If anything other than that cat moves, you run as fast as you can back to the car, you hear?"

"Got it," I told him.

We moved forward slowly, half-crouched and looking all around. Brice stopped at the open door and turned his head slightly. "You stay here."

I nodded, and moved aside to huddle against the stucco. "Please be careful," I whispered.

Brice crept forward through the door and disappeared. A moment later I heard, "FBI! Get your hands in the air!"

And then I heard nothing else. The abrupt silence was so eerie that after several long seconds I couldn't take it and finally crept to the door. Very slowly I poked my head through, wondering if it was a good idea or a very bad one to call out to Brice. Finally I decided to risk it. "Brice?"

No one replied. I gulped. Chancing another few steps, I moved in through the back door and found myself in the kitchen, which was a disaster. The place had obviously been tossed, and most of the contents in the cabinets had been pulled out and strewn about, but there was no sign of Brice or Michelle. I grabbed a frying pan off the floor and held it in front of me protectively. Inching forward through the kitchen into the living room, I searched the place with my eyes. It closely resembled the disorder of the kitchen, except that between the couch and the overturned ottoman I saw a prone figure lying facedown. The carpet under the figure was soaked in blood.

"Oh, no," I mouthed. The spiky black hair had to belong to Michelle. "Brice?" I whispered again, shaking in fear. Why wasn't he answering?

Taking a deep breath and summoning my courage, I moved toward the hallway that had to lead to the bedrooms. As I came up to it, I stopped in my tracks. At the end of the corridor were two figures, locked in a kiss.

"Oh, *thank God*!"

Brice and Candice unlocked their lips long enough

to look back at me. "Hey, Sundance," Candice said. She looked so tired and frail. I was glad Brice was holding her up.

"How's it going?" I asked, not especially wanting to interrupt the romantic reunion, but . . . um . . . there *was* a dead body on the floor.

"Not so great," she said. "I see you decided that instead of flying back home, you'd ask Brice to come here."

"Seemed like a better plan."

"Ah. I should've figured you wouldn't listen to reason."

I shuffled my feet and motioned with my shoulder behind me. "Sooooo, about the dead woman . . . ?"

"She was dead when I got here," Candice said.

My lie detector backed her up. I pointed to the mess all around the home. "Somebody seemed a little angry after they did her in, huh?"

"Maybe not so much angry as frustrated," Candice said. She was still leaning heavily against Brice and I badly wanted him to take her to see a doctor.

"Should we go?" I asked him, using my sleeve to wipe my prints off the handle of the frying pan and place it back on the floor.

"No," Candice answered before her husband could. "Whatever the person who killed Michelle was looking for, I don't think they found it. She had something worth killing for, something that would've put Saline in danger, and I have to find it."

My brain flooded with questions, and I wanted to sit Candice down and hear the whole story, but I knew that now was not the time, and definitely not the place. "Candice," I said gently. "Honey, if someone heard the gunshot or even the sound of this place being tossed, they could've called the police. We're sitting ducks here the longer we stay."

"Abby's right," Brice said, and he hugged her closer and began to try to walk with her down the hallway.

Candice wasn't having any of it. "If you two want to go, then go," she said, digging in her heels and refusing to be pulled along. "But I've come way too far and been through way too much to give up looking now."

Brice and I exchanged a look, and I sighed. "How do you know Michelle's killer hasn't already found it?"

Candice motioned with her chin to the doorway right next to her. "Come here and take a look," she said. I moved down the hallway and peered into the central bathroom. Every drawer had been pulled out and turned over. The bathroom floor was littered with toiletries and the like. Even the medicine cabinet had been swept onto the floor. The only neat corner was the kitty litter box by the toilet. Once I'd taken in the room, Candice said, "When you toss a place looking for something, you start with the big stuff, under furniture, in a closet, up on shelves. When you still can't find it, you'll toss the bedroom, living room, and eventually the entire kitchen. When you *still* can't find it, you'll get frustrated and impatient and tear up carpeting, pull pictures from the walls, and toss the attic or basement. Whoever tossed this place ended his search by yanking open the medicine cabinet and tossing pill bottles onto the floor. See how they landed on top of the towels and other toiletries? There's no way Michelle would've hidden what he was after in the medicine cabinet. He did that out of anger right before he left."

"What was she hiding?" Brice asked her.

Candice sighed. "Something Saline wanted to keep well hidden." And then she started from the beginning and told us all of it. Much of it we'd already guessed at, but it was good to hear her tell it.

Taking up Brice's hand, she said, "A few days after we got married, my ex-husband called me on the room phone at the Bellagio. At first I just hung up on him, but he kept calling and begged me to hear him out. He threatened to introduce himself to you if I didn't agree to meet with him, so I did.

"Anyway, Lenny said that he'd been hired by someone to investigate a woman named Saline Hamon, whose real name was Olive Wintergarden. I knew right away that Lenny was head over heels for her the second he mentioned her name. He told me that Saline was in trouble. Big trouble. She'd recorded something she shouldn't have on her phone, and she'd done something she shouldn't have, and she'd likely be dead before the end of the month if someone didn't intervene.

"Lenny also admitted that he was having an affair with Saline. He was ready to leave Michelle, but he wanted to make sure Saline was safe before he did anything that might alert his wife to the affair. I'll admit I nearly got up and walked out of the restaurant right then and there. I mean, what the hell did I care if Lenny wanted to screw up yet another marriage? But then he mentioned Sal Kato, and that was a game changer for me. I've known Sal since I was nineteen. He'd always been good to me, and I owed him one. Big-time. So, when Lenny showed me proof that Saline was actually Sal's biological daughter, I knew I couldn't just walk away.

"I agreed to meet with Saline, and then with Kato, who by now knew that Saline was his daughter. He also knew what she had done and to whom, and he wanted to protect her by sending her away, but she refused. Now that she'd found out who her father was, there was no way she was leaving. Kato offered a solution that might work on a couple of levels. His longtime friend, a retired plastic surgeon, was in a financial jam, and he'd declined all offers to let Sal help him, so Kato instead offered to hire him to alter Saline's appearance enough so that she could take on a new identity. Saline wore my exact size, even down to my shoes, and, as I already had a fake ID here in Vegas, it seemed like an easy fix. Kato supplied me with some cash for both my trouble and to set Saline up with her new identity. He told me none of it could be traced back to him, so I got to work arranging the apartment and setting Saline up with a company credit card for an LLC that I created online. Then, when I was back in Austin, I hunted for a discreet place to have the procedure done.

"What I didn't know then was that during all the time I was in Vegas working to help Kato hide Saline, Michelle had become suspicious of Lenny, and she'd started her own surveillance on him. She showed up at our final meeting together and accused us of being back together. It was laughable and I stupidly shrugged it off. What I also didn't know at the time was that Michelle worked for Kato, who'd taken her under his wing much like he'd done with me a dozen years ago.

"Michelle learned about our plans, and I believe she saw Saline as a credible threat to her close relationship with Kato. Once she got it into her head that Lenny and I were having an affair, well, she knew she could exact her revenge on all of us. She waited and watched for an opportunity, and took out Lenny first. I didn't even know he was dead until after Saline arrived in Austin and told me that they'd found him dead.

"For all her faults, Saline had been crazy about Lenny, and I don't know that I could blame her because I'd once felt the same way, until I got smart and left his ass."

"Did you know Michelle murdered him?" I asked.

Candice shook her head and stared sourly at the prone figure on the floor behind us. "I completely underestimated Michelle," she told me. "And at the time I didn't know of her connection to Kato, so I assumed Lenny had been murdered by any one of a number of enemies he'd made over the years. Anyway, I had other things to worry about, namely, meeting Robinowitz at the airport and getting him situated. I left Saline at the hotel and went to pick up the doc, and that's when Michelle jumped me." Subconsciously, Candice raised her hand and gingerly touched the back of her head. "She pistol-whipped the hell out of me, and I blacked out. The next thing I knew, I was waking up in the back of my own car, covered in a blanket with my hands and feet bound, tape over my mouth, and the sounds of a gun going off. Immediately after that, Michelle got into the car wearing my clothes, a wig that was styled just like my hair, and drove us out of a parking garage. Muddlebrained as I was, I knew exactly what she'd done.

"She then dumped me half-naked off Highway Seventy-one. Out in the boonies. The last thing I remember before she laughed in my face and took off was her throwing me my phone. She knew the police would try to track me through the GPS, but she also knew it would be my only means of getting help. That's when I called you, Abs, and left you that voice mail. I had to get you to get that file before the police found it."

"But why?" I asked her. "What was in that file that was so important?"

"Evidence that I'd been trying to protect Saline," Candice said. "Nobody knew that she was Kato's daughter, and in the wrong hands, that file would definitely mark her as a target. Plus, I figured Sal would protect me and back me up when I came forward and explained the story. Little did I know that Michelle had been the one to escort Saline to Austin, so she knew exactly where to find her.

"Meanwhile, I know Michelle was also feeding Sal a story about having delivered Saline into my waiting hands before heading back to Vegas. I'll bet she made sure to show him the video of me supposedly shooting his best friend in the face, and telling him she couldn't reach his daughter to further make it seem like I'd suddenly gone psycho on him."

I knew that was likely exactly correct, because when

I met with Sal, he knew his best friend had been murdered by a woman who resembled Candice and he also seemed quite surprised to learn that Saline was in the hospital.

"As for me," Candice continued, "by the time I stole some clothes and a couple of bucks from a house off the highway, and got back to the hotel, Michelle had already kidnapped Saline. I think that it took her a few days to torture the truth about what Saline was hiding, and where Michelle could get her hands on it. That's why she came back to Vegas. To retrieve it and use it to her advantage. Michelle's big flaw, however, was that whatever Saline was hiding, someone else knew about it, and wanted it back. They probably figured out the whole frame-up too, and knew who'd really killed Robinowitz. That's when they came here and killed Michelle, only they must've done that before they could get it out of her where she'd hidden it."

Candice paused and we all looked around again at the mess. I was just making up my mind that there was nothing here when my radar pinged. Sometimes, I make a great bloodhound. "Hang on," I said, stepping carefully into the bathroom, careful to disturb as little as possible while I made my way over to the toilet. "You know the one place he didn't look?"

"Where?" Candice asked.

I bent down and picked up one end of the litter box. Underneath was a file sealed in plastic. I smiled. "I had an aunt who used to hide cash under her litter box. She told me that no thief wants to put his face close to cat poo."

"Well, I'll be damned," Candice said.

Using my sleeve again, I carefully picked up the file and brought it with me to the doorway. "Now can we go?"

Candice leaned forward and hugged me tightly. "Yes," she said. "Now we can go."

We left the house the same way we'd entered, and once out in the yard I searched for Michelle's kitty, but other than a few bloody footprints, I couldn't find him.

"What do we do about the cat?" I asked. Candice pointed to a water dish and a bowl on the side of the patio. "I coaxed him outside with food and water," she said. "We'll call a cat rescue after we alert the authorities. I know of a good one that's dealt with cases like this before. They'll have someone out here working to catch the kitty before the sun goes down."

"How're we going to alert the authorities without implicating ourselves?" I asked.

"Have you been in touch with Robert Brosseau yet?"

I smiled as Brice held the gate open for us. "We just came from his substation," he told her. "We didn't let on that we were headed here, though."

"Good." Candice moved ahead of me and Brice, stopping at the small rock garden just in front of the house to pick up a good-sized rock. After looking around to see if anyone was watching, she pitched it through the front window, then walked quickly away.

Brice and I were a little stunned, but as soon as we got in the car, Candice said, "Okay, Abby, call Brosseau and tell him that you went over to interview Michelle, and when you arrived, you saw that her house may have been broken into. He'll send a car, and they'll find her."

"Should we wait for them to come?" I asked.

"No. We have someplace else to be."

Brice turned to her. "Where's that?"

"The man that killed Michelle didn't find this," she said, holding up the file wrapped in plastic, "but I'm pretty sure he found the evidence that would clear me of Lenny and Robinowitz's murder. I want to make a trade, but first we need to call your friends at the Vegas bureau."

Brice's brow furrowed. "Why do I think you're getting ready to do something really stupid?"

"Because I am," Candice said bluntly. "And because there's no other way to clear me of murder and get us all back to our lives."

I didn't want to say anything, but I had a bad feeling about what Candice might have in mind.

Several hours later Candice was standing in front of me with her arms raised, angrily telling me how I could . . . um . . . shall we say, "pleasure myself."

"You're just mad because I talked the Feds into letting me go with you."

The female tech finished inserting the tiny microphone on the underside of Candice's bra and turned to me. I unbuttoned my shirt while she handed me a new one with a camera placed in one of the buttons. I draped that over my shoulders before raising my arms just like Candice had so the tech could affix the microphone.

"There's *no* way I'm letting you do this, Sundance," Candice spat. Clearly that bump on the head had brought out her temper.

"Oh, there is a way," I told her. "The Vegas bureau has already cleared me, and Gaston's even on board. No one here trusts you, Cassidy. Me, at least they sorta trust, and as I've already met the man in question, I'll only add legitimacy to your request to see him."

Candice rounded on her husband. "Do something!"

Brice had his eyes shielded by his hand and was trying hard not to look at my half-dressed self. "If I had my way, I'd never let either one of you go in there."

Candice clenched her fists in frustration. "Abby, you are *not* going!"

"Oh, I am *so* going!" I yelled back.

"Hey!" Agent Oppenheimer shouted. We both turned to see he'd poked his head through the curtain separating us from the other agents. "Quit it, you two. You're both going or the deal's off."

I crossed my arms over my torso. "Hey! This isn't a peep show, you know!"

Oppenheimer indulged me by putting a hand over his eyes. "Sorry."

He said that like he wasn't one bit sorry. Just then my cell rang. Caller ID showed it was my husband. I palmed my forehead. "Crap on a cracker!" Perhaps Brice and I had neglected to call Dutch and assure him that we'd be home soon and that we weren't up to *any* shenanigans in Sin City. "Hey, cowboy!" I sang, all breezy and relaxed.

"Where are you?" he demanded. "I just heard you'd

been rehired by Gaston, and that you're involved in some crazy undercover op out in Vegas."

"I'm *fine*, honey. And how're *you*?"

"Don't be cute."

"You make it hard to be otherwise when you're mad."

"Edgar . . . ," Dutch growled.

"What's that, Brice?" I said, looking meaningfully at Brice. He started to shake his head. Vigorously. "Oh, you want to talk to Dutch and explain everything? Sure! Hold on, Dutch, here's Brice."

I held out the phone to Brice. He continued to shake his head. I gave him my best "I'mma kill you if you don't take this phone from me *right now*!" face, and reluctantly, he took the phone.

Candice and I got back to arguing with each other while the tech finished up with me. Twenty minutes later we'd settled down. A bit. Candice was still pissed off, and Brice looked like he'd gotten a pretty good lecture from my husband. He'd tried to hand the phone back to me a couple of times, and eventually I took it and simply hit the "end" button before turning off the phone. Dutch couldn't yell at me if he couldn't reach me. I'd probably have to put out several times over the next few days to get him to forgive us, but if making love to my incredibly hot and oh-so-sexy husband was what it took, well . . . I *suppose* I'd take one for the team.

"Okay, now let's go over this again," Oppenheimer said. "You go in there and request a meeting. You meet and get him to admit to killing Michelle Fusco. You then trade him the file for the evidence to prove Candice's innocence, and then you get the hell out of there. You do not, and I repeat *do not*, leave that hotel to go to any other location. We've got the place surrounded, but his surveillance team will be working from the inside, and if they're alerted to our presence, they could definitely run interference with us. The code word if you get into trouble is 'canary.'"

"That's a stupid code word," Candice said. I suspected she was angry enough at me to take it out on Oppenheimer.

"How about 'pizza'?" I said.

Oppenheimer sighed and rubbed his face. "Fine. The code word is 'pizza.'"

"Uh, no. I was a little hungry and I was hoping for some pizza." Oppenheimer glared so hard at me that I actually backed up. "Kidding!" I said, raising my hands in surrender. "Gee, you Vegas guys need to lighten up a bit."

"*This* is why I don't think she should come!" Candice snapped.

I knew she simply wanted to keep me out of harm's way, but she was starting to hurt my feelings. So I turned to her and said, "What you fail to understand, Cassidy, is that I've already pointed my radar at this little meet and greet, and without me, you have *zero* chance of survival. With me, the odds are significantly better."

All eyes in the room widened in surprise. "You didn't tell me that when you asked me to get permission to go along, Abby," Brice said, alarm in his voice.

"Yeah, well, some things are just better left unsaid."

"You're making that up," Candice said, squinting at me.

I looked her dead in the eyes. "No. I'm not."

There was an awkward silence after that, and finally Oppenheimer said, "Well, at this moment, Candice, you're still officially under arrest for the murder of Dr. Robinowitz, and the attempted murder of Saline Hamon. You either cooperate under the terms we've negotiated, or we call this whole thing off and you go directly to jail."

Candice glared at both me and Oppenheimer. I could tell she wasn't happy about any of this, but it was the only way to clear her name. There was concrete proof out there that Michelle had framed Candice and we had to get it from the person who'd killed Michelle before he destroyed it.

Also, the FBI could use the file we'd gotten from under the litter box to reel in a big fish, so they were sorta chomping at the bit for us to play nice and get the meet and greet going. We'd be on a short leash, but at least we had a chance.

"Fine," Candice said through clenched teeth. I gave her a winning smile, even though, on the inside, I was shaking like a leaf.

I had a terrible feeling about walking into the lion's den. I knew we'd be protected to a point, but it didn't feel like we'd thought of every contingency. Of course, this plan had been put together on the fly, so it was more than likely that we'd missed something important, but we were committed and there wasn't really another choice available to us if we ever wanted the charges against Candice dropped.

At ten past five, we were given the green light, and Candice and I went down to our new rental car and drove the short distance to the casino.

I parked in the same area I'd parked in before, and led the way to the entrance. We made it through the casino and up to the lobby level by way of the escalator. I gripped the railing on the way up; every nerve was on edge and my Spidey senses were tingling with warning.

As we got off the escalator, we were met by a familiar figure. I had a feeling he'd greet us, especially after I'd put a few more of the puzzle pieces together since my close call at the apartment. "Arlo," I said. "So sorry I couldn't hang out with you at the apartment last night, but you seemed a little tied up."

Arlo's eyes narrowed and his lip curled in a snarl. Moving aside his jacket slightly to reveal the gun holstered at his side, he said, "I'm free to hang out now."

Candice moved closer to me and her posture suggested that she was ready to karate chop his ass if it came to it. "Aww, that's sweet of you," I said, patting his chest. "But we've got an appointment to keep. Maybe next time."

He gripped my elbow much the way he had before. "The boss told me to personally escort you two upstairs," he said.

I cut my eyes to Candice and subtly shook my head. I didn't want her to get into it with Arlo. He was the smaller fish in the pond. We'd deal with him later.

She frowned but relaxed her shoulders a bit. She didn't like it, but she'd play along.

Arlo "escorted" us over to the elevator and we waited for the doors to open. At last the elevator pinged and we headed inside. We rode up in silence and I felt my underarms become slick. So much for the extra deodorant I'd slathered on. I wondered if they made a formula strong-enough-for-meeting-a-Mafia-killer-but-made-for-a-woman. I'd have to inquire about it if I made it out alive.

The elevator slowed, then stopped, and with a ping the doors opened. We stepped out into a corridor and headed to the end of the hall. Arlo then let go of my elbow, and knocked on the double doors. "Enter!" we heard a voice command.

Arlo opened the doors and then reached behind the two of us to push us forward. The second we were through the entry, he closed the door behind us, locked it, then gripped both of our shoulders tightly. "Thought I'd spare you the public pat-down, but I still gotta put you through it," he said.

He started with Candice, feeling along every limb and the small of her back all the way down to her ankles. She took it without complaint. We both knew Arlo wasn't about to find the wires we were both wearing. They were tucked into our bras and the tiny battery pack was hidden in the clasp at the back. Sometimes, being a girl has its advantages.

Arlo moved on to me and while he touched me, I read his energy. I kept the information to myself, but I knew he was the kind of guy that made the wrong choices. How ironic that he'd gambled in Vegas and was about to lose big-time.

Once Arlo was done patting us down, he motioned with his arm and we stepped forward. Candice had to be running on adrenaline at this point, but her steps were sure and I could tell she was alert and ready for anything. "Frank Garafolo," she said. "Saline's told me all about you."

Big G pulled out a Big Gun and pointed it at us. "Where is she?"

"She's dead," Candice said simply.

I hadn't expected her to lie about that.

Big G and his gun stared hard at her. "Did you kill her?"

"Nope," Candice said before turning sideways and motioning to Arlo. "Your friend Arlo here did."

Arlo's jaw dropped and he drew his own gun. Pointing it at Candice, he said, "That's a lie. Tell him the truth, you bitch."

"Oh, but it's not a lie," I said, ready to holler "PIZZA!" at a moment's notice. "You did kill her, Arlo. Because you were in on Michelle's scheme, and you didn't warn Frank here."

Nobody moved or spoke for several seconds. Finally Big G said, "Arlo, put the gun away. Fusco, talk to me or I'll kill you myself."

Candice motioned to one of the chairs in front of Big G's desk. "May I?"

G waved his gun nonchalantly. "It's your funeral."

Candice took a seat, but I felt like standing. Okay, so I felt like bolting, but I managed to stay put and watch Candice play this thing out.

"I'm going to tell you a story," Candice said. "And

you tell me if it matches up with what you think went down."

Big G leaned back in his chair. "Amuse me."

"A little over a month ago, my scum-sucking ex-husband was hired by you to investigate your girlfriend, Saline Hamon. Saline had you thinking seriously about marriage, but before you went down the aisle with her, you wanted to make sure there were no skeletons in her closet you didn't know about.

"You knew Lenny from the days when he came in here and blew a couple grand in cash. He was flush with you, thanks in no small part to me, but you felt he was trustworthy because he knew what you'd do to him if he ever double-crossed you.

"Unfortunately for you, Lenny wasn't as smart as you gave him credit for, and certainly he wasn't as trustworthy. He discovered pretty quick that your girlfriend had a false ID. Her real name was Olive Wintergarden. We now know that her mother had once been the girlfriend of Salazar Kato. By Saline's account, her mother had never told her much about her father, only that he'd broken it off with her a few weeks before she even knew she was pregnant, and because he'd headed off to America to find his fortune, she'd never tried to track him down to tell him about the baby. Lenny managed to obtain Olive's birth certificate, listing her father as Salazar Kato, and he wondered if she could be his daughter. Somehow he obtained DNA samples for both, and sent them off for testing.

"Meanwhile, he also discovered that Saline was ripping you off. You added this wing of the hotel for condos, and Saline handled the title paperwork. You thought with her background in real estate she was the perfect person to execute the docs. What you didn't know was that Saline was onto your methods for selling the condos during a time when the real estate market is, shall we say, less than robust, and yet, all the condos were sold lickety-split." Candice snapped her fingers for effect. Big G seemed annoyed, but he let her continue.

"You tended to target a specific type of person to give the sales pitch to. You looked for regular guests of the casino, those folks who were starting to struggle with the compulsion to gamble. Maybe their credit was also starting to suffer a little, and you offered them a convenience that was hard for them to resist. If they lived right above the casino, they could ride that lucky streak any time they felt it coming on. You were exceptionally good at talking them into this, and once they were living here, you were also exceptionally good at coaxing them downstairs to lose more and more money. Eventually they started to default on their credit cards, and their car payments, and even their mortgage payments. And then you offered them a way out; you suggested that you could write them a new mortgage, and you would become their lender. You'd charge them very low interest for the first six months, until they could get back on their feet, and then you'd jack up the rate to nineteen, twenty, even twenty-five percent. They'd make a few payments to you after those first six months, because they wouldn't dare risk missing a payment to *you*, now, would they? And then they'd slip, and you'd foreclose. That was a little item in small print that most of them missed, wasn't it, Frank? That line about foreclosing after thirty days? You'd bring the hammer down so swiftly they wouldn't even know what happened. They'd shuffle off to work one day, and come back to find out they couldn't even get into the lobby. Within a day you'd have the place back on the market, ready for another hapless sucker. Oh, and you'd still make the old owners responsible for the balance of the remaining mortgage. And every once in a while you'll send out a thug to remind them that they still owe you, right, Frank? Who says loan-sharking is dead?"

Candice paused to study Frank, who was still holding his gun as if he might like to get in a little target practice. Candice seemed amused. "Now, we all know these mortgage terms you set up were super illegal," she continued, "but Saline was handling all the paperwork, and somehow whatever she was filing down at the county recording office didn't set off any alarm bells, so win-win, right?"

Frank's eyes narrowed. We'd learned some of it by Candice's conversations with Saline, and the rest by looking through the file we found under Michelle's kitty litter box, which held an example of one such mortgage and a flash drive with all the other docs on it. It'd made for some interesting reading.

"Did Saline tell you all this?" Frank asked Candice.

Candice waved her hand as if to shoo his question away. "I'm getting to that," she said to him. "The part I want to talk about now is the part where you didn't realize that Saline was actually recording the condos in her name. Slowly, one by one as you wrote out a new mortgage to cover the bank-owned one, Saline was putting herself exclusively on title, and then she'd tuck in a lease agreement into each of the closing docs, which meant she was only leasing these places out to your next victim. You'd collect the rent, of course, but Saline didn't care about the cash payments. What she cared about was the value of each condo as it was transferred from the bank to her. With each new mortgage you thought you were setting up, Saline was gaining a share of the value of your casino. All she needed were twenty-five condos, plus the one you outright gave to her when you proposed. Once she had that number, she'd be the legal owner of fifty-one percent of Big G's. She'd be *your* boss, Frank. And she could assign those condos to anyone she wanted. She could even assign them to her father, Salazar Kato, who would then effectively own your ass. Which is exactly what she planned to do. She told me personally you were smothering the crap out of her, and actively working to bring down her dad. She also knew about the other women. For a while, your loving fiancée had you so fooled, Frank."

Big G's jaw clenched and his free hand formed into a fist. The room became very tense and I wondered if now was a good time to throw a pizza party.

Candice, however, appeared unfazed by the tension she was creating. "I don't know when you caught on to the plan, Frank. And I'm not sure how you recruited Arlo and Michelle to work for you. Maybe you promised them each a condo. Michelle was in the middle of selling her place when she was murdered; maybe she'd planned to move in here?"

Frank's mouth became a thin line. "You've got nothing," he told her.

Candice smiled at him like she thought he was being cute. Looking over her shoulder at Arlo, she said, "The problem with sending Arlo to do your dirty work, Frank, is that he jumps the gun—no pun intended. True, he killed Michelle before she could tell him where she'd hidden all that fabulous evidence that could land you many, many years in federal prison . . . but we found it." Candice pointed back and forth between her and me, and when Frank turned his mean eyes on me, I gulped. He then turned that hostile gaze on Arlo.

"G," Arlo said quickly. "I swear. There was nothing at that bitch's place. I tore it apart! No way was there anything there!"

Candice tapped her fingertips together casually. "Did you think to check under the kitty litter, Arlo?" she asked him with a sly smile. "Cuz we did."

Arlo's face drained of color, and both he and Frank knew we weren't fibbing.

Frank pursed his lips and rocked back in his chair. "It's hard to find good help these days," he said.

"Well, he did one thing right," Candice told him. "He collected the evidence Michelle had stashed, which would've cleared me for Robinowitz's murder. Am I right, Arlo? You grabbed that just in case I got my hands on Saline's file."

Arlo glared at her before brightening slightly. He

thought he had his leverage back. "You mean the wig, the gun, and the coat with all that blowback on them? Yeah, I found it. I've tucked that someplace safe, though, so you better play nice with Mr. G."

Candice smiled and turned her attention back to Frank. Pulling out a small flash drive from her bra, she handed it to Frank. "That's a duplicate. I have the original, and the FBI on speed dial. If you want that, and for me to keep my mouth shut and walk away, you'll give me the evidence Arlo found at Michelle's place that'll clear my name."

Frank took the flash drive and opened up the laptop on his computer. Sticking the drive in, he pulled up the images and there was murder in his eyes.

He stood up with clenched fists and said to Arlo, "Take them to the evidence, and bring me back the original drive or I'll kill you, and anything else you love." Turning to us, he said, "If you ever breathe a word of this to anyone, you two will end up like Saline."

I gulped again, but Candice casually got to her feet and saluted. "Got it, G. Nice doing business with you."

I then looked at Arlo, who motioned with his gun toward the door. "Move," he growled.

Once we were outside in the hallway, Arlo put the gun directly into Candice's back and said, "Go."

We walked forward like good little soldiers, but with every step I felt a more immediate sense of danger. "Arlo," I said, knowing he had murder on his mind. "I think you should consider that if you kill us before we give you the original flash drive, Frank's not going to stop until he hunts you down and kills you too."

Arlo grabbed my shoulder and squeezed till I squirmed. "Shut it, bitch!"

He then pushed and shoved us to the elevator and we were forced inside. Arlo hit the down button and I opened my mouth, ready to cry out, "PIZZA!" when Candice put a hand on my arm. She knew I was close to panicking, and I could tell she'd wait until the last moment to call for help, which would hopefully be only one second after she had the evidence to clear herself.

We rode the elevator all the way down to a level that felt belowground. The doors opened to a parking garage, and Arlo put the gun to Candice's back again. "Move!" he repeated.

We walked forward with Arlo so close to us that he felt on top of me. I could feel the steamy heat of his hot breath on the back of my neck. "You hid the evidence down here in the parking garage?" I asked loudly.

"Not exactly," he said, shoving me forward.

"Where're you taking us?" I asked next, hoping the Feds were hearing the alarm in my voice.

"Shut up!" he said, giving the back of my head a good whack.

Again I opened my mouth, ready to call for help, but Candice grabbed my hand again and squeezed. I could see the pleading in her eyes, but my radar was sending so many alarm signals that it was hard to decide what to do.

Arlo stopped us in front of a big white van. "Get inside," he said, reaching over us to pull open the side door. My mind filled with the image of that van, kicking up dust in the desert, and I knew for certain Arlo wasn't about to hand over any evidence in exchange for the flash drive. He was going to take us to the desert, kill us, then go to Salazar Kato and tell him that Michelle had been working for Frank, and on his orders, she'd killed Robinowitz and Saline. It's how he planned to save his own skin. I could see it all so clearly, it was like reading his mind.

"We're not getting in that van," I said, putting my arm out to stop Candice from even thinking about it.

I felt the cold muzzle of the gun up against the back of my head. "Yes, you are," he growled.

"What kind of a van is this anyway?" I asked. "A *pizza* delivery van? It looks like something you'd deliver *pizza* in!"

Arlo grabbed my neck and shoved me forward. I tripped and fell half in the van. Behind me I heard a scuffle, then the sound of a gunshot, and I scuttled out of the van to spin around. I saw Candice struggling with Arlo—he was trying to point the gun at her, but she was fighting him with both hands wrapped around his wrist. She was losing and the gun was slowly turning toward her head.

I leaped forward and got Arlo around the middle, but he was big. I pushed with all my might and managed to shove him several steps to the side. Another gunshot rang out, and I jerked at the sound, but wouldn't let go. I pushed and shoved and kicked at him, praying that he hadn't shot Candice. I tried to get my head up to see, but Arlo's elbow blocked me. And then the big thug tripped, and all three of us went down. I heard something clatter and realized it was the gun. I scrambled forward, clawing at the pavement while I heard Candice grunt and lots of slapping behind me. I reached out as far as I could stretch, my fingers almost touching the metal when I felt something slam down on my back. My chin hit the pavement and my teeth clinked together so hard I knew I'd chipped a tooth. At the top of my vision I saw Arlo's big hand wrap itself around the gun and he rolled over to point it back at me.

I froze and at that exact moment a car came zooming up to us and screeched to a stop as doors flung open and an army of men jumped out all shouting at once, *"Drop your weapon!"*

"Drop it now!"

"Get on the ground, facedown, scumball!"

Arlo raised his arms, dropped the gun, and rolled over facedown. I let go of the breath I'd been holding before turning my head this way and that, searching for Candice. I found her lying on her back with a bloody lip, looking more spent than I'd ever seen her.

I crawled over to her and took her in my arms, never more grateful to hug my best friend. "We did it!" I said.

She hugged me back limply. "We almost did it," she said. "He still never gave up the evidence."

I let out a small laugh. "Uh, yeah, he did, Cassidy." I then got both of us up and moved her back over to the van. "See that black garbage bag with the blond hair sticking out of it?"

Candice crawled into the van and grabbed greedily at the bag. Out spilled the coat Michelle had stolen from her the night she'd killed Robinowitz, the blond wig, and a gun. "Oh, thank God!" she whispered right before Brice crawled into the van with her and hugged her to him like he was holding on for dear life.

I turned back around to give them some privacy, and when Oppenheimer approached, I spread my arms and legs to block him from the van. "Nothing to see here," I said. "At least, not for another minute or two."

Chapter Fourteen

Candice, Brice, Dutch, and I sat around the fire pit on our deck, enjoying the beautiful weather and relishing the return of normalcy. On the grill, four thick, juicy steaks steamed and hissed. Brice was in charge of ensuring that Dutch had the biggest, juiciest steak on the barbie, and that his beer was always cold.

I'd be in charge of Dutch's needs later that night. Something I was seriously looking forward to. "But why did Michelle keep the gun, your coat, and the wig?" Dutch asked. "I mean, that was a stupid move if you ask me."

Candice nodded. "Michelle could be cunning, but in a lot of ways, she was often overly confident. Still, I think she kept the stuff because she knew that eventually I'd be caught and brought to trial. It'd be just like her to plant the coat and the gun at my old office or somewhere near the condo and send an anonymous tip to the police, making sure to suggest she saw either Brice or Abby dumping it."

"The bitch," I said. I didn't usually speak ill of the dead, but in Michelle's case, I decided I could make an exception.

"So how did Kato take the news about his daughter?" Dutch asked next.

I grimaced. I'd gone with Candice to that meeting too, as had Brice, and he'd worn his badge in plain sight just to make sure Kato knew whom he was messing with. We needn't have worried. Kato had already learned of Michelle's betrayal and that of Arlo, and once Candice explained the whole story to him, he'd been more than contrite about his contribution to all our woes. He'd even taken some responsibility for Saline, suggesting that if he'd been there as a father for her, maybe she wouldn't have tried such a scheme against such a dangerous man as Big G.

Candice told all that to Dutch and he said, "Well, at least Saline is making progress. She still has a long road back, but the doctors are optimistic."

"Her dad is coming in tomorrow," Candice said.

"I can't believe you still like the guy," I said to her. "I mean, he was ready to feed you to the coyotes, honey."

Candice smiled, like that made him all the more dear to her. "Sal's all bluster," she said. "He would've let me tell my side. And you know he didn't send Arlo after you. Arlo went because he was trying to get to me before Michelle could finish me off. He thought I knew where Saline had hidden the file."

"Still," I said. "I think when Kato comes to town, I'll

skip having lunch with him. How long is he gonna be here, anyway?"

Candice leaned back in her chair and sighed. The bruises were starting to fade and she was looking much more rested and healthy. "He said he'll stay as long as it takes to see Saline well enough to take her back to Vegas."

I reached out to stroke Dutch's arm. "Back to Vegas isn't a phrase I think I'll ever use again."

"Hear, hear," Brice said, raising his beer.

I raised mine too, and Dutch followed suit. But Candice seemed to hesitate. "It's hard," she said softly. "Because my sister's buried there."

All three beer bottles lowered. I leaned over to squeeze her hand. "You know that Sam's spirit isn't tied to that grave, right?"

Candice smiled sadly. "Yeah. I do. But it's still a place with her name on it. A place I can go and sit and talk to her. I need something like that to memorialize her, Abs."

My heart went out to Candice. She was looking better now that she'd seen a doctor about her head injuries, and it turned out she'd suffered a pretty severe concussion, which the doc had said could make her more emotional than usual. We were all trying to be sensitive to that.

So I didn't try to argue the point with her. Instead I looked out at our yard, where a newly arrived vitex tree, ready to be the yard's centerpiece, stood in a pot. It was a beautiful tree, and was already covered in purple blooms. My radar pinged and I said, "Hey, Candice?"

"Yeah?"

"What was Sam's favorite color?"

She cocked her head at me. "Her favorite color? Why do you ask?"

"Indulge me."

"Purple. She loved purple."

I nodded knowingly and motioned with my beer to the vitex tree. "See that tree?"

"Yeah."

"That's Sam's tree. The landscapers are coming by tomorrow to plant it, and I'm going to order a nice stone bench to sit underneath it, and I'm gonna have it engraved. I'm gonna call it Sam's Place. From now on, every time you want to be close to your sister, you come on over and hang out under that tree, so that you can let what happened in Vegas stay in Vegas."

Candice's eyes misted and she turned from me to stare for a long while at the tree. At last she squeezed my hand back, raised her beer, and said, "Hear, hear."

Read on for an excerpt from
Victoria Laurie's next Psychic Eye Mystery,

Sense of Deception

Coming in hardcover from
Obsidian in July 2015

There was chaos in the courtroom as I was dragged kicking and screaming from it by two beefy bailiffs. After landing a pretty good kick to someone's kneecap, the number of bailiffs "escorting" me out of the courthouse increased by two. It would've been humiliating if I'd paused long enough in my struggles to consider it. Mostly I yelled my head off and wrenched my limbs back and forth until one of the big and beefies put a can of mace right next to my nose and threatened to let loose. I piped down quickly after that and settled for glaring hard at my captors before being handed off to a couple of deputies. The deputies made quick work of handcuffing me and placing me in a van for a short road trip to a large loading dock, where I was taken out and moved to a big ugly building. After that I was put through the process of getting my butt thrown in jail.

On the plus side, there wasn't a strip search (thank the baby Jesus!), but I did have a panicky moment where I seriously regretted my decision to go commando that morning. Some days it just pays to wear underwear.

Still, I had to give up my dress slacks and blouse for an orange jumpsuit, and I don't care what anyone says: Orange is *so not* the new black.

After demanding my right to make one phone call for the eleventh time, I was handcuffed and led down a dark, narrow, claustrophobia-inducing hallway to a bank of phones attached to the wall. The husky woman in uniform who'd led me there growled, "You have ten minutes," before moving a little way down the hall to eye her watch and then glower at me.

Charming.

After squinting meanly at her retreating form, I turned to the phones and called my hubby. "Rivers," he said when he picked up the line.

"Hi, honey, it's me."

"Edgar," he said with honeyed tones, using his favorite nickname for me. I love the sound of my husband's voice. So rich and seductive. It soothes me like a morning cup of coffee, heavy on the cream and sugar. "How was court?"

"Oh, you know. Not quite what I was expecting."

"Was it tough on the stand?"

"A bit."

"Yeah, this defense counsel of Corzo's . . . he's a slick bastard. Did you get beat up a little?"

I swallowed hard. "Um, yes, actually. You could say that it went exactly like that."

"Aw, dollface," Dutch said. "Don't let 'em get you down. You did great on this case. Gaston even pulled me aside yesterday to say how happy he is with the work we did to nail Corzo. And, between us, I think he's especially proud of you."

I winced. Dutch's boss's boss was Bill Gaston. Regional director for the Central Texas FBI office. Former CIA. Totally great guy, until you got on his bad side. Once on said bad side, you might as well pack a bag and leave town. Quickly. "Speaking of Gaston," I said, trying to keep the waver out of my voice, "could you maybe get him to come down to the county jail for me?"

There was a lengthy pause; then (after adopting a slight Cuban accent) my hubby said, "Edgar? What did you do?"

I took a deep breath. "I sorta outed the judge to a packed courtroom and then he attacked me and then I was thrown in jail for contempt of court."

Another (longer) pause. "Please tell me you're kidding."

"I'm kidding."

"Really?"

"No."

There was a muffled sound where I suspected my husband was trying to quiet a laugh. "Tell me *exactly* what happened."

I opened my mouth to give him the 411, but at that

moment the guard tapped her watch and gave me a stern(er) look. "Actually, honey, maybe you should just call Matt Hayes. He can give you the play-by-play. But please also call Gaston. I have a feeling we're going to need his clout to get me out of here."

I thought I heard my hubby stifle another laugh with a cough in the background. After clearing his throat, he said, "I'll call Gaston and Matt. We'll have you home for dinner, sweethot."

Dutch had slipped into his best Bogie impression for that last bit, and it actually made me feel a little better, even though he thought my getting tossed in the clink was high-larious.

After hanging up with Dutch, I shuffled down the hallway to the waiting guard, and she led me by the arm back down the corridor, to a window with a red-headed, freckly-faced inmate standing ready behind a counter in a little enclosed room with lots of neatly packed supplies behind her. I was pushed up to the window, and a pillow, sheets, a thin blanket, and some toiletries were shoved into my chest. "We're out of toothpaste," she said, as if I'd already noticed and had copped an attitude.

"Okay," I replied.

"Are you on your period?" she asked.

I felt heat in my cheeks. I'm a bit modest when it comes to discussing bodily functions. "Not presently."

"Good. We're out of tampons, too."

"Got any aspirin?"

"Yeah. You got a headache?" she said, reaching behind her for a one-dose packet of Tylenol.

"Yep."

"Here, but that's all you get," she said firmly before jotting down the added item on a clipboard in front of her.

"Thank you very much."

She rolled her eyes and turned away. I wondered if we'd end up braiding each other's hair later.

Stern Eyes then led me to a set of doors, which required us to get buzzed through. Once we were through the doors, the conversations and shouts and jeers on either side of the hallway from the inmates currently jailed there echoed and bounced off the concrete walls like a mad game of Pong.

I tried not to tremble as Stern Eyes pulled me along, but I might have let out a whimper or two.

I'd been in jail before. Trust me on this: It's not a place you *ever* want to be. It's loud, it's jarring, and it smells like a mix of Pine-Sol, BO, and perhaps a soupçon of desperation.

Plus, it's dangerous. I mean, it's *literally* wall-to-wall criminals. Think about that the next time you want to jaywalk. (Or out a federal judge to a packed courtroom . . . ahem.)

Stern Eyes walked me down the length of the open section of the jail, and I ignored the catcalls and whistles from cells to my right and left. I suspected that new prisoners got paraded in front of the other inmates like this on a regular basis. It was meant to scare the newbies—and make them easy for the guards to handle initially—and I can tell you for a fact that it's effective.

About midway down the length of the open section,

Stern Eyes gave a tug on my arm and directed me to the right. "You're here," she said, coming to a stop in front of a closed cell door with only one inmate inside. Using the radio mic at her shoulder, she ordered the cell door to be opened, and after a rather obnoxious buzzing sound, it slid to the right. She didn't even wait for it to get all the way open—she merely gave my back a hard shove and I stumbled forward, barely able to stop myself before my head hit the top bunk on the right side. "You have a new roommate," Stern Eyes said. It took me a minute to realize she wasn't talking to me.

I turned cautiously to look across the cell at the other inmate and did a double take. She wasn't at all what I was expecting.

Tall and willowy, she had very long, very curly blond hair, big blue eyes, and the kind of heart-shaped face that would break a man's heart. (Or a woman's, depending on which team you're playing for.)

She considered me without a hint of expression, and I wondered how I measured up in her mind. I tried to square my shoulders to show her that I was cool, yo. All she did was blink.

The guard then turned to me, and with a thumb over her shoulder to the inmate across the cell, she said, "That's Miller. Play nice with her or we'll send you to solitary. You missed lunch, so dinner's at six. When the doors open, move out into the corridor and stand to the left of the opening to wait to be counted by one of the COs. Then move single file to the cafeteria. It'll be your only chance to eat for the rest of the day, so make it count. Lights out at nine p.m. Sharp."

With that, she motioned for me to raise my arms, and after dumping my assigned goodies on the metal frame of the top bunk, I held my hands out so she could undo my cuffs.

After pocketing the keys, Stern Eyes got up in my face and glared hard at me, as if she alone could scare me straight (good luck with that), and then she simply turned on her heel and walked out.

A moment later the door buzzed and slid mechanically closed.

I looked meaningfully at my new bunkmate and said, "Well, she's not getting a holiday card from *me* this year."

The corner of Roomie's mouth quirked, but there was no real humor in her eyes. Instead, I noticed for the first time a rather profound sadness there. Like all the mirth had been sucked right out of her, and what remained was something hollow. Broken. "So you're one of those, huh?" she asked me.

I stiffened. "One of what's?"

"One of those people who makes a joke out of everything as a coping mechanism."

I laughed and waved my hand. "No. I definitely have a serious side."

"What'd you do to get in here?" she asked.

"Used my charm and quick wit when I should've used diplomacy."

That quirk came back to her mouth. "Well, whoever you pissed off, they must've been high up the food chain. I'm on death row and I'm not supposed to have roommates."

I stiffened again. "Death row? I'm on death row?"

"Relax," she told me. "I'm down here from Mountain View for my appeal. Normally they'd put me in solitary, but that's full up from the last fight in the cafeteria, so they moved some people around and I got the luxe digs here."

I gulped. The urge to ask her what she'd done was heavy on my tongue, but I wasn't sure that was (a) polite or (b) a question that could get me shivved in my sleep, so I simply nodded and said, "Well, I shouldn't be here long. My husband's gonna get me out, hopefully before dinner."

Her brow rose skeptically, but then she went back to a rather blank expression. "So, what do you do when you're not expelling lots of charm and quick wit?"

I struggled with her question for a moment; no way was I gonna reveal that I worked with the Feds, especially not in here. But I also wondered if it was a bad idea to let her know that I was a psychic. I mean, maybe I was bunking with the only serial psychic killer in all of Texas. "I'm an accountant."

She squinted at me. I had a feeling she could smell the smoke from my liar, liar, pants on fire. "Ah," she said. And then she sat back on her bunk and picked up a paperback. In jail only ten minutes and I'd already failed my first test.

"Actually," I said, taking a seat on the lower bunk, "I'm not an accountant."

"_Quelle surprise,_" she said flatly. She didn't even look up from the book.

"Okay, I deserved that. The truth is, I'm a professional psychic."

Her gaze slid over to me, as if she were waiting for my orange jumpsuit to actually explode in a ball of flames. I made sure to hold her gaze. "For real?"

"For real."

"You make a living at that?"

"Yep."

"So . . . what? You just look into a crystal ball or something?"

I grinned. "No. Crystal balls, head scarves, and lots of bangles are for amateurs. My technique is to focus on a person's energy—their electromagnetic output, if you will. We carry bits of our future in the energy we expel, and someone like me can focus on that energy and tell a person about what's likely to happen in the future."

I waited for her to ask me what I was picking up about her, but she surprised me with her next question. "Can you look back at something?"

I cocked my head. "Back? You mean, can I look back in time?"

She sat up and put her feet on the ground, resting her elbows on her knees after setting the paperback aside. "Yeah. If I told you about something like a break-in, could you see who did it?"

"That's actually a more complicated question than you'd think," I told her. "If you're asking me if I could see how a crime unfolded, and give a description of the offender, yeah. I could do that."

Tears welled in her eyes and I couldn't imagine what I'd just said to upset her. "Have you ever worked on a crime before?"

I thought about lying again, but her sudden display of emotion and those sad eyes got the best of me. "Yes."

"How many?"

"Several dozen."

"You work with the police?" she asked, a hint of suspicion in her eyes.

I was quick to shake my head. "My business partner is a private investigator. We work quite a few cases together." And that was not a lie, albeit not exactly the whole truth either.

My roommate took a deep breath and looked away from me to stare out the bars of the cell. It was a long moment before she was able to compose herself. Putting a hand on her chest, she said, "My name is Miller. Skylar Miller."

I got up and extended my hand. "I'm Abby. Abby Cooper. Rivers. Cooper. Cooper-Rivers."

She took my hand and that small quirk at the corner of her mouth returned. "You sure?"

"I still can't decide if I want to take my husband's last name or not."

"How long you two been married?"

I returned to my side of the cell. "It'll be a year in November."

She nodded. "Keep your own name," she said. "Don't give up your identity."

"Word," I said, and put my fist out for a bump, but she didn't raise her hand or acknowledge the banter.

My hand dropped limply back to my lap. "You okay?" I asked her after an awkward moment. She still looked so sad, and she hadn't asked me about this break-in she'd mentioned earlier. I'll admit that she'd more than piqued my interest.

"Yeah," she lied. Then she reached under her pillow and pulled out a Twix. Opening the wrapper, she shook out one bar and offered it to me.

As someone who never turns down free chocolate, I was quick to get up and retrieve it. "Thank you."

"Can I ask you something?" she said, looking thoughtfully down at the remaining candy bar.

"Sure."

"How much would you charge me if I wanted to ask you about something that happened a while ago?"

"That break-in you mentioned?"

Her gaze lifted to mine again. Her expression was still so sad, but for the first time since meeting her, I swore I saw the smallest glimmer of hope. "Yeah."

I took a good bite of the Twix and held what remained up. "You're in luck today. I'm running a special. All glimpses into the past are priced at one Twix bar."

"I'm serious," she said.

"So am I."

She nodded, but she didn't rush to ask me her next question, and I thought maybe a demo of what I could do was in order. "You've been in jail for . . . ten years, right?"

She squinted at me and nodded slightly.

I assessed her for a bit before continuing. "This is your last appeal."

Again she nodded.

"You don't think it'll go well."

"No."

"You're right. Your lawyer is shit."

"He came cheap."

"When's the appeal?"

Skylar sighed. "It was supposed to be today, but it got postponed to the nineteenth."

I nodded. That wasn't even two weeks away, and in Texas, when your last appeal doesn't go well, you'll have an IV filled with lethal toxins in your arm by midnight.

As I sat there, I took in all of Skylar's energy, which was extremely complex. She carried a whole lotta baggage and it was tough to riffle through it all. "You've had a pretty tough life," I told her. "But a lot of it you brought on yourself."

She squinted skeptically before waving a hand to indicate the cell we were in.

I ignored that and kept going. "You struggled with addiction. It got the best of you for a lot of years, but then I feel like you worked really hard and overcame it."

Her expression softened. I'd just struck a chord.

"You're divorced," I said next. "And your ex is still *really* angry at you."

She gave me one short nod.

I closed my eyes to better concentrate, feeling my way along her energy, looking for bits of information that I could talk about. "You lost someone," I said. I didn't know why I hadn't touched on it sooner. It was the loudest thing in her energy. "Someone very close to you was murdered." And then I gave a small gasp and opened my eyes. "Your son?"

Her eyes had misted again, but she didn't look away from me. Instead she asked, "Can you see who murdered him? Can you tell who it was?"

My brow furrowed and I stood up. The energy from my roommate had shifted dramatically; it was as if the floodgates had been opened and there were now waves of guilt rolling off Skylar—an ocean of regret filled the space between us and it was so intense that I had to withdraw my intuitive feelers. "Skylar," I said, because I needed to get her to close those floodgates. "What are you in here for? Why are you on death row?"

"Cooper!" someone yelled at the door to our cell, and I jumped a whole foot. Stern Eyes was back, handcuffs dangling off her index finger. "Step forward with your arms in front of you and put them through here." Stern Eyes was indicating a small square open section of the bars next to the lock, where she wanted me to stick my hands.

"What? Why?"

"Someone's here to see you," she said. "Someone with big brass balls and a whole lotta pull, so hurry it up."

Gaston. It had to be him. I gulped. God, I hoped Dutch was with him. Especially after what I'd pulled in court. I shuffled over to the door and put my wrists through the small window so she could slap the cuffs on me.

Glancing over my shoulder, I saw that Skylar was

staring at us, and I tried to offer her an apologetic look. "Let me go meet with this guy and when I get back, we'll talk," I said.

"What if you don't come back?" she asked, and that small glimmer of hope that I'd seen in her eyes vanished.

"I will," I promised.

"All right, Cooper, step back and I'll have them open the door," Stern Eyes said.

"I will," I repeated to Skylar as I moved two steps back and waited for the buzz.

It came and as the door began to slide open, Skylar said, "That question you asked me about why I'm here?" I nodded. "You know why, don't you?" I nodded again—reluctantly, though. She was here for her son's murder, and those waves of guilt still sloshed around the cell. I didn't quite know what to think about that.

Skylar studied my face for a moment before she turned her gaze to the wall. As the door clanged to a stop, I turned to face Stern Eyes, still feeling the sticky residue from the Twix bar heavy on my fingers.